# FOREST GATE

## A NOVEL

\* \* \* \* \*

PETER AKINTI

FREE PRESS
New York London Toronto Sydney

FREE PRESS
A Division of Simon & Schuster, Inc.
1230 Avenue of the Americas
New York, NY 10020

First Free Press trade paperback edition February 2010

FREE PRESS and colophon are trademarks of Simon & Schuster, Inc.

For information about special discounts for bulk purchases,
please contact Simon & Schuster Special Sales at 1-866-506-1949
or business@simonandschuster.com.

The Simon & Schuster Speakers Bureau can bring authors
to your live event. For more information or to book an event,
contact the Simon & Schuster Speakers Bureau at
1-866-248-3049 or visit our website at www.simonspeakers.com.

Manufactured in the United States of America

1  3  5  7  9  10  8  6  4  2

Library of Congress Control No.: 2009047592

ISBN 978-1-4391-7217-9
ISBN 978-1-4391-7296-4 (ebook)

For William Oluwayeni Akinti, my father
In memory of Lucia Ekunola Akinti, my mother
and
for Simone Akinti, my daughter

## Acknowledgments

I am more than grateful to: Ellah Allfrey, my editor, who may well be an angel; my U.S. editor, Amber Qureshi, I am indebted to you for your hard work, and for the belief you have shown in my book from the start, thank you; Kathleen Pyne for putting up with me; St. Charles Borromeo church (Ogle Street, London) for strengthening my wavering faith; The Arts Council of England—thank you; Bidonville where I sit and write; Miranda Pyne for inspiration, friendship and love; Michael Fountaine, for always waving the flag; Cheryl Henderson for doing that stuff; Joyce and Susan Akinti (love you both wherever you are), Don Smith and Dej Mahoney, kind, generous men; Taponeswa Mavunga, for your patience; my early readers for their kind words and encouragement: Agnes Kuye, Lynne Butkiewicz, Bomi Odufunade, Donna Williams, Regine Zamor, Aissatou Minthe, Nadine Rubin and James Berry . . . Thank you all.

A special thank you to my wife, Kelly, who somehow manages to make everything all right. God bless your nutty little African-American heart.

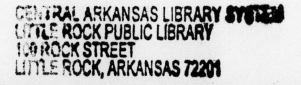

I know what the world has done to my brother and how narrowly he has survived it. And I know, which is much worse, and this is the crime of which I accuse my country and my countrymen, and for which neither I nor time nor history will ever forgive them, that they have destroyed and are destroying hundreds of thousands of lives and do not know it and do not want to know it.

James Baldwin, "My Dungeon Shook," *The Fire Next Time*

# FOREST
# GATE

# ONE

# MEINA

"Yes," I said, my eyes fixed on the dead body. "Yes, it's him."

I stared at the policewoman, at her almond-shaped eyes and her slow-moving mouth. I swallowed and tried to clear a stubborn glob of phlegm from my throat. My heart stalled at a solid memory of my brother, Ashvin, laughing at the ceremony of my third marriage to a forty-year-old with rotting teeth and a bunch of rowdy kids.

"How long do you think you'll be away this time?" Ashvin asked at the wedding.

"A week," I said. "Maybe two."

After the ceremony, the two of us spent the entire day hiding away from all the others in a stinky chicken pen with hungry mosquitoes and the burning sun shooting through the holes in the roof. We laughed so much at that old man. I remember laughing until dawn as we feasted on meat from the dowry I had been sold for: a few goats and a bull the size of a truck. We were like soil and grass, my brother and I. Whenever my aunt married me off, my brother would never leave me alone. It seemed he knew how I felt even before I found the words to say.

He would walk for miles, sometimes twice a day. Sometimes he would sit silently outside the compounds of the men I had married, not saying a word. He would not leave until he had seen me. And when he saw me, he would say nothing, just get up and trek back to my aunt and her rum-drunk lecherous husband, just like that. That was before he came up with the blind beggar routine—you would be surprised at what a few strange-tasting meals, odd noises at night and a cat-eyed boy can do to the psyche of a Somali husband. Believe me, I know. Divorce worked for me six times.

"It's him." I repeated.


I am Meina. Armeina. I'm named after the river that runs through Baidoa, a city south of central Somalia. "It glistened," she said when I asked Mama why. "It was a long glistening river, never disturbed." I lost my parents at the beginning of the fourteenth civil war and between the ages of seventeen and nineteen I was married off six times by a jealous aunt, an old uneducated village woman. My life has never been undisturbed. So, I prefer to be called Meina.

What I know of this story begins in the autumn of that dreadful year, 2006, the night my only brother, Ashvin, took his life. He wanted to be a doctor once but he had lived with real pain. I know what I know about that fatal night because James told me. I guess you could say James's life, our lives, began the day after my brother's death. You see, he (James) almost died too. But I'll begin at the real beginning, on the dilapidated rooftops on an ordinary estate, in an ordinary neighborhood in London. I owe that much to my brother; this is his story too. I understand that now. What I will never understand is why my brother killed himself then, why he waited until that night to leave me. The way I saw it, for the two of us, all the bad stuff, the real tragedy, was over.

Coming to London should have been our fresh start, our new beginning. I remembered how very happy we were because we were going to Great Britain. I remembered the shock of finding ourselves alone in a small council flat in east London. Truth was, in many ways we lived better in Somalia, where despite years of war we were around familiar things that at least made life seem constant. In London, we had to start all over.

If you look at a map of Africa, you will see my country wrapped around the horn between the Red Sea and the Indian Ocean. I have a clear memory of my last moments in Somalia. It was *jilaal*, the dry season. I remember taking time to pause and inhale deeply on the steps of the plane. I remember staring at the horizon and at the fierce sun as though my heart knew I would never see my country again.

Things were different from the London I had read about or seen in pictures. Until I arrived here after a six-hour flight, I imagined a different universe of street parties, white girls with ponytails—and boyfriends—who ate chunky chocolate bars while jumping rope on lush, green grass; ice cream and fine wines and homes with tended hedges.

I had never heard of bipolar disorder. Those were the words the coroner used to justify my brother's death. It wasn't a term ever used where I was from—where we learned to recite the Holy Qur'an before we learned to walk, where we were taught to work like immortals, to pray and to trust in Allah as if tomorrow was the last day.

The *Oxford Concise Medical Dictionary* describes people with bipolar disorder as being under the darkest of clouds. Somalia has been through fifteen years of war. People walked under these darkest of clouds, oblivious to beautiful things. But we did not have words for this state of mind.

Back to that night. It was cold and velvet black. The moon had risen early, it looked like dripping wax and cast eerie judgment over the oaks, sycamores, and bare hornbeams and over the twin towers of Wanstead Flats, Forest Gate, east London.

James and Ashvin, best friends, stood on two separate roofs of the towers, aware of the danger of leaning so close to the edge, the impetuous energy of death pulled at them like the high tide from the shore. Both rooftops were wide and dirty with piss puddles and sprays of overgrowing weeds.

The binmen were expected; that muscular smell of refuse made it difficult to breathe. The smell drifted everywhere, covered every-thing, like concrete in your developed world. It mingled with the tightly coiled smell of stale urine and frying bacon, together they made the air dank and thick like camel stew. The horizon, as far as the eye could see, was enveloped in the gritty fabric of the London skyline at night, traces of the permanent stench, the stooping rhythms of failure: aerosol cans, empty plastic carrier bags, orphaned toys, rubbish everywhere—a three-wheeled pram, a sodden mattress with orange foam hanging out of it, a fashionable construction boot with no laces, trampled cigarette packets, a slashed rubber tire, empty Scotch bottles, half-full condoms; all scattered relics from battered lives.

A sudden burst of static from a semiprofessional walkie-talkie bought less than a week earlier from Currys, Stratford, a closing-down sale that had been going strong for eight months.

"You ready?" James's rasping voice. He sat on the edge of the roof of John Walsh Tower, a thirty-one-story block of high-rise council flats as oppressive as the environment within which it was built. James waved his right arm at his friend.

Another burst of static. "Like Freddy." My brother Ashvin's voice, a refugee with an evasive Somali accent, a sullen tone. He was lying. He wasn't ready to die at all. If only he would have talked to me.

Ashvin sat on the edge of Fred Wigg Tower, an identical block opposite John Walsh. He stared down blindly at his trembling hands. He put a hand in the knee pocket of his combat trousers, fished around, took out his compass; the needle directed him and he faced the Middle East. Then he washed his head and his hands and feet with icy bottled Volvic water. Slowly, he began to recite his *sura*, his face dripping wet. Despite being taught, he only remembered one of the seven beautiful verses from the opening of the great book.

Ashvin could only see James's silhouette on the opposite building. When he completed his prayer he returned James's wave and then checked his watch. Almost time.

James and Ashvin. Teenage boys dressed mournfully in black. Friends who some might have said shared the same looks: the same wide flat noses, full lips, hair cut short enough to see the scalp and recently enough to feel the sharpness of the bristle. James had soulful black eyes while my brother's were firefly orange—like the desert sands. They were good-looking boys in an African fashion.

They encircled their necks with rope, nooses tightened with well-practiced slip knots. And then they held the slack from the rope in the palms of their hands, training their thoughts, allowing for no further doubt. They looped their hands through the rope leaving enough room for slight movement of their wrists. And

4

then their final preparations were complete. There was a moment's pause as they both took a final glance down at the lights across the vast city—to the west, Leytonstone; Wanstead to the north; Manor Park and Ilford to the south and, to the east, Forest Gate. I often put myself in his position. I feel as though I know my brother's last thoughts. When I close my eyes I see it all clearly.

In that moment, Ashvin let his gaze fall down on the head-lights from a car traveling toward Ilford, down a long dark road far below. He became giddy as his thoughts turned to the driver and where he was headed. To a beautiful home he owned? A bed with clean sheets? The warm breasts of his wife? The sound of laughter from his kids? Ashvin wanted to be the car driver, but he wasn't. In five minutes, he would be dead. He suddenly felt unspeakably weary, his hands trembled, realizing the terror he felt coursing through his veins. He blew a long sigh and tried to remember the words to another prayer. He couldn't. He bowed his head and allowed his tears to spill.

On the other roof, James was trying in vain to focus his last thoughts away from death, trying to sharpen his dimmed senses. But, as always, dark thoughts lurked, a heavy, silent presence like a stalking python. He thought of his own funeral and then he thought of Ashvin, of their conversations that went long into miserable nights when they smoked chronic and spoke with rage about human nature and global economies, about a future world they felt was stacked against them and about other old, jumbled resentments.

The trouble with my brother and James back then was that they were possessed with what they thought was the truth but they both lacked imagination. My brother was an extreme, a fighter, but he thought too much, if that is possible. When we first arrived in London he allowed himself to become angry and he forgot what we were taught by our parents about the well-being of the spirit and the heart. He said he wanted to fight, but London was different. Where we came from we knew the faces of the enemy. In London, there was no one to aim for. In London, he said, you never saw who kept you down. He spoke of the relent-less rhythms of machinery and mechanisms that acted like the wind, swept you up high in the trees where you swayed and you swayed until one day in the autumn you lost your grip, you fell and you closed your eyes and hoped, even prayed, for a soft landing. But, in London, you knew you wouldn't land well because everything, everything around was so hard.

James could hardly breathe up on the other roof and he was beginning to panic. Far down below in the stink of the backstreets he caught a glimpse of a pack of boys he recognized. Gangs. The Forest Gate Man Dem had been warring recently with the Paki Panthers from Ilford. He stared down and thought of the boys filled with perpetual rage, want and hunger. Some of them were wearing masks. He knew they would be armed with knives and wooden bats, as they rode pedal bicycles like delirious locusts, guarding a crumbling territory they would never own. The boys in the gang watched the high road in both directions for anything, scanning for prey to close in on. Sometimes, James hated those boys, sometimes he understood them.

He looked out across Leytonstone, down by Forest Gate. So quiet. James hated the houses, the shops and the streets. He hated Forest Gate. More than anything James hated his life. He could never grasp the point of it all. He wouldn't ever quite become the person everything around him told him he was supposed to be and, for as long as he could remember, he felt he had been born at the wrong time, into the wrong family, in the wrong place. That night he would put it right.

James felt his forehead grow cold. He was tired. He remained stiff in contemplation, slipping into a familiar place within, where he could not be touched. It was Tuesday. He had thought the day of his death would feel different, special, but it began like any other. He woke with the same deep despondency and, as always, he dreaded getting up.

He thought of the day before when he and Ashvin had inspected both rooftops one last time. They had watched a man—one of those middle-aged, new-money types with a fresh haircut and Italian slip-ons whose profession you could never quite tell. The man stood with a delicate-looking woman with an unattractive, angry face. She had lush hair, wore pendant earrings cut from jade, and a loose milk-white dress, silk, mottled with red. The couple quarreled.

"Stop calling me at home. She knows it's you. You knew what this was about when we started." His English was clunky, his accent Slavic. He wore a smile as he spoke, but it did not hide the malice in his words.

She looked at him and nodded, but her eyes revealed her suffering. Then she struck his face in fury and tore his cheek with her nails; he struck her back, and with contorted faces they stood slightly crouched and held each other for what seemed like a long time.

In the quietness of that tender moment, James's eyes met Ashvin's. Both boys remained still and watched closely, hypnotized. James wished the couple would go away because they were white people like ghosts and for him, because of the things he knew, their pain, their reality could not be identified as the same as his own. Watching the couple argue was like watching unbelievable characters from some American B-movie.

Without saying a word, as if reacting to some signal, the woman hitched her dress and popped the buttons on the man's fly. She stroked his prick until he was stiff and then she straddled him. The boys made an effort not to look but they couldn't remove their eyes.

The closest James had ever come to seeing between a woman's legs was at Starbucks in the Angel, Islington, once, when he saw one of those carefree-type Englishwomen with bushy armpits. She wasn't wearing any knickers, she sat opposite him with her knees wide apart while she read a gossip magazine. And there was that awful girl, Natasha Dixon, who he had messed with once in a lift, but that was different. Natasha is an old bike, everyone in the neighborhood has had a go. Half-Scottish, half-Jamaican—one of those girls who is first at everything but so messed up she doesn't know the father of her two kids. It's either Danny or Robert Pollin who live two doors down from her on Leybourne Road. Natasha doesn't care because she gets half of each of their checks. I saw her last week showing off her tattoos on the number 25 bus, her own name tattooed on her scrawny neck. "It hurt like fucking hell," she said, "but not like the one on my toes, that shit was like, murder." When she looked at me and knew I had been listening I turned away and she and her friends laughed.

"I swear, Elena, you have the devil in you," the man on the roof said.

Elena did not hear him. She moved, up and down, looking like a completely different woman, her face flushed, her arms tightened around his neck, legs clamped around his waist.

The man did not move much at first, he remained still as she shifted her weight on him, up and down, but his expression was that of a man who was trying not to show how he felt. It didn't last. In a moment he was furious, his half-closed eyes gleaming with lust and anger. He used a heavy arm to support her head as he forced her back and leaned over her, tugging at her dress. He kneaded greedily at a soft white breast and pounded her body. Each thrust buried deeper, his knees moved wider apart. She— her expression turned menacing—tossed her hair, abandoned one of her shoes and called for the devil. It was like watching a battle. He was much stronger but she was much more skilled. When she came she bit his lip so hard she drew blood. He made that unmistakable grunting sound that comes from a man who has reached his climax too soon. And in the tension that came with their unexpected stillness, they suddenly looked like a living picture of beauty.

"Now we know what it is like to see a grown woman come," whispered James, but when he turned he saw Ashvin throwing up. Ashvin heaved violently and his puke splashed the silence when it hit the ground, spread with flecks of blood like a pink porridge. The couple heard and turned their heads.

"Tell me, Borys, why is it you can only perform in front of strangers? You fucked me good like a true Bolshevik." She laughed as she turned to look at the boys. She wiped slime from her thighs with a handful of crumpled pocket Kleenex and laughed at their frightened, unblinking eyes.

"You have the devil inside you," repeated Borys, buttoning his fly.

Still laughing, the woman took a pull from her cigarette, exhaled into the cold night air and then flicked it, but it didn't go as far away as she intended, so she took a step toward it and crushed the stub with the sole of her red patent shoe. She smudged mascara across her face when she wiped it.

"I'm sorry. I didn't want to call your house," she said flatly, like she meant it. "When you didn't show yesterday and your phone was off, I didn't know what to think."

"I'm sorry even more, and you'll be sorry too if you ever call my house again," he said looking steadily at her, his hands clasped behind her back. She pressed her short blonde curls into his chest. He raised his face up to heaven in triumph.

"James? James? . . . Are you still there?"

"I'm here, I'm here," said James into his walkie-talkie but he had forgotten to press the push-to-talk button.

"I'm here, I'm here," he said again.

"I want to tell you something."

"Course. Go on."

There was a long pause.

"I want to tell you about Somalia and their fucking war."

"Right now? It's nearly time."

"They ain't worth shit. I told you I saw what they did to my mum and dad. I told you, I told everyone that I hid. Well, they heard me. They heard me, and they did some shit to me, man. Three nasty motherfuckers took my honor. That was the last image my dad saw of me before they cut his neck. When I screamed, they told me to shut up and I did. And then they cut my mum. She was still alive when one of those fuckers took me again. I'm haunted by shame."

A loud burst of static.

"Ashvin? Is that why you raped Nalma?" asked James.

"Rape? I didn't rape him," said Ashvin.

"I saw," said James.

"I was getting him back for what his people did."

"His people?"

"Ethiopians. Those evil sons of bitches."

Static.

"Since you are coming with me," said Ashvin, "you should know. In case you are afraid of the repercussions, y'know, from God like, for what we're gonna do. You don't have to do this, is what I'm trying to tell you."

"Don't do that. Don't reduce me like that. I have my own reasons for being up here."

Another long pause.

"Do you remember Kenny Doughnut?" asked James.

"Course I remember Kenny, fattest kid in our class. Fattest kid in the school," said Ashvin.

"Fattest kid in the wooorld." They said it together as they had a thousand times.

"Yeah, well," said James, "I heard his mother got three years for repeat shoplifting. Turns out she used to sell whisky she stole from Tesco's to her local off-license for his dinner money and stuff."

"So? Poor Kenny, but so what? We all got problems."

"He hadn't been showing up for school. That welfare woman, Miss Tetherington—"

"Tetherington? I had to see her twice a week. I hate that big-nose bitch."

"Yeah, well, anyway, Tetherington goes to Kenny Doughnut's house and finds him starved. He spent the whole of last term on his own. Nobody thought to tell him that they'd locked up his mum. They're putting him up for fostering."

"Fat fucking chance. Who's gonna want him?"

"Why d'you have to be that way?"

"He's a lump, you know it, and his mum was on crack anyway. Everybody's got problems, some worse than his."

"Yeah. I guess."

There was another burst of static and then silence as James thought of his own mother and tears filled his eyes.

"It's time to set your watch and check the rope." Ashvin's voice brought James back to his senses.

"Okay, okay," said James as he eased along the chilly bricks, holding on to two narrow shafts closer to the edge.

They had synchronized their digital watches, also bought at Currys, Stratford. They did one final check of the thirteen coils on the nylon ropes. Each boy could see the faint outline of the other. They looked across the tower blocks, trying to find some way back, but there was no hope. At 11:57 p.m., they were quiet as they emptied their minds, as they tried to forget life, to blend with their frail place in the universe.

They waited, listening to their own breathing. Three more

minutes, fumbling with rope—their destiny—with hands numb from the cold. The pace of their heartbeats slowed and their breathing quickened, deepened, but brought little air because of the fear clogging their lungs. In cold sweat they squeezed shut their eyes and in silence their throats sickened. Everything went black and silent, an icy sort of truce. Then after two slow, careful steps, over the edge they went like two stone-filled sacks. They jumped.

There was a sound of a low thud and in less than a second my brother, Ashvin, was dead. Gone to dust. Free to begin again. His neck broken, his body swung effortlessly from side to side by force of a howling wind.

James's neck did not break. He was alive but remained neither conscious nor unconscious in a place where the pain was of such proportion as he had never felt before. The silence of the night was broken by his terrible cries, cries that saved him in the end.

James's mouth foamed while he gasped for breath, his legs kicked involuntarily, vehemently from the burning report he received from his throat. As his body swung, he thought of his father. He saw him quite clearly, smiling, rolling a joint. His heart pumped wildly. He looked down at his legs and he began to panic when he saw them thrashing wildly back and forth, kicking the wall of the great concrete monstrosity with his heels and at the air with his toes. His thoughts turned to the air being squeezed from his body and in the same instant there was another thought of a new and immense fear of death, an instant lust for life. Instinctively, he wedged the palm of his hand between his throat and the burning rope. He began to claw at his throat. This meant life. Then, under gold stars that sparkled in the sky, his thoughts became remote from his body, he stopped struggling and fell into a truly comfortable, satisfying sleep.

# TWO

# MEINA

IT WAS SECOND PERIOD, during English. We were discussing "Wine on the Desert," a short story by Frederick Faust. It was about the slow demise of a runaway murderer who plans to escape by traveling through a desert on horseback only to find wine in his flask instead of water. It showed that scheming actions lead to doom. The story was so vivid that I felt the physical detail of what it would be like to die slowly, in dire need of water. It was flawless, first the horse, then the mind and finally the body, all succumbed to thirst.

Someone interrupted our class with a message from Mrs. Kelly, the head teacher. She had come to get me. It was Bertha Stewlan, a gangly girl, with braces across her teeth. She was head of the student body and looked like a cross between Lauryn Hill and Angela Davis: tall, pretty and aggressive in a natural sort of way. Messages sent via the head girl meant one thing. The girls in my class immediately started speculating, excited to be part of potentially juicy gossip. The whispers about my imminent expulsion began before I left my seat, even among my "friends." I couldn't think what I had done.

"She's going back to Africa," said somebody really smart. I turned to see who it was, ready to throw my ocean-freeze stare. I think it was Shirley Farquhar, a bizarre-looking girl the color of blended Scotch whisky who seemed to be growing inwards from the hunched way she walked. Practically the first thing she told anyone about herself was that she was a third Indian. She was funny, odd. I had never met a black person like her before. She said weird things to me like: "Why don't you eat bacon?" On my first day of school she asked me what it was like to be starving because whenever she didn't finish her meals, her mum always said, "Think of all the starving kids in Africa." During Ramadan, it would be her who'd talk about how stuffed she was after lunch. The day before she had asked Fuzia why the Indians in the Forest Gate post office didn't ever employ black people.

"I dunno, Shirley. I'm from Morocco," said Fuzia, bewildered.

Once, Anastasia, a Turkish girl from Tottenham, went for Shirley's throat when Shirley asked her how come her dad didn't own a kebab shop instead of a fruit shop.

"There are at least ten fruit shops on the same stretch of road," she said. "My brother says you're all selling hash and that the police know it and that they wouldn't allow that shit if it was blacks. I mean, come on, how many kilos of seedless grapes do you think a person can eat at two in the morning?"

That was Shirley. She had a boyfriend, an older boy who called her "Sweet Mama" when he picked her up from school in his flashy red sports car. I tell you, she was just stupid. Always talking about how some rapper was marrying a girl from her island and she had the most annoying ringtones (always, always soca tunes). And God alone help you if you were near her in the corridor when her phone rang, she'd be all hips and arms and winding waist.

As I passed her desk I wanted to say something unforgettable about her peanut-head brother who kept sending me gifts and e-mails without capital letters but I couldn't focus my mind.

"Shhhh," said Miss Diaz to the class, looking over the rim of her specs as she pressed her index finger against her thin lips.

My mind froze, overloaded with half-thoughts and fears. I followed Bertha's immaculate back, looking at her big arse that made me feel good about my own and her God-awful weave, gathered in a ponytail. I looked at the rubber heels of her shoes and then at the hem of her skirt, way above her knees, and I suddenly thought of home. In my country, a girl would do anything to avoid being exposed to the gaze of men. Bertha would not make it home if she ever wore a skirt like that. In Somalia, gunmen ruled the cities and they would rape girls like Bertha and they would say she asked for it because of the length of her skirt. I remembered the stories. They would use long, sharp knives to slice open the walls of the tin-shack homes and snatch daughters away. Girls would return, sometimes, in the morning, cast off from a traditional society that demanded virginity at marriage. At home in Somalia, I always wore a hijab or headscarf outside the house and I used to wear long, dark dresses, *direh*, and colorful cloth over my shoulders and around my waist, they followed behind me everywhere like a shadow. I don't cover my head in London but I always wear trousers. I looked down and tried to remember the last time I had seen my own naked legs.

I tried my best to match Bertha's brisk stride. I liked the funny sound her steps made on varnished wood. She turned her freshly made-up face on mine just once at the mouth of the long entrance that led to Mrs. Kelly's office, the only carpeted corridor in our college. Bertha fixed my tie and turned the collar on my shirt so it didn't show at the back. Then she put her hands on my shoulders and gave me a long, searching stare.

"Do you want to tell me anything before you go in?"

"Huh? No."

"Well, in that case," she said, "the police are in there waiting. If you have any shit on you, get rid of it now." Her cloying smile was like a gulp of chocolate mousse and then she swiveled and bounced off. I had heard she could be a real bitch at times, Bertha Stewlan, a real snob, but I'll always be grateful to her for that moment.

I walked through a heavy wooden door into the calm office. There were piles of thick books on a solid oak rack and a moon-shaped teakwood desk littered with papers. Mrs. Kelly was dressed in a pleated blue suit and watched me steadily as I entered the room. I couldn't stop her favorite phrase from entering my mind: "Newham girls are always mindful of their diction." First-term girls would be given to repeating her phrase along the corridors after assembly. It got on everyone's nerves, like tourists saying "Mind the gap" on the Central Line at Bank.

The female police officers sat facing Mrs. Kelly on two stiff high-backed chairs, with a third vacant chair to their right. When I was called in they looked at me with the same hard expressions, like two white masks. I stood still for a moment, my knees

weakening and then, without being asked, I sat in the
hoping Mrs. Kelly wouldn't notice my blue for black

Mrs. Kelly was a redhead with a pale freckled face.
her syllables around her tongue. I liked her—she had gi
chocolate bar once for winning a short-story competiti. The
other girls said I only won because I was from Africa.

As I sat down she uncrossed her long, thick fingers, rapped
them on her desk and said, "I'll spare you any more suspense and
get straight to the point. There has been an accident. Your brother
may have been involved. You live with your brother, correct?"

"Yes, Mrs. Kelly."

"Speak up."

"Yes, Mrs. Kelly!"

"When was the last time you saw him?" asked a policewoman
with an arched left foot for a jaw.

I shrugged. I thought of the last time I had seen Ashvin, at
breakfast the day before last.

"Google keeps eighteen months' worth of search history and
sells it to the highest bidder behind our backs. When we search
the Internet we leave a trail of all our needs, all our desires," he
had said.

"You'd better lay off 'YouPorn' then," I'd said without looking
up from my bran.

"Just don't Google, smart mouth," he said.

*Don't Google . . .?*

"Was he at home last night?" The policewoman had to repeat
herself, but her tough voice did not go with her softening face.

"No," I said.

The three women looked at each other and each gave a tiny
nod.

What? I thought and Mrs. Kelly must have read my mind.

"These police officers would like you to identify a body," said
Mrs. Kelly gently.

She paused for my reaction. I gave none. Instead, I feigned a
cough and made a weak show of covering the expelled air from
my mouth with both hands.

"The welfare officer, Miss D'Suza, is off sick. I'm not sure I
approve of you going alone. You're not under arrest or anything

ıke that, so you don't have to go, you understand? You have a choice," she said. "But it may be for the best if you do."

"Yes, Mrs. Kelly!"


Green. Amber. Red. We left my school at eleven in the morning as it started to rain. I was feeling dazed in the back seat of the Ford Fiesta police car with a bright orange stripe driving through the world to Whipps Cross hospital. All the houses we passed were two-story terraces with nothing really to set them apart. The streets were teeming with people weaving, playing chase, criss-crossing paths. I opened the window but the drone of car engines was overwhelming. I looked up at the sky. It was rat gray. I tried to ignore people peering in at me but there was this one old couple—they looked like Mr. and Mrs. Bennet from that Jane Austen book—who pulled up in a new Volvo the color of an avocado and they were looking at me, talking about me in my face like I was a monkey or like they'd already made up their minds. I stared them down. The way they looked at me was so English, so imperial. I wanted to stick my middle finger up at them and poke out my tongue but the light changed and vroom, they were gone, back to their universe, back to Longbourn House.

It was at the third set of traffic lights when I noticed him. Old Larry Bloom, my guardian. He pulled up on my side in a very businesslike silver Jaguar. He kept his eyes facing forward so that I could see most of his gray ponytail and not much of his face. But I knew it was Bloom as soon as I saw the red of his florid skin against his silver hair. For a second, my mind eased. He wore his gray suit well with a thin club tie on a wide-collar blue shirt. Mr. Bloom had known my father. I was eight when I first met him. He looked like the typical white man in Africa from the American movies: red-faced, flash jeep, reeking of built-in authority.

Yet, over the years, things changed. Apart from my father, Mr. Bloom was the only man I trusted. It was Mr. Bloom I had called the morning after my parents were killed. He had picked us up, Ashvin and me, and after everything, arranged our flights. I remember him seeing us after we had washed the blood from our parents' bodies, the way he lowered his gun and then began to curse, unable to stem his anger, the way he walked around my parents' bodies carefully and quietly as though the realization broke slowly within him like the cold, the loving way he embraced my father. Mr. Bloom remained speechless. He just stared at the two of us for some time—I was slumped in a corner not having seen, until then, the amount of blood I had on my dress. Ashvin sat in an old plastic chair by the window. Mr. Bloom was the reason we were fast-tracked into Great Britain. Red. Amber. Green. It was only as I watched the plume of smoke and the drips of fuel that fell onto the asphalt from the corroded exhaust of Mr. Bloom's car that I knew Ashvin was really dead.

There were police outside the mortuary. Death stained the walls of the building like rust clutching at iron. They led me down a narrow flight of stairs to a drab, tile-clad room that felt like it was directly underneath the entrance. The small, gray room was a place outside the rush of time. The two long windows had been darkened and gave me the uncomfortable feeling that I was being watched. There was a strong smell of sulphur. I turned and noticed a third basement window with a roller blind that was half closed so it looked like a giant eyelid. There was a crisp white sheet half covering a body on a metal slab. All the majesty of life gone.

"Take your time," said one of the policewomen.

I felt a dull thud in my head as I searched for the desert orange of my brother's eyes but the eyes of the corpse were closed. It looked as though his upper lip had been bitten off. The neck was ravaged pulp. I looked at the face and I thought if I looked for too long anything could become familiar. I froze when I saw his navel. His had not been cut right, my brother's, it had swelled to the size of a tangerine, tumorlike. It was him.

His forehead was lined with creases. He had large bags under his eyes. It was hard to believe he was still just a boy. My sixteen-year-old brother.

His skin was pallid, his face swollen. It carried no expression save for a quiet snarl that did not belong to him; his arms looked flabby. There was a track of outraged flesh and coagulated blood around his throat and lacerations on his face where he must have scratched himself involuntarily. I felt my insides coil and reverse on themselves. I looked from the body to the police out of the corner of my eye and I thought of our father. I had asked him once why he didn't call his friend Mr. Bloom by his first name. He looked at me as though I should have known. "Because he is a white man, and despite what they say, they like us to remember our difference. You will do well to remember this, daughter," my father said.

"Well, miss?" asked the officer with the boyish haircut who hadn't spoken to me up until then.

"Well, what?" I said without removing my eyes from Ashvin. I wondered why it was that in Somalia people did not have surnames in the Western sense. To identify a Somali, three names must be used: a given name followed by the father's given name and the grandfather's. Women don't change their names at marriage. Nearly all men and some women in Somalia are identified by a public name, *naanays*. There are two kinds of *naanays*: overt nicknames, similar to Western nicknames, and covert nicknames, which are used to talk about a person but rarely used to address that person. I remembered my father called us fireflies on account of our eyes. And then I heard my father telling us that he loved us more than his own life. And then I wondered if coming to London had been worthwhile, if there was ever such a thing as escape. Since life is ultimately what you carry around in your heart.

"Well, is it him or not?" She pointed her chin at me.

I could do that.

I had first noticed something strange happening to my brother a few months earlier. He would get very happy and then, mid-sentence, become irritable and start talking too fast, too much. He began coming home to our flat to shower and change clothes only when he knew I would be at school. He hardly ever slept. Some nights, I would listen outside his bedroom. He would be having conversations with himself, as though he were two people. At first, I would knock and go in but then he stopped letting me. When he wasn't around I would sneak in and try to work out what he saw in all the newspaper clippings he kept. He would circle words like "Pope," "UN," "asylum," "oil" and "Ethiopia" always, always in red. And he kept a list under his bed with all the names of leaders of African countries and he put numbers next to them, numbers that made no sense, like Y2B8 or Zd29. We didn't speak about what he did in his room or about the bits and pieces of conversation I heard him having alone. But his gloom had come between us; it settled in our flat uninvited like a squatter. There were many things I had no idea about. At first I asked him questions but finally I gave up. I missed the days when Ashvin thought he was my protector, when he talked to me about everything as though he understood.

"Miss?" asked the policewoman.

I nodded my head but fought off my tears.

I began to wish I were dressed native, in black with a golden headtie. I didn't feel right somehow, dressed in a school blazer and a tie. The officer who had sat with me in the back of the police car looked at me soberly, inspecting my face.

"I'm very sorry," she said softly. With pursed lips she handed me a shopping bag full of belongings I barely recognized. When I extended my hand to take the bag I felt my fingers going dead from cold. The other policewoman, the driver, seemed happy with my discomfort.

"Were you aware of your brother's medical condition?" she said.

I nodded.

Then she opened a large Manila envelope with her knuckle. "Do you know this man?" She pulled out a black-and-white photograph. I looked at it for some time.

"Course I know him," I said. "He's that dead Ethiopian guy in all the papers."

She sighed. "Apart from what you have seen in the papers, have you seen him before?"

"No."

"Well, we took a few fluid samples when we examined the body, before we established who he was. Some interesting revelations have come up."

I turned back to look at Ashvin.

"Your brother is now a prime suspect in a murder inquiry."

I took a deep breath, looked up at her and I laughed.

"Glad you find that funny," she said.

"But he's dead," I said, tears blurring my sight.

"DNA doesn't lie."

"What does that mean?"

"Was your brother involved in a gang? We believe these deaths may be the connected result of gang-related violence."

"A gang? My brother was not in a gang."

"Secrecy is a big part of gang culture," she said philosophically.

"I don't want to answer any questions right now. Where I come from we give relatives time to honor their dead."

"As I understand it, you came here to escape where you come from." She said it as though she had known about me for a long time. I looked down at my feet and remained silent, suddenly feeling a hot wave of shame. I wanted to explain that I had no choice in coming to Britain. That term, *political asylum*, stole my bearings. I suddenly missed my parents, my friends. But inside I knew the policewoman was right. I should be grateful. I felt the resentment the policewoman saw when she looked at me.

"I am a human being," I said, or something just as daft.

Much later, I felt angry and wished I had punched that policewoman, but in that moment I realized, instinctively, what my brother had done and I hated him for being weak, for leaving me alone. Then I remembered the words to the old Somali song we sang whenever there was a death. My aunt sang it on top of a steep hill at the burial of my parents. That was when I tore open my school shirt and wailed.

I couldn't go back to school. The policewomen dropped me off at our estate. The one-pound shop was overflowing with people, the chicken restaurant was closed but the smell hadn't wandered very far, it blotted out the smell of freshly cut grass from the park. I stopped off at Mr. Khan's and bought a loaf of bread and a newspaper. I took a long soak in a hot bath and read the celebrity news. I wrapped my hair in a towel and after I dried myself, I fell into the sofa where I curled up with an arm propping my head and watched the dust beams of sunlight coming through the windows.

I remembered the first day we arrived at our flat, dressed in our church clothes. The first day of a new life. The sun was out, several children were playing freely without fear on the streets. In those first weeks we hardly left the flat, fascinated and contented as we were with the TV, radio and the new Ikea furniture supplied by Mr. Bloom. But you know, thinking about it, I realized how much I hated watching the news on television. The way it brought so much agony into our living room, so much of what I tried to forget.

I ate a bowl of 25p ramen noodles, the sort that you add boiling water and red dust to, astronaut food that never disappointed. I loved the meat and rubber smell and the wild-thyme taste of steaming hot noodles. When I had finished eating, I closed my eyes and tried to sleep. I couldn't. A phone was ringing somewhere deep in my mind. When I answered, I heard the loving voices of my mother and my father. They were together and they were happy. I slammed the phone down but couldn't rid myself of the sound of their soft voices floating out from the dark. And then I saw their beaming faces surrounded by love and filled with the joy of our past lives. I used all my strength to push them out of my head, to block out their images. But there was this one that got through.

Once, when I was small, the police burst into our house on a Sunday and took my father away because of something they accused him of saying against the government in an article he had written for a local journal. Enforced disappearances were widespread and systematic. Armed men would block roads, search towns and raid homes in the middle of the night. He was missing for a week. It was one of the few times my mother took to embroidering and she also canceled her Friday-night salon. I remembered listening to her calling her friends, the artists and poets who filled our house with cigarette smoke and grand hand gestures. In the background of their meetings there was always gunfire, sometimes intense, but they would continue to talk, as if to say everything was normal, under control. I remember her eyes seeking bad news. She told her friends she felt "lifeless." I couldn't understand this expression "lifeless" at the time. She agreed to move their planned discussion to the following month. Every day while he was missing my mother would burn charcoal and herbs inside a *haan* and she would shake it around the house; white puffs of smoke oozed out and sailed behind her with her prayers along our faded walls and a heavenly smell would spread. Every day my mother would send Ashvin to buy the *Shabelle Times*, the local newspaper that published the names of the men wounded or found dead. But mostly we found out what was happening by listening to the radio. We would huddle together listening to the voice of Muhad Ahmed Elmi on *HornAfrik* while people cried and prayed.

Boys were generally banned from listening to the radio by their mothers because once they understood what was happening they would want to join their fathers, brothers or cousins and go to war. There were never enough men in families to protect the women and to do the work that needed to be done. Boys and men would return crippled or blind, some of them with missing limbs—but at least they were alive. When my father came home his hair was dirty and messy, he was bruised and skinny and his eyes were splashed red. But when he saw us all together he smiled, white teeth on smooth chocolate skin. Despite looking haggard he was still very handsome and my mother laughed even as she wept. I remember watching her tears splash onto her black muslin dress and when I touched her eyes the water that came from them was hot.

"How can you cry when you are happy?" I was young and confused.

"Because they are tears for love, they are tears to make you better."

My mother squeezed my face between her palms and we all tucked ourselves under my father's open arms as if we were one body and he winced and laughed at the same time, never taking his eyes from my mother's. I felt safe in my father's arms. He was like a big Higlo tree with long roots and leaves that always remained green. He didn't speak much but the little he said kept me busy. Neighbors would frequent our house: "What should I do about this or that?" My father was very practical, he told the truth no matter what because, he said, it was all he had.

That day when he came back to us we ate warm bread together just before sunset in our small living room that overlooked Damal trees in the highlands under the Karkaar Mountains where the grass grew tall. By then, the ICU had declared jihad on Ethiopian troops who were crossing into Somalia. The Ethiopians, recipients of US military aid, invaded Mogadishu and installed a new Somali interim government with Abdullahi Yusuf as president. All the ICU soldiers regrouped to Ras Kamboni, the oldest al-Qaeda training camp in Africa. But, every day, the Somali insurgents— mostly frightened, vengeful young men and homesick boys— fought with the installed Transitional Federal Government for control of Mogadishu.

Many of the roads were blocked with families fleeing. Our part of the city was relatively calm but the streets were empty during the day, only a handful of people could be seen and the market, which used to be the biggest in East Africa, did not function because of the assassinations linked to robbery. People were scared. Who would risk their life for the sake of a few vegetables? It felt strange to be in London so far from home, to be all alone. I remembered the muffled sound of the shelling and I thought of crowds scattering like birds and of bullets penetrating soft skin.

The memory of my father returning home stopped playing in my head but the sound of gunfire went on and on, haunting me. I had lived with the sound for so long it had become bearable. All you could do was hope for silence, for still air. It all seemed like such a long time ago, long before moving to live with my crazy aunt and the six husbands who touched me at night.

An ice-cream van arrived in the neighborhood. I could not place the name of the nursery rhyme; it was way out of tune. I stood for some time naked in front of the mirror. Spots had erupted on my forehead. I wiped the moisture from between my breasts. In the possessive silence I felt a longing for someone to hold me. I was still for a while, staring at the hair between my legs as a ball of heat began to rise. I thought of Shirley, from my school, the way she spoke about having a Brazilian once a week, how smooth she said it was. I scraped the last of the noodles from the black bowl. And then decided to shave my pubic hair. As I spread shea butter delicately over myself I laughed when I thought of Shirley going on about her Brazilian during class. It is standard practice for a Muslim woman to remove all her body hair, especially just before marriage, we just don't ever talk about it.

I felt empty, my mouth dry. The overwhelming need for release was overtaken by images of my brother that came flashing one after the other. In the quietness of the room I felt something strange; not an idea, a notion. A warm sensation spread over me and I smiled. All of a sudden I became very clear about what I was feeling. I decided right then that I wanted a baby.

I couldn't bear to be on my own. It was okay being home alone when I knew Ashvin was coming back, but now it felt different. It was almost two o'clock when I left the flat. I wanted to be seen. I dressed, opened my front door and stepped outside just as a white lady and her daughter walked by.

I let them pass and then I walked slowly up the road as the wind blew leaves and sweetie wrappers around my legs. I passed a mother a few doors down sitting on a chair on her doorstep plaiting her daughter's hair. The smell of singed hair from a burning-hot comb came out of the house along with Gladys Knight's voice. I smiled at the little girl's stubborn expression. She was dressed for a party and had a pink towel wrapped tightly around her neck. Half of the child's head was already done in tiny neat rows while the other half, undone, looked like a cloud of brown candyfloss. I remembered leaning my head against my mother's thighs, one arm raised, holding a tub of Dax while she plaited my hair. I have always suffered from a dry scalp and my mother would use the sharp edge of her comb to scratch the dry flakes out of my hair and then she would rub aloe vera and Dax between the lines of my thick plaits. It only hurt a little but I would act like I was having a heart attack. "Who is my beautiful little girl?" she'd ask tickling me with her knuckles until I said my name. That was our "doing my hair" game. I still used Dax in my hair after all these years. I shook my head and inhaled to try to catch the smell of my hair grease but my nose filled with the smell of my deodorant and of the yellow fabric softener I used on my clothes.

I walked past a group of boys who were always hanging around on the estate. They were dressed in denim with shiny belts and gleaming trainers and hats worn at many different angles.

I recognized Jimi Hamilton who had once driven a stolen car through my neighbor Helen's living room. She was a supply teacher who Jimi held responsible for getting him excluded. What was funny about the incident was that Jimi didn't run. He stayed because he said he *needed* to get arrested. When the police eventually arrived, he told them straight. "Here what," he said to the officers, removing his hood, "I'm gonna do it again because she ruined my career, blood."

Helen walked around visibly shaking for a week. She was only twenty-two. She told Crimestoppers she was having a crisis of conscience and one day, about a week after the incident, she was gone, traded her one-bed for a two-bed in East Ham.

Those boys. Always standing in the same spot. Sometimes at night I watched them out of my bedroom window. I have been doing my own private psychological study of them and I still can't work out what it is they do on their corner. I call it the poverty effect and they have immersed themselves. They don't sell drugs or fight. They just stand there talking real fast into pretend microphones. Maybe being bums is the best thing for it. Perhaps that is what happens when adults screw each other indiscriminately. At some stage, everyone becomes part of each other and then we just all hang out. Get along like a faded Benetton ad or the Jolie-Pitts. I tried to think what my brother would have been like if he had not been up to his neck in the turmoil of current events. And then I thought of what I would have given in that moment to see my brother on the corner with those other boys just shooting the breeze.

I wore a white blouse. It was covered with blue fluff from my wool jumper. For the first time, I did not cross the road. I walked straight through the group of boys but inside I was shaking. Two of the Staffordshire terriers wore hoodies; one of the boys wore all black except for his white trainers. He looked like a tall upside-down glass of Guinness.

"Yo, sis. Wha' you saying?" he said and then he pushed another boy in the back and they laughed. It was a soft and polite voice but how was I supposed to reply?

The boy who had been pushed approached me, bouncing as he stepped, his chest puffed out like a pigeon's. He was a sandy-colored boy with bright eyes and a round face. He wore a T-shirt that said "Dreams of fuckin' an R&B Bitch, Badboy Inc." He looked at me like a lizard might look at a small, meaty rat. Once he was away from his friends all he said was "Hi." I hardly heard him and kept my eyes fixed on the weeds growing in the cracks in the pavement and did not open my mouth. I felt him looking at my tits slowly and exactingly. I looked up at him when I felt my nipples harden and his cheeks flushed. He walked away with his head bent, so that I could see the raised bumps of his spine.

None of the boys were particularly handsome and all of them looked like they spent too much time in front of the mirror for my taste. They would never know—nobody would—but I would have fucked any one of that group that day if only one of them had said a kind word. I would have invited him home and given him sweet kisses on his mouth and let him touch my beautiful places and I would have given him what my husbands always took by force. I would have held him and told him how handsome he was and how strong and I would have made him feel golden sparks, if only for a little while.

I stared at the group. They reminded me of the teenage boys—a mixture of Islamist fighters and militiamen from the Hawiye clan—at home who, in protest over the presence of Ethiopian troops, blocked the roads with trees and threw stones and rocks at the armored trucks. Ultimately, the boys offered no resistance. Mostly, they were like a great blot of incompleteness, shadows merging together to speak about dreams and girls in some poor attempt to supplement a meager existence. As I passed, I began to feel differently about the boys standing around. I began to think that maybe they huddled together to keep hold of their dreams. I thought of all the hidden emotions of boys. Maybe they were right to disengage from the world.

When I was at home I would visibly shake around men, any man who so much as looked at me. When I arrived in London I thought the world would change, that men would be different. I was wrong. I guess men are the same wherever you go, like mosquitoes always ready to suck blood from any available vein.

# THREE

# MEINA

I GUESS I SHOULD say how Ashvin met James. They were in the same class, 4T, but they didn't even notice one another to begin with. Ashvin had started the term late on account of our visa restrictions. The teacher, Miss Raisa Bukolov from Gomel, decided to stand him in front of the class to give him a proper introduction, one of those ruinous decisions that teachers are remembered and hated for. With a flicker of amusement she mispronounced his name and sent him off to his seat. There was a pause as the boys in the class stopped talking among themselves. Their adolescent interest nudged, a rare and complete stillness took hold of class 4T. And then they started to laugh.

Ashvin lifted his chin, trying his best not to make a sound as he crossed the room to a seat at the back, in the darkness. He slumped into his chair, pulling at a thread on the frayed edge of one of the holes in his orange jumper, thinking about how popular he had been at home; how the teacher would always hand him the cutlass and ask him to lead the boys out to cut the thick grass that grew in front of the school where he used to play while he waited for our father to finish his lectures and collect him. Strange that, the way happiness only works in retrospect.

Class 4T was a different case altogether. They teased my brother relentlessly from then on. James, who was in class that day, heard the laughter but did not notice what had taken place, such was the distance between him and the rest of the boys.

At that time Ashvin owned one pair of trousers—it took a while for his size to come in at the shop that sold his school uniform. At home—I mean in Somalia where even those of us with private cars were poor—it wouldn't have mattered. In our

27

village, girls sweated in the same frilly dresses for months at a time and boys were grateful for whatever they were handed down. But it was different here in London. For boys, anyway.

I went to a sixth-form college. I was in all the top groups, even mathematics, which I found odd since I had never been considered anywhere near brilliant at home. I fitted right in with the popular girls because of my waist-length hair. The thought of me fitting in with all those eighteen-year-old Caribbean girls just because of the length of my hair makes me shudder, but at Ashvin's school, it seemed his clothes were the only thing about him considered of any importance. Initially, they teased him because he always wore the same orange jumper and baggy blue corduroys. When he started wearing his school uniform they jeered because the waist on his trousers was considered too tight. Then slowly they moved on from his trousers to his "no name" trainers. Then they laughed at the way he walked, the way his voice differed from theirs. After weeks of almost constant teasing, Ashvin despised them all.

In Somalia, Ashvin loved to go to school, he really did. Forest Gate Community School for Boys changed all of that for good. He told me once that he spent hours locked in the toilets, stitching up holes in his trousers with green thread and trying to readjust his belt. He said the kids always laughed at him, but only in packs. James thought they were afraid of Ashvin really. He told me there was something frightening about the flicker in my brother's narrow orange eyes.

The first time the two of them took any notice of each other was 18 March of this year as James walked home from school. How would they know where it would lead? James had felt guilty about doing nothing about the gang of boys—the "Scare Dem Crew"—who that day teased Ashvin all the way to Hoe Street, near Walthamstow Central tube station. "Paki liar, Paki liar." Their taunts were uninspired.

James stood and watched as the bullies began throwing things: stones and bottles lying around at first but then fists and kicks started to fly. When I asked James about it he said he could tell Ashvin was furious about the bullies' taunts, but on the outside he remained strangely calm.

28

"I'm not a Paki. I'm not lying. I *was* born in Africa," said Ashvin. Then he swung a fist and landed a decent punch that changed everything. It made James think differently about Ashvin, made him think he was brave. It made him want to be his friend. He watched one boy, thick and tall, who was caught on the nose by Ashvin's wild punch, pull a gun, a Baikal, and put it to my brother's head.

"Hit me? I'll kill you," said the boy through clenched teeth.

"Shoot me. Go on, do it," Ashvin said and then he laughed.

He had seen war. It was the reason we were here.

The boy cocked the gun but he did not shoot. He froze for a long moment as though waiting for the voice of God, and then in the prickly silence he smashed the butt of the gun across the bridge of Ashvin's nose. Ashvin hit the ground, curled into a ball and soaked up more hammer-blows. But he was still laughing. My brother could be very stubborn.

James remained hidden until the beating stopped and then he watched the boys run toward the tube station shouting obscenities as they fled. When Ashvin was sure he was alone, he made a solemn effort to prop himself against a wall, taking slow breaths in the rain. His eyes gleamed as he wiped himself down.

From his hiding place behind dustbins, James watched Ashvin as the rain abated, feeling pity and something else that he couldn't quite describe until much later.

As time slowed, the only sound came from gentle rainwater filling street drains. James watched Ashvin until the street lights awakened and the brightening moon cast a hideous glow over the East End. He said he felt ashamed. When I pushed for more detail, James said he would have cried but he remembered staring directly into Ashvin's eyes looking for tears, and they only glistened in triumph.

Ashvin made for a lonely sight. Blood seeped from the split on the bridge of his nose and yet he sat very still, staring at a pigeon. Every now and then he would shiver because of a sudden icy breeze. It was like watching a scene from a poem. "I will never forget the look on Ashvin's face," he said, "the way he hunched his trembling shoulders and glared across at the traffic, the tower blocks, the run-down council houses and the unkempt front gardens."

I loved my brother dearly. Thinking about him now invites only pain. He had a brilliant mind and I imagine what kind of life he could have had, the wife he would have chosen, about his kids. Ashvin was slightly built and had a serene face, smooth cheeks with cinnamon skin. I clearly remember the day those boys put a gun to his head—the thoughtful look on his face when he returned home. His orange jumper was covered in dirt and his curly black hair full of dust and dried blood.

"Where have you been?" I asked him.

"I made a friend," was all he said. And he smiled.

When James came out from hiding, Ashvin had walked briskly in his direction, shadow-boxing while holding his belt and mumbling in his raspy voice.

"*Suffer, poor Negro, the whip whistles, whistles in sweat and blood.*" He often recited random lines of poetry, my brother. His delivery was serious and natural. He wasn't showing off, just practicing, he would always say. At school in Somalia we learned to recite poetry and Langston Hughes was one of my brother's favorites.

"What?" James asked him when he emerged from behind the hedge. "What did you just say?"

"*Suffer, poor Negro, the whip whistles, whistles in sweat and blood,*" said Ashvin.

The only poet James knew by heart was Lil' Kim.

"Suffer, poor Negro? Who's that?" asked James.

"That's Langston Hughes," said Ashvin.

"Langston who? Old or new school?"

Ashvin smiled as he squinted his eyes at James incredulously and pulled his lips in a grimace. His teeth were stained red; he had a gash above his right eye and the split on his nose widened. He looked up at the brownish sky.

"It's started again. It's not going to stop," he said.

James turned his face upward and flinched as he was pelted with cold rain.

Ashvin continued shadow-boxing on his way. "*Suffer, poor Negro.*"

Intrigued, James followed.

James knew Ashvin lived on the Lumumba estate that was just

behind his. They took the long way, past Stratford cinema. There was a long queue and people, adults, saw Ashvin's blood and beat-up face but no one met his eyes. Stratford Picturehouse was showing *The Queen*. Ashvin held up two of his fingers and spat blood loudly when he looked up at the poster of Helen Mirren as Her Majesty. James, smiling, spat too.

They did not speak much to begin with. They walked steadily, coming to terms with each other's presence.

"Why didn't you run home?" James asked.

"What? So they can know where I live?" Ashvin said.

"Look," said James thoughtfully, "I've watched you in class and wondered why you don't just change your trousers, get some new shoes?"

"I have got new trousers. My sponsor bought me expensive jeans, same as everybody wears, with the red sign on the back pocket. He bought me trainers, too, Air Force 1s," said Ashvin.

"Good for you. So why not wear them?"

"Why should I?" asked Ashvin as he spat a fresh glob of blood. "I don't want to be friends with you people."

"You people? Don't lump me in with everybody else. I hate it when people do that. I'm different."

Ashvin lowered his eyes to James's feet, threw a hateful gaze at his footwear.

"What?" asked James. "I like Air Force 1s. It don't make me the same as everyone else. Seems to me you want to fight with everyone."

"Beats following the crowd," said Ashvin.

"Trying to be different is like vanity, no?" asked James.

"Makes me feel free."

They were both quiet for a while as James watched Ashvin walking clumsily, wincing now and again as he struggled not to put weight on his left leg. James put his arm around Ashvin's shoulder to support him across Leytonstone High Road.

"What's your star sign?" Ashvin asked, catching his breath.

"Gemini."

"My mum's a Gemini."

They talked all the way to the corner of York Road where they had to split up to get home. But they didn't part. They stood and carried on talking. Ashvin had an air of authority that appealed to James. They talked about unsettling things, of war and of charcoal and diamonds. Ashvin spoke of artists whose music our father knew by heart. Nina Simone and Fela Kuti. Ash said their music "set him free." He told James about writers he loved, Zora Neale Hurston and Aimé Césaire. Mostly, James listened, absorbing new things with unusual intensity.

They had eight pounds cash between them and at about nine o'clock they decided against going home, preferring to share a meal. It was beautiful and fatal—their immediate friendship was innocent, but they were tormented boys with troubled hearts. They shouldn't have been brought together. Not then.

Together, they were emboldened by thoughts they discovered they held in common. I have often wondered how different things could have been if they had been two teenage black girls blessed with peace and the hope of most women. Perhaps two girls would have accepted who they were instead of complaining about life and the things they couldn't change. Instead, like two old philosophers, Ashvin and James spoke of the ruin of their lives, their unfulfilled needs, their unanswered prayers and ultimately—over pizza topped with black olives, green peppers and sweetcorn—they were seduced by the phantom call to death by suicide: its science, its poetry, its violence, its art.


Forest Gate Pizza Hut had recently been made over. It smelled pleasantly of baking dough and was full of bright colors and angles like a snakes-and-ladders board. The restaurant was very busy for 9:15 on a week night. A tattooed waitress with hair plastered to her forehead made a "you're so lame" face when James used his Sean Connery voice and asked for his usual table. But the two boys bent over with laughter. They followed her to a middle booth between a Polish couple looking ill at ease and an elderly black man wearing a London Underground uniform who looked as though he had been born with a frown, and sat reading a tabloid while he ate.

Directly opposite Ashvin and James were another two booths. A teenage couple huddled together in one. The boy wore a cool pair of sneakers with three fluorescent stripes. While his girlfriend ate garlic bread and cheese noisily, he masturbated his laces. Two women in their midforties with thick braids and thicker Bajan voices sat in the other booth. Every now and then someone would shuffle past the boys' table, different people, wearing a loud scent or using a mobile phone. At one point during their dinner, their waitress, a delicate Eritrean girl who James had been eyeing, interrupted to hand them both crayons. That had them both in stitches.

They spoke intimately that night. I don't know all the exact details but I can just imagine how the conversation went:

"Do you think it can get better?"

"Not for the likes of me and you."

"What about religion? Do you have any faith in God?"

My brother would have laughed. "The night they killed my parents," he would have said, "while I hid under the stairs, I called to Allah and then to Muhammad and then to the God of Abraham, to Jesus Christ. I asked them to save my mother. She was old school. She'd been religious her whole life, fasting and praying, genuinely devout. She never put a foot wrong. But while she suffered, God and all His prophets remained silent."

"What is all the fighting about in your country?" asked James.

"I asked my dad about this once. He said it began with the collapse of the Ottomans, the last Islamic empire. The Europeans met in Berlin in the 1800s and carved Somalia into slices like pizza. Some slices went to Italy, others to Britain and France. Menelik II, Emperor of Ethiopia, was also a Christian, and he begged his fellow Christians, saying that his country was a Christian island in an Islamic ocean. And so Ethiopia was also given a slice of Somali pizza—Ogaden. This territory has remained the cause of much of our fight with Ethiopia."

"I didn't understand a word of that," said James and Ashvin would have almost spat out his pizza when he laughed.

"My father sold drugs. He used them, too," James told him. "In the end he was shot by men he thought were his friends. Two years ago, my eldest brother returned from prison with years of his memory erased." James held his head in his hands and his voice became tense. "I saw my dad in hospital the night he got shot. He said he was going to be all right. He promised. I was only young. You might think he was bad because he sold drugs but he wasn't. He tried to go straight. The night before my dad died my brother made me kneel down while he prayed. I'd never prayed before, not really. I always felt stupid talking to myself in the dark but not that night. My brother said some words that I thought would make everything all right. Of course, it didn't. My father died. God didn't even answer my one simple prayer. I never pray, not now. I don't ask for anything: happiness, beauty, love, power, order, money, all the world's possibilities aren't worth the sorrow and suffering it seems you have to give in return. Things keep getting worse."

James told me he hadn't spoken so openly to anyone else before. Not someone who understood.

After that they seemed to spend all their time together, sitting in Internet cafes, going to the movies, enjoying bus rides, roaming Oxford Street and sitting in the park. Yet I often think back to James and my brother together in that Pizza Hut in Forest Gate.

James had five brothers. He said he didn't want to be like them, amoral men whose exploits normal people read about in the *Evening Standard* on the Tube on their way home from work.

While they ate Ashvin remarked on the features of their wait-ress: She was tall with honey-brown eyes. He called her over and James asked for her phone number and email address. She laughed and gave the two boys another set of crayons and a sheet each of plain paper. "I don't date black men," she said.

"But you're African, I can hear it in your voice," said James.

"That's why I don't date black men."

They didn't understand the girl, but I would have given her a high-five. James took the crayons and paper and drew a picture of a satsuma with two green leaves still attached to the top and my brother wrote "Death is Art" in red and they both laughed more than they should. The man in the London Underground uniform peeked over the booth. He kissed his teeth loudly when he saw the picture. He got to his feet cautiously and tucked his crumpled blue shirt into shabby black trousers. He smoothed the rough fabric on his coat resolutely, all the while watching them with disgust. Then he held up his newspaper and offered it to James and Ashvin.

"Lickle shits," he said.

"Excuse me?" asked James.

"You think you want to die. You aren't even ready to shave. Lickle shits, get a fucking job like everybody else," said the old man in an incongruously pleasant tone.

"What, so we can end up like you?" said James. "Eating stuffed-crust pizza all alone on a Monday night?"

The old man slammed a meaty fist on their table, spilling a glass of orange juice and sending a fork clattering to the floor and causing heads to turn. The restaurant quietened as he waved the newspaper at them.

"I got sons older than you. If you were my boys, I'd kick your cursed arses. Join the army if you don't got nothing to do. Get yourselves fucking jobs, you stupid black boys. You gotta work. Stop killing each other, making us all look bad. I been here forty-six years. Never been arrested, much less seen a gun. In my day we knew about hard work. What happen to y'all? Go to school and get a job like everybody else. Lickle shits."

The old man tossed the newspaper on their table. The headline was about the murder of a black boy; the article said he was in a gang.

"What the hell is y'all doing?" A neon light illuminated the sweat on his face and his eyes were wide. "I bet you can't even read."

When the waitress and her manager asked the man for calm, he pushed past them and headed toward the glass front door. He turned and pointed a finger at my brother.

"One day you'll wake up and you'll be sorry for your sins. You mark what I'm saying. Get a job, stupid lickle shits." The old man opened the door, pulling the zip on his coat. He grimaced at the stiff breeze and then left. James and Ashvin accepted the manager's gesture of free ice cream and a small discount from their bill. They were both rather embarrassed when they left.

When I think back to James and Ashvin's first encounter I worry about the inner promptings of our souls and I get confused about

35

whether we are ever in control of our own actions. Ashvin and James were reserved and private, but both full of wit. They had a deep distrust of people and they regarded themselves as outcasts.

Before that night with James, Ashvin had never spoken about the deaths of our parents. Not even with me. But he found himself speaking freely to James. He told James all about our father, who was shot dead, about our mother who was also shot after she was raped by the same armed gang.

Our parents loved each other, and our upbringing was a reflection of that love, our home a simple one. My mother had grown up in Scandinavia, where her father had fled after leaving Somalia. She had a PhD in art history and she loved to paint although she wasn't very good. My father would joke that he spent more money on paint than on food. What made our father stand out from his peers was the way he expressed the love he held for our mother. They met in the Royal Library in Copenhagen, studying for the same paper on English literature. My father was strong-minded and fearless and he was so handsome he was almost intimidating. He was a professor of English at Mogadishu University and regularly published essays in political journals; he was a contributing reporter for *Waayaha Press* and the only Somali stringer for the *New York Times*. His constant and unabated criticism of sharia law, warlords, corruption in big business and other general government internal policies eventually led to his death.

They whipped my father and then shot him in the legs and made him watch while they mauled my mother. Most Somali houses have only two rooms. Ashvin, hiding in our third, saw the whole thing. I was late home from school. I am slowly forgetting the events of the day my parents died, but I have a vivid memory about that night. By the time I had returned, Ashvin had put our parents' bodies beside each other and we lay silently with them until morning. We slept together as we had on many previous occasions, only that night our parents remained still. My brother wept with such lack of control it seemed almost primordial. I followed his lead but although I was older and in just as much pain, he was vastly more complex than I was. I did not really understand the magnitude of our loss. Ashvin cried long after I had fallen asleep. Anything that has hurt me since has only been an echo of what I felt on that night. As for Ashvin, I believe his soul left along with theirs at dawn.

As Ashvin and James walked home after their pizza they met a man dressed in a faded black *djellaba* that reached the ground, carrying business cards he normally handed out in Stratford mall. He approached them, gave them each a card.

Sheikh Ali, spiritual healer
Wash away your troubles
Solve any problem
At work, relationships, money, exams
Call 24 hours
07988 885902

"You are troubled. The spirits trouble you both. Come and see me tomorrow. I can help you."

The man rolled his r's. His teeth were brown, his lips thin and he smelled of incense.

"Help with what?" asked Ashvin.

"You are troubled. Troubled," said the man. His tone was grave.

"I know who you are. We don't have any money for you. Now fuck off," said James.

The man laughed defiantly. "Take my card. Be sure to come and see me tomorrow."

"We're all right, thanks," said James.

"Not all right," the man said, shaking his head as he blocked their path. "I can help you. Free of charge. Free of charge."

Both the boys became suspicious.

"Are you a griot?" asked Ashvin.

The man looked weighted by what was on his mind. "Why are you so afraid?" he asked. "The two of you are strained by life. Why are you so afraid of life? You need my urgent help."

The man turned. "Come and see me," he said. "Tomorrow at three," and walked briskly across the street in the opposite direction into an alley between a brick house and a playground.

It was almost midnight. James and Ashvin walked home in the dark.

"So listen," said Ashvin, "shall we go together?"

37

"Go where?" asked James.

"To the other side."

They turned and looked at each other, searching for any crack of humor.

Then, there was a screech behind them and they both froze as an unmarked car with a blue flashing light stopped directly in front of them.

"Stop. Police."

Instinctively, my brother raised his hand in the air. James did the same.

Two uniformed policemen wrapped tightly in bulletproof vests got out of the car.

"Put your arms down and step toward me, lads." The officer walked backward into the alley where the market traders locked up their stalls at night.

"What do you want?" asked James.

"Step over here, I said." The officer had a wide forehead and close-cropped hair. He didn't look like he should be messed with. "We've had reports of a street robbery in the area. You two fellas fit the description, so I'm going to have to search you guys, okay? If you have any drugs on you, it's best to let me know now, lads. You won't get nicked if you've just got a little bit of weed."

Once the boys had entered the small dark alley, the two officers stepped closer. "What are your names?" one said as he held Ashvin's wrists firmly.

"Ashvin."

"James."

"Nice names," said the other officer with a mocking sneer.

"Where are you from?" asked the officer who had gripped James's wrists. He was a heavy, mean-looking man with pasty skin.

"London. You're hurting me," said James.

"Could you spell your surnames for me, please?"

They did.

It was pitch black. At that point, Ashvin and James were only a few steps apart with their backs to the officers and their hands against the cold metal shutters of the lock-ups. They were growing suspicious but didn't dare say anything.

The first officer spoke up. "Any drugs? Last chance."

"No dlugs," said Ashvin. His accent was always thicker when he was afraid.

"No drugs," said James.

"No drugs, eh? What do we have here then, the last of the Lord's black disciples?"

The other officer laughed. "Let's have a look, shall we, lads? Spread your legs."

While their hands were still against the shutters, the officer searched the boys' pockets, pulling out the lining.

"Have you been fighting?" the first officer asked as he went through Ashvin's back pocket.

"I fell over playing football after school."

Ashvin tried to tug at the waist of his trousers, pulling them up but the officer yanked them down and then pressed a thick hand against his throat. Ashvin squirmed as he felt a thick finger poking at his anus.

"Hold still," said the officer.

"I wasn't fighting. I fell over," Ashvin protested.

"Yeah and my girlfriend, Kate Moss, gives great head and she swallows."

"Where you coming from?" The other officer patted James down. He put a hand in James's front trouser pocket and tugged at his penis and felt the weight of his balls.

"Pizza Hut," said James, trying his best to struggle free.

"Pizza Hut, eh? What did you fellas eat?"

"What you doin'? Get your hands off me," said James. He tried to pull away but the officer held him by his throat and squeezed his windpipe until he was still.

"You're blushing. I didn't know you blacks could blush," the officer leered.

"What did you eat?" demanded the officer with his finger in Ashvin's arse. He removed his finger and then spat on his hand loudly and slid his finger further inside Ashvin. Ashvin winced and then let out a low moan.

"I said, what did you eat? Don't make me repeat myself."

Ashvin's eyes widened and he snorted. "It's none of your business."

"A pizza," screamed James when he thought his windpipe was about to crack.

"What type of pizza, sparky? Tell me all about it," said the officer, still milking James.

"It was a deep-pan with double cheese, olives and green peppers."

The officer closed his eyes momentarily. His voice started to falter. "What . . . c-color were the . . . olives?" He held James's dick tightly and rubbed faster until it grew hard.

James moaned. "Black. The olives were black."

"Very romantic. So, if we were to take a little stroll back to the Pizza Hut the manager would be able to verify your story, would he?"

The boys shrugged. Their attempts to wrestle free were useless.

"Where are we going this time of night?" asked the officer now draped around Ashvin's waist slowly stroking his dick as he moved his finger in and out of his arse.

"Home," said Ashvin grimacing, sickened at his body's response.

"That's good. Go ahead and come, don't be embarrassed," whispered the officer, his breath hot against Ashvin's neck. He began mumbling, his strokes became faster and harder.

"Where is home?"

"I live on the Lumumba estate," Ashvin stammered.

The officer gripped Ashvin's shoulder with his right hand and continued, unperturbed, pulling on his dick until it became slick, almost oily.

"What about your friend," he said.

"Mandela estate." James's heartbeat raced and he was ashamed to find he was crying.

He watched as Ashvin rocked slightly from the balls of his feet to his toes. When Ashvin came in the grip of the policeman's fingers his anguished moan made James's skin crawl. James's officer looked him in the eye as his wrist became frantic, rising and falling, his face red and mottled. James tried to shield his eyes but the officer told him to keep his arms down. Instead he looked to the top of the buildings. Against the night sky he could see the admin offices of the Department of Social Security, DSS in big black letters: a six-story boxy building, a looming black monster with bright yellow trimmings along the large plate-glass window that reflected the glow from the moon.

James, who had been refusing to acknowledge what was happening to him, gasped. His thighs began to jerk, his pulse throbbed and he erupted.

"You fucking bastards," he sobbed, without much conviction. He fell to the ground, his back heaving as he sobbed, but he pulled himself together when he saw Ash, his face set in a glare, adjusting the buckle on his belt. The silence was broken by a loud crackle and a female voice coming from one of the officers' radios.

"No previous, sarge. They're clean."

"Well, well, well. There's a surprise. Perhaps you two really are disciples. Be sure to go straight home, ladies, and stay out of trouble."

The officers returned to their vehicle. "Whoa," one of them shouted out of the window, as they sped off with their lights flashing.

Ashvin and James did not look at each other. They didn't speak. They continued on their way home, regaining their composure with each awkward step. They walked along empty streets. Over toward the Docklands a green laser light beamed into the hollow of the sky. To the east a blue light emitted from number 30 St. Mary Axe, London's second tallest building or something, the Gherkin—the financial district's big dick. Beyond that, far, far in the distance, the London Eye, fitted snug in its place like a treasured plate of porcelain.

When they returned to the crossroads on York Road at the back of their estates, Ashvin spoke slowly in a funny voice he thought sounded German.

"Do you have any last requests?"

"I want to have sex with a girl and I want to see something breathtaking. What about you?" asked James.

Ashvin laughed, but there was no trace of humor on his face. "I'm going to kill that guy who hit me today. I want to take my sister to an art gallery. I want to see something breathtaking, too."

"What do you mean, kill that guy? Like murder?"

"Yes, sparky. I mean like murder."

They both laughed.

"I know him," said James. "His name is Nalma Kamal. He's Ethiopian."

"I know," said Ashvin.

"I'll help you get him if you like."

They shook hands and then walked their separate ways.


James wasn't at school the following day, but he turned up on Wednesday, two days after their pizza. When they saw each other in class, James asked Ashvin to sit at the desk next to his. Ashvin turned his fierce eyes on James, looked him up and down and crossed his long, skinny legs.

"What for?" he said. "Why would I want to sit next to you?"

"They'll leave you alone," said James.

James told me he'd always remember the way Ashvin laughed, showing all his teeth.

Weeks later, during a geography class on a day when a supply teacher was talking—to himself mainly—about sustainability and the earth's resources, Ashvin whispered, "Thank you."

"What for?" James asked.

"Ever since I've been sitting next to you they've stopped following me and no one laughs at my trousers. Who are you, Peter Parker?"

James turned from the window to look at Ash in that innocent way he had mastered. He didn't say anything because he didn't want to spoil such a beautiful day by talking about his brothers.

"'S cool," said James.

Ashvin and James shared the same hatred for the area we lived in. So, when he found out about them, Ashvin said James was lucky to have older brothers. James didn't feel lucky.

"I'm afraid," he said. "Everything we own comes from evil. They sell drugs and guns. Everything always goes wrong around here. People get greedy and jealous. Failure is like the wind and it's only a matter of time before one of my brothers won't be at breakfast. Do you know what I mean?"

For a long moment they held each other's gaze.

"I know exactly what you mean, man," said Ashvin. "In the end, death is the only winner."

# FOUR

# MEINA

AT THIS POINT IN the story I had not yet met James, but I'll tell you about him. He was the youngest of six boys. They all lived together on the Mandela council estate in east London, three doors down from the flat where that five-year-old girl was shot in the back with her father, in a flat where they earned their living selling crack. James did not have much of a past, but he was always certain of his future. He was convinced he was going to die young.

James's mum told me once that he was shy but always imaginative. I knew different. James wasn't shy. He was solitary by nature, with an honest outlook on things. He saw that in his neighborhood teenage boys turned into soul-shattered men who ended up in miserable jobs. Or went insane or became unwilling fathers or crack-pipe criminals. He said he was different from those boys and from his brothers. From everyone. At sixteen, he decided against allowing the system to beat him. Then, he and my brother just gave up.

In the beginning, what I felt for James was a purely maternal sort of affection, he was a year my junior but it didn't feel that way and once we finally accepted we were in love, he told me everything. He described how once, at home, when he was dying to pee, he pushed the bathroom door open without knocking. He said he was rushed by the combined smells of burning plastic and forest-green Radox bubble bath. He saw his mum in her short white nightdress (the one she always wore, smudged with age), just sitting there with her knickers on her knees, behind a veil of steam that came from the rushing tap. She was smoking crack. He waited for her to scream at him for having invaded her space, but she didn't. She just sat there with her glazed eyes barely open, looking at him with a sad smile on her face.

"Claws se hucking door," she said.

I had never known anyone who used crack, so I asked James not to spare any of the details which he didn't particularly like since it was his mother I was asking him about. But I reminded him of all the times he had pressed me about my parents, so he told me everything he could remember. He was frightened, seeing his mother reduced like that, her face blank, her far-off eyes. He looked at the bubbles formed like a pyramid beneath the tap, took slow exaggerated breaths and did as she asked: He backed up and closed the bathroom door. He told me that for a moment he felt as though he had betrayed her in some way. After that, James was unsettled and felt the need to talk so he went in and sat with his brothers, Number 1 and Number 2, while they played on their PlayStation console, a racing game where two imperishable sports cars, yellow and silver, smashed through a deserted city at night. James had little time for video games; he had tried but he just didn't understand them. Neither of his brothers spoke to him until halfway through an account his brother Number 2 gave of a "battery operation" he and his friend, Imperial Wiz, had performed on the same girl, Tameka Brown. She was a little whore who'd sleep with anyone, anywhere for twenty English pounds. Number 1 and Number 2 must have seen James's frown as he tried to imagine what a battery operation was.

"Is a battery operation when more than two guys take turns on one woman and it goes on and on like a Duracell?"

"You make it sound disgusting," said Number 2.

"It kind of is disgusting," said James.

"What do you know about it? Furthermore, get out," said 2.

1 and 2 raised their voices together. "Get out," they said.

Before we met, that was the only way James learned about sexual matters—from the advice he gleaned from his brothers. He once asked his brother Number 3 how he would know when he met the right girl.

"Remember when we bought paint for the front room and you chose the color?" 3 said. "Remember when we got home and we all started painting and you got into a panic and made us stop

44

because you said the color didn't feel right? It's the same with girls. When you kiss her, somehow you'll get to know how she feels, right or wrong."

A pillow hit James's face so hard it almost knocked him over. "Get out."

James didn't often cry, except when he got frustrated. He was frustrated that day when his brothers threw him out. Everything in his home felt unsafe. His eyes itched and tears blurred his vision. He felt an ache in his chest, but it had faded by the time he reached the front door. He remained still, alone, and felt he wanted to die. He could hear the distant tick, tap and gush of the central heating system. He stared at their front door. He said he wanted to open it and go outside and never come back. But when he unlocked the bolts and opened the door the air outside was calm. Everything out there was unknown and that made James feel vulnerable because, he said, outside there was nowhere for him to go.

James's father died years ago. He'd had a girlfriend at the time, a white woman from Essex, called Pat, someone he'd been seeing off and on for years. James has a half-sister from that relationship. She lives in Cornwall, and sends him birthday cards occasionally. She will be seventeen on her next birthday. Sometimes, he'd try to imagine what she looked like. He planned to send her a birthday card this year. He and Ashvin planned to leave a letter to everyone they loved. In the end, they didn't send anything to anyone.

James's brothers, 1, 2, 3 and 4, left school with nothing by way of formal qualification (his eldest brother 5 was the only one to complete school) and over the years he had seen their declining grades, read horrendous school reports and watched their fist-fights. During his own schooldays he had a sense that he had lived it all before. Always a fast learner, James decided against going to school in the end. He and Ashvin didn't see the point. "There isn't even one teacher in my school who could give a shit," James said. His class teacher of the last six months was Miss Bukolov. She looked like the princess in the first *Star Wars* movie and made James blush.

"You boys need to start wearing deodorant," she would say and James made her right. Sixteen-year-old boys had bad habits and they stank like wild goats, especially at 3:20 in the afternoon in summer months.

Brother Number 3 had picked him up from school once that summer, showing off in a stolen sports car (the type with a go-faster spoiler that you only saw in east London). James was livid when 3 and Miss Bukolov exchanged telephone numbers. Turns out, Miss Bukolov had a brother, Andrius, a vet by profession, who made his living importing second-hand cars and low-powered Baikal pistols from Lithuania which he converted to discharge live ammunition and sold with Number 3, from an Internet cafe in Leyton. Once she started going out with his brother, James studied his teacher carefully during classes. He said she smiled at him in a peculiar way during lessons and she began to pin all his drawings up on the wonderful-work wall.

One Friday morning, the day the BBC reported a new study released that claimed 600,000 Iraqis had been wiped out since the invasion and the mayor was threatening Londoners with wind turbines, James sat down at the window with his back to his mother, twirling a pencil and a sketch pad while a big white man with cropped blond hair banged on the door like only men with clipboards did. He wore a dark suit and shouted through their letter box.

"Mrs. Morrison, I know you're in there," he said.

James peeked out of the window. Many of the neighbors' curtains twitched, too.

"There's another man out there sitting in a white van," said James.

"Ignore them," his mother said as she picked at the scab on the nasty cut under her left eye. "They'll be sorry if they wake your brother, 4."

"Mum, I'm not going back to school."

She watched him in silence for a moment, crossed her legs and nodded wordlessly.

"Someone bullying you?" she asked. "Talk to one of your brothers. They can sort anything."

James's brothers, especially Number 4, were known as psychopaths with a readiness for violence.

"No."

46

"You're my youngest. You know I want the best for you, right?" She kissed him gently on his forehead. "You have to talk to your brothers, they are . . . well," she sighed, "they're your brothers."

Her mobile phone—the one no one dared touch—sounded, a Jimmy Cliff tune. She looked around trying to locate it. James closed his eyes when he heard the sound fondled leather makes as she plunged the sofa for the phone. She answered, speaking quietly.

"Skeets, give it ten minutes, then come up 'round the back."

As she spoke James looked at the black-and-white poster his mum had stuck above the futon on which he'd always slept. There had been four posters once, all black men. James had pulled three of them down but he'd kept this one, not because he trusted in the words, "by any means necessary," or the symbol of the automatic weapon the man in the poster held firmly in his hand. He told me he left that particular poster up on the wall because he recognized the way the man looked out of the window at the world, poised in anxious expectation. "He looks truthful to me in every way. Whenever I look out of our window at home, at the mosque and the church towers that block my view of the world, whenever I look squarely at my surroundings, at my small futon sandwiched at an awkward angle between the living room door and our dining table, I know exactly how the man in the poster feels."

# FIVE

# MEINA

IT WAS 2:30 P.M. The afternoon I had identified my brother. I walked along the main thoroughfare of our estate, past all the small East Asian businesses. The only shop out of the ordinary was a sauna, an odd building which had just opened. Sauna? Everybody knew it was a brothel. Cars roared by, the green on the grassy park was stirred by the wind. To the left was the road that curved passed Lea Valley all the way to Hackney. To the right, the long winding street went uphill onto the new road where the houses fell away and returned with a clamber of damaged cars in the slope and rubble of Bow. A silver-colored Jaguar pulled over close to the curb. Mr. Bloom leaned out of the open window.

"Where are you going?" he asked. His voice had an African lilt.

I shrugged my shoulders.

"Get in," he said and he opened the passenger door.

The car shut off all the noise outside. From inside the wind sounded like a soft moan. The air in the car was slightly stale; there was a whiff of tobacco smoke and the leather seats were soft and smelled new. It took less than a second for me to recognize the slow, buttery voice of Sarah Vaughan. The half-full ashtray under the blue light of the radio reminded me that old Mr. Bloom smoked Marlboro cigarettes.

"You look different."

"It's the suit. I'm back in an office unfortunately. The flash car isn't my idea either. Nice, though." He shrugged.

An awkward silence.

"I'm sorry."

I said nothing because if I had I would have started to cry.

"How are you doing, Meina?" he asked, squinting his wide eyes.

"I don't know," I said finally.

The first time I met him, Mr. Bloom had come to our house to pick up my father. Ash and I followed them to the Alibi, an illegal bar. I must have been about ten then. I remember he wore cowboy boots. I would stare at his shoes with admiration and delight. That first night, he sat in our living room and didn't smile once. After that, he would visit our home and sit for hours, drinking Johnnie Walker Blue Label with my father and his friends, arguing about Thatcher and Reagan and reminiscing about the sixties. He said he worked for the UN, as an emergency aid official. But I knew better. I knew he worked for a British government intelligence agency, just like 007. Only I didn't know which one. I wondered what it would be like having a job where no one knew exactly what it was that you did. I always liked the idea of Mr. Bloom constantly trying to justify his movements to girlfriends, his boss, to anyone he met.

"I don't have too long. I just need to know if you want to stay."

"Stay where?"

He put his hand on my bare thigh but quickly removed it when he saw my frightened expression. "Here in London," he said.

I couldn't tell whether he touched me because he cared or because he was taking advantage of me. I wanted to be sure I could tell the difference.

"I've lost my balance. I can't think just now," I said.

"It will take a few weeks. Try not to do anything extreme."

"Extreme? Like what?"

"I don't know. You will feel very vulnerable. Take it from an old man. I know. I thought you might want to leave the area?"

I shook my head. "Where would I go? Don't worry, none of this is your fault. No matter where we went, we wouldn't have got away from ourselves." I closed my eyes and listened to the calm singing voice and the slow deliberate sound of my own breathing. A truck roared by and my side of the car rattled. For a moment, we did not speak.

"You didn't come in to see him."

"I thought you'd want to be alone. You knew I was there, right?" He didn't meet my eyes.

"I guessed you were watching."

"I was going to give you a list of options but I can't remember anything. I'm sorry. You have been through so much," he said. His voice was uncertain.

"Did the police tell you what happened?" he asked.

"Yes."

"Do you know the other boy?"

"What other boy?"

"Bastards," he said. "The other boy who jumped off the roof at the same time."

My head felt light as though I might topple like one of those palm trees you see on television bent over backwards in the grip of a megastorm.

"No. They didn't tell me anything about that. But I can guess who he was."

"His name is James Morrison. Some old biddy heard him on the roof and called the police. He's in intensive care."

"James is my brother's best friend."

We remained in silence for a moment, and I smiled when I glimpsed Mr. Bloom's suede boots. Seeing them reminded me of my father.

"Does Google sell our search history?" I asked.

He didn't look at me as he replied, his eyes focused on some far-off thing. "I rarely touch the Internet. I read somewhere that in one month alone the five leading sites recorded nine billion searches. Some smug little bastard somewhere knows what the whole world is thinking, all our intentions, everything. None of those technological giants have morals. These people are dangerous. I've been saying it for a long time," he said.

"Do you use the Internet to look at porn? I mean, do all men do that?"

He looked at me and shifted uneasily in his seat. "Did you hear anything I just said?"

"Yes, but don't most men look at porn on the Internet?"

"I don't use the Internet," he said. "If I did use it for porn I wouldn't tell you. Why do you ask?"

I shrugged.

His eyes were on me as if he knew what I was thinking. He puckered his mouth and inhaled deeply.

"You're not thinking of doing anything stupid?" he said.

I knew he would ask me that. I thought for a second. Would I commit suicide? I didn't really have any ideas of my own, none strong enough to want to die over. He began to talk about how important life was. "It'll turn out all right," he said, his voice heavy with worry. "I know that sounds ridiculous after all you've been through, but it will be okay, I promise you."

His words barely registered.

The sun filtered through the leaves of a nearby tree and I passed my eyes over rows of cinnamon-brown rooftops. Suddenly, the pavements were filled with freed children in scruffy uniforms, mothers with prams and sprightly grandfathers in flat caps. None of them seemed real. I remembered how excited I would get the few times my father picked me up from school. Some of the children could not help staring inside the car as they passed, as if expecting to see someone important. I loved the innocence of the children, their lack of preconceptions, the way they interacted with each other and exaggerated all their facial expressions. It made me think about how much we learned to keep tucked away as adults.

"Is there anything I can do?" Bloom asked. "I owed your father a considerable amount of money. If you need anything, just say."

"What did you owe him money for?" I asked. I knew he wouldn't answer.

He let go of the steering wheel and handed me a credit card— green with white dots—with my name on it.

"I've written the pin number down. Can you read my writing? Four, three, two, two."

He put his hand on my thigh again. It felt warm. I looked directly in his eyes. I tried to use my eyes to show anger but I knew they betrayed me, so I shut them tightly. I was confused because I always had a great respect for Mr. Bloom. When my father was murdered his friends all disappeared, out of fear I guess. Mr. Bloom was the only one who seemed to care. He didn't remove his hand. Instead he began to rub inside my thigh gently. I thought I would melt with the tingling sensation that spread along my spine. I breathed deeply and closed my eyes as Mr. Bloom used his other hand to touch my neck.

For a moment, I wanted to cry because I remembered being dressed up by my aunt, Shifa. I wouldn't dare use her name, not even in my thoughts—in Somalia all elders are called "uncle" or "auntie," even strangers. It is a mark of respect. She was wildly spiritual, my aunt, but not godly. She took an immediate dislike to me right after I told her the things her husband tried to do to me whenever we were alone. I don't know what I expected.

My aunt dressed me for the men she would bring home to come and look at me. She would put yellow beads around my neck, a middle parting in my hair and dress me in a slinky white *diriic* like my mother's, which hung low on my shoulders and revealed the top of my back. The men always came in the afternoons. We would assume our positions in the center of her living room like stage actors, while my aunt's husband lay flat on the folding table in the kitchen—the worse for drink—with his mouth open wide, dribble coursing through his stubble.

Their house was an unfinished two-story building of brick. One of those houses somebody started building but then ran out of money or was killed. My aunt and her husband took possession in 2002. It was a common thing to do. She wasn't poor, my aunt, but she wasn't rich either. She scraped by. When my parents were alive I remember she often came over to our house to ask for help. When they died, she thought about moving into our house—I heard her discussing it with her husband. They decided it was too dangerous, they were afraid of being so closely associated with my father. Our house was lovely, especially at night under the glow of moonlight. It was surrounded by grass that felt like carpet to walk on, even barefoot—when I close my eyes I can remember the feeling of warm soil pressing against my toes. It was always cool and when there was no gunfire you could hear the sound of flowing water.

The men my aunt brought to look at me were all old. Cattle herders mostly, covered in sweat, with naked arms protruding from voluminous cloth. We Somalis called it *aroos fahdi*, arranged marriage. My mother did not agree with *aroos fahdi*. "It could make you think you were indifferent to the power of true love." When I think back on those men in that living room with its makeshift bamboo shades on the heavily framed windows, its empty-beer-bottle smell and its ugly walls, it all seems very sad to me. In my memory the men all look the same—wide lips, dead eyes. Up close, they smelled of cattle or desert sand or fresh khat, a mild stimulant they liked to use to speed up time.

My aunt would burn incense in my hair and use *khidaab*, a plant-based dye to decorate my left foot up to my ankle. I hated that incense smell in my hair. It was too old for me.

"Wirgin?" the men would ask candidly. They often spoke English to feel like the wealthy men of the West but they could never pronounce the English letter "V."

"Straight from heaven, not even circumcised," my aunt would say.

My mother was circumcised. My great-grandmother held her down and cut her when she was nine. Strangely, she was not bitter like most of the girls at my old school. She put it down to culture rather than male domination. Ashvin was circumcised when he was three years old. My mother made a big deal about being progressive. She waited until I was thirteen and she gave me the choice. She sat me down with a human biology picture book.

"What is it?" I asked.

"It is a Muslim ritual."

"I know that. But no one ever says *what* it is."

My mother put the book on my lap. "In Sudan they remove the clitoris," (point) "the labia minora," (point) "and the labia majora," (point) "and then they stitch the sides together." (Point, point, point, point.) "In Somalia we only remove the clitoris." (Point.) "It takes forty days to heal. It's part of your ancestry. Would you like to have it done?" She smiled because she already knew the answer.

I was in shock. I can't remember my exact words but it was Somali for "Hell, no."

We laughed. But I was frightened because I thought I would be forced. When I started to cry, she hugged me. "Armeina," she said, "you will never be forced to do anything."

I miss her.

"Enough touching. You want more? You have to marry." My aunt was the color of coffee without milk, all bosom and no heart. She was fat, old and wasted like a big slice of stale fruit cake. She wore colorful headscarves and liked to pencil her eyebrows into a perpetual enquiry. On the few occasions she smiled, usually when my prospective husbands were in tow, her big upper lip would fold over itself.

Sometimes the men would show off their guns to prove that they could protect their land and their livestock and, by association, their women. They would stand in front of me salivating and my aunt would slowly spin me round in the middle of the living room. I remember there was an overriding smell of goat's pee in the room, mingled with the fearful smell of male desire.

The room was painted a smoky blue and the ceiling was covered with fake wood. One dust-encrusted window looked down onto the gravel street. Up and down the street on a steep hill was a mass of modest houses with sun-faded bricks and rows of breeze-swept trees with reddish-brown leaves. There were noisy children playing and a barefoot old woman in a faded blue apron displaying wares nobody was willing to pay for: miscellaneous kitchen implements, empty jars, pot holders and rubber bands. She had eyes dimmed by cataracts and hairs on her chin, that old woman. My aunt thought she was a spy for the government-sponsored militia because somehow she always had money.

Everything seemed to freeze as I was twirled in my white robe like a figure from an old English fairy tale. I'd ask myself, "Is this who I really am?" I would be touched intimately over my dress, between my legs, on my breasts and my backside. It was some time before I realized it wasn't the flimsiness of the material of my dress that gave me goosebumps. Every nook of the room filled with my fear and my heart charged with sorrow—my father would be so ashamed.

I would remain rigid, sometimes searching the faces of the men but usually I would close my eyes, my heart racing. My belly would tense involuntarily like it often did when I lowered myself into a hot bath. With my eyes closed, I could see the blood in my eyelids on account of the sun. I would count the slowly passing seconds in my mind. I was a butterfly free to flutter away in search of a new home.

All eighteen of my suitors said yes after seeing me and touching me. But only six came up with the dowry. Those men would say yes to any woman because of their interpretation of marriage.

Or perhaps they all mistook my childish bafflement for modesty. I don't suppose you can call it rape if you are married, but for what it is worth I never once gave my consent to any of my six husbands. But with the formality of daylight over, and without prompting, each of them would begin pushing and pulling my body into peculiar angles. I always fought them off until I had no strength left, and after disentangling myself I would weep because I would be left with a strange stillness and the sense of having failed my father.

They would always bring some gift on those first visits. Never chocolates or fresh-cut flowers as men did in my books. Always slabs of boneless camel meat that my aunt and her husband would eat while they drank alcohol from my mother's best glasses and the two of them whispered and laughed like it was all a big joke. By then, Ashvin would have been let out from the room at the back where they'd locked him up so the men couldn't hear him protest. I can still see him now, sitting in a plastic chair with his head bent low.

Ashvin's face showed off his emotions; back then he could never lie to me. Whenever they unlocked him, he would have a look of hatred beyond all argument and stony eyes. Seeing Ashvin so angry reminded me of something my father used to say when we were afraid of the "cack-cack-cack" sounds of gunfire, when it was so loud and seemed so close it prevented us from sleep.

"Close your eyes, fireflies," my father would say as though he commanded the night. He would tell us stories about a peaceful Somalia, before the war interrupted everything. "Do you know that before Somali men were known for war, we were known as Africa's greatest poets?"

"Really? Is it true?" I remember Ashvin asked and his eyes lit up.

"Really," my father said. "When I was your age we used to compete. The best poets were called *afmaal*, mouth of wealth. The Somali poet was considered a person of prestige and power, once feared only for the words from his mouth." My father would whisper the words of some old poem as Ash and I fell asleep.

Living with my aunt was a bad time for us but my brother would always find his way to me. My aunt regularly fed us what she called *maraq*. But it was just a watery vegetable soup. We would have to eat it because we were hungry. Ash would be seething, tense with rage.

"These men could have AIDS," Ashvin said once.

"She says she makes them take the test," I said.

He looked at me as if I was an idiot and I could see anger puffing his cheeks.

"Did you slip and bang your head?" he'd ask.

"*Afmaal*, remember?" I would say, to try to calm him down.

"Screw *afmaal*. They're making a business out of you," he'd say. But even though he was furious, I know he remembered my father because Ashvin would bow his head and after a few moments he would squeeze my hand. "Okay, sis?" He would play games to amuse me; once he brought me flowers and made me a paper toy. He sang Somali folk songs at night and recited poems he half remembered from our childhood. Sometimes he would stroke my cheek. "It's going to be all right," he'd say. It reminded me of the Ashvin I knew from before our parents' funeral. Then we went everywhere together. He would recite poems as he walked me to school, he would only ever give up his seat to pretty girls on the bus, and he would eat the leftovers on my plate to prevent me from getting into trouble with our parents. In those days, *I* was Ashvin's best friend.

The Ashvin I knew before was long gone and he never came back. He never cried during the time we spent with my aunt. He must have been slowly boiling inside—like water inside one of those old kettles. I never thought about it, not until today. Now, I wish he had. I should have known there was something wrong inside him because he seemed so unsurprised at anything.

I told Ashvin I had seen Mr. Bloom in the bar we had once followed our father to.

"He still goes to that bar?" he asked. "You went there alone? Have you lost your mind?"

I told Ashvin I had only spent about ten seconds staring through the cracks in the wood at the back, same as we did before.

"What did you see?" asked Ashvin.

"I saw men dancing together on that wooden board they use for a dance floor. They were drunk, singing at the tops of their lungs to Madonna ('Like a Wirgin') or Cyndi Lauper, I can't remember which. I saw Mr. Bloom sitting on a chair directly opposite the back wall. He was alone, looking worried. He was leaning forward on his elbows with his sleeves rolled up, huge empty glasses in neat rows on his table."

Ashvin shrugged his shoulders. All he said was, "Okay."

I didn't hear anything more about it until the day we finally left my aunt's house forever. I don't know how or when my brother met Mr. Bloom. He must have gone to see him at the bar. It's a detail we never spoke about. One night, almost morning, two uniformed men, who Mr. Bloom had paid, kicked open my aunt's front door waving guns. They dragged us out of our beds. My aunt and her husband were too frightened to notice that Ashvin had a packed bag with our belongings.

We had been living with our aunt for almost a whole year. Until October, when we went back to Mr. Bloom's in Kismayo. We were only with him there for four months before he arranged our papers for London.

I'll probably never see my aunt again. She had the same shaped face as my mother. It used to trouble me, the way we have no control over who comes in and out of our lives. Not that I care about my aunt. It just makes me wonder what people give or take from each other. Why.

I opened my eyes and looked at Mr. Bloom, his hand on my thigh. He had that same look as the cattle herders when they touched me, a look that said he knew he was doing something wrong. I looked down at his cowboy boots, and again they brought me a clear picture in my head of my father and this time my eyes did not let me down. Mr. Bloom removed his hands. I thanked him for the credit card and I smiled as I got out of the car.

I walked around for hours in a fog and then I went to Zudzi. From my first visit, it had seemed familiar to me because I recognized so much about it from home. It was a small storefront restaurant filled with the permanent smell of cardamom. It was only three stops away on the tube.

I put four pounds on my Oyster card. I hated traveling by tube even before what happened with the terrorists. Being stuck underground with strangers, united by the tugs, rumbles and throws of the Central Line. I hated the way people looked at me, at what

I was reading, what shoes I wore. I hated the way I felt I was being appraised by quick sideways glances. I like to imagine people's characters, it has become something of a ritual—Ashvin called it one of my twisted habits. I had tried to stop, but always found myself giving in to impulse. I often wondered what people thought they saw when they looked at me.

I counted twenty people packed together, like we were in a sauna with people from all over the world. Twelve of us sat in two neat rows of six. There were eight people standing, trying to look like they didn't want a seat. I heard at least seven different languages; five people had on white earphones; nine were reading the *Metro*. On the cover was the face of a sixteen-year-old black boy who had been stabbed to death that weekend. A fat woman sat next to me, eating chicken from a greasy red box. A young couple in matching cheap sportswear and gold jewelry with a baby in a pushchair; an important-looking white man with silver-framed eyeglasses and a fitted chalk-stripe suit. He eyed a young man sitting on his left and I imagined what he was thinking. "Would you mind lowering the volume on your iPod, there's a good man?" The important-looking man ate a wrap from Pret A Manger while reading a John Grisham. There was a wannabe fundamentalist with a long beard—he knew he was freaking everybody out even though he wasn't doing anything. He was laughing at us in a way. I stared at him for a while but I figured that a real terrorist wouldn't wear £180 Air Max. It didn't fit somehow. I turned to my left. A spotty young City worker in a shiny suit and pointy designer shoes. He had spiky hair and I could tell he spent all his money on the first Friday of the month at the pub. There was a blonde in a Marks & Spencer coat, clutching an expensive handbag like it was an automatic firearm. She wore an engagement ring. I guessed that her fiancé was a welder with a Chelsea football club season ticket. There was a black woman in her thirties; she wore a blue raincoat clasped with a bronze buckle at her middle, skinny jeans and powder-blue flats with a pretty bow. She sat with her back straight. She was a single parent and a bank teller, probably recently born-again, praying fiercely for a drama-free white man to stabilize her life. There was a young African with a sharp new haircut, dreaming of being granted asylum, wearing all the right gear but still not fitting in. The woman next to me with the chicken had a book in her hand, *Basic Nursing*. She'd be the last person whose face I would want to see if I was sick. I couldn't look at her directly but I watched the reaction of the people who got on as they noticed her stuffing ragged pieces of meat in her mouth. I wanted to move, but I'd have felt embarrassed. So I remained still, and shut my eyes as the screeching of the train got louder. The driver announced we would be held in the tunnel. When I finally got out, I inhaled the fresh air deeply. And then I made my way along the crowded street.

Zudzi is painted yellow, with mismatched Formica counters and tie-dye tablecloths. It is quiet, one person cooks, serves and washes dishes, and no one ever speaks English—the restaurant is run and owned by a business co-op of Somali women who were in the local paper recently for their hot-sauce deal with Sainsbury's supermarkets. There is a sign on the register written in Afar and Somali:

> Listen, friends. No more food loan—cash only.
> More blessings to big auntie
> When she give tips.

The clientele are exclusively Somali women; most of them are, like me, refugees granted political asylum. Although a few non-Somali neighbors have started to trickle in—you know, the shea-butter set, blacks that come as part of their perpetual search for Africa, and the type of culture-hungry, hippy-looking white person who wants a slice of everything. There isn't a "No Men" sign on the entrance but there may as well be. There is always a deep thread of anxiety about men for all of us. Sometimes a stray who thinks he owns a pair, that "highly bred" mold of Somali man with disgusting candor, will enter. All the women will watch him with suspicion. From the moment he walks in the place will clam up tight and you can feel the white-hot tension because we can never trust what might erupt from him at any moment. It would take a brave man to eat comfortably in a place like this.

"How are you today, Divorce?"

It took a while before I got used to her calling me that. She is Sister Ashar but I have heard them call her Star Trek because she escaped by trekking from her home town to the Dagahaley refugee camp in the north-eastern province of Kenya. She was housed in a tent made of branches covered with patches of plastic and cloth, among thorn trees and scrubland swamps. Since Ethiopia invaded Somalia, I have heard of thousands who ran away from Mogadishu to the camps. Sister Ashar said the Dagahaley camp sheltered more than twenty thousand people, mostly women and children. It became the target of armed troops. Sister Ashar was raped at gunpoint seven times.

"God is great," I said.

There was a menu, not all of it was available every day, and it took me months to try most of it. The portions were generous; the most expensive thing, *mufo*, cost three pounds and when I first tasted it it was so delicious, just like my mother's, that I almost wept. I sat in the same spot on each of my visits, just on the edge of the room where most others gathered to chat.

"One and a Half," said Sister Ashar. "Don't forget your change."

I was slightly embarrassed for the woman who hobbled from her table on one leg to collect her change.

"They are giving her too much disability allowance so she can afford to throw money away," said Sister Ashar loudly.

All the women—Landmine, Machete and Soft Touch—laughed at that, especially One and a Half herself.

I asked for the chicken *siquar*, a stew of diced chicken, green peppers, onions, carrots, a fair amount of celery and a few chunks of potato. It smelled like coriander but it was like eating fire, and the burn from the peppers lingered on the tongue for hours. Sister Ashar lowered her eyes from mine and sadness crept over her face.

"Don't you feel well today?" she asked.

"Me? I'm fine."

"Maybe when you eat you feel better."

She had a gentle way of speaking. She studied me closely while I searched for the right thing to say.

"Divorce, you don't look right. What has happened?"

I felt a balloon expanding behind my chest.

"My brother," I said calmly. I paused momentarily and then I abandoned all pretense and I stood balanced on the verge of something, tears or collapse. She glided around the counter, stood beside me. She held the nape of my neck and led me to a table where she sat down with me. I watched the soft sway of her head-scarf, green with gold trim. Her lavish scent enveloped me, causing a warm pleasant sensation.

"My brother is dead. He killed himself." And then I told her everything, except about Mr. Bloom.

"Eh-yaay," she said. She furrowed her brow and began to rub her hands along my back.

She told the other women and my mouth went dry on account of all the eyes that fixed on me. Most of the women carried the vacant expressions of those who have endured the same loss. Zudzi normally has a soothing atmosphere, but not that day. My truth crashed it open like a box and transformed it into some murky place, small and gloomy with dark furniture, bereft of happiness, where the air is heavy and damp with tears. I glanced fleetingly at some of the women who had come over to comfort me, their colorful robes and headties reminding me of some ghostly market clan. The women said sorry with their eyes in that distinctive Somali way none of them seemed to have lost despite their escape from home. I tried my best to avoid their sad gaze because I could feel homesickness trying to overwhelm me. I looked around at the empty tables, examined the beautiful paintings hanging on the walls and the photographs of missing family members stuck wish-fully above a Bible in the window as though they might be wandering the streets of east London. Then I imagined Ashvin sitting next to me, there he was beside me slurping over pepper soup and then he vanished. Zudzi seemed immense. After some time an old woman with a long face who had lost her five daugh-ters came over. She looked at me and held my hands in hers.

"Allah gives what you can bear," she said with the authority of her years. As she wept a black gas filled my head. I couldn't breathe but I did not want to cry. Then some of the women began to sing that old mournful song they always sang in my country when someone died and finally I wept, safe in the weird comfort of their eerie lament.

# SIX

# JAMES

JAMES HAD TAUGHT HIMSELF to tie a slip knot. He thought it was the most solid knot and chose it specifically so that when he killed himself there would be no mistake. He wanted it to be simple, unsentimental. And when he was gone, he hoped his family felt they were to blame. He hoped they wouldn't find a doctor who would console them by saying he was suffering from some chemical imbalance. He wasn't.

He did his research. According to Google, divorced or separated men were more likely to commit suicide than any other group. Men were 4.8 times more likely to do it than women, rates of black men that did it between the ages of fifteen and nineteen have increased 114 percent and recently suicide rates among Australian male Aborigines has shot up by 35 percent.

But James didn't die. When he opened his eyes he saw them. All of them. Nothing had changed. There was a Chinese-looking doctor—he might have a little dab of black running through his veins—with brown eyes that appeared heavily lined with mascara. His arms were bare and covered with fine hairs. His thick upper arms looked strong beneath his ribbed undershirt, like his face. There was a lot for him to deal with. James's brothers, 1 and 2, were playing furiously on their PlayStation PSPs. Number 3 was whispering in the ear of some white girl he had just met in the emergency room, 4 was simultaneously on the phone and searching in his bag and number 5, the eldest, held a Starbucks coffee and sat staring at James.

There were cut flowers in a glass vase on a shelf opposite the bed; a half-eaten bunch of grapes in a deep bowl, a copy of *Vibe* magazine, a bottle of original Lucozade and three get-well-soon cards with the transparent wrappers still on. Propped slightly apart from anything else on the shelf was an envelope with his name, and a first-class stamp.

The scene reminded him of *Central Station*, a Brazilian movie with English subtitles about a woman who works at Central Station, Rio de Janeiro, and who is paid by illiterates to write letters. She witnesses the death of the mother of a boy and together they travel through Brazil on a bus in search of the boy's father. At the end of the film he wakes up in bed with his two brothers and the woman has left him. James used the back of his hand to examine his neck, closing his stinging eyes and trying to make himself invisible.

"He just opened his eyes," said 5.

His mother jumped from a low chair on his opposite side; her head came into his line of vision. She wore blue jeans, Reeboks and a long black coat that James hated. Slung over the back of her chair were some clothes he recognized as his own. They hung stiffly, like dead skin.

He couldn't believe he was still alive.

"Where?" said his mother and she stuck her head in his face. "No he didn't. He's still in coma."

"Mum, please," said James. "Do you have to shout like that?"

James felt his breath stank like rotting meat. His heart pounded and his stomach churned. He couldn't tell whether he was hungry or whether he was going to be sick.

"Oh, thank you, sweet Jesus," said his mother and she began to sob, stroking his head. "How could you do this? Don't you know how much I love you?"

"Where am I?" James asked. In the distance he could hear the faint sound of sirens.

"Newham General, you prick," said 1.

"Shhhhhit," said James, inhaling deeply. He winced at the pain in his throat.

"Shit? What were you thinking, dickbrain? Were you drunk?" said 4.

"He don't drink," said 2.

"Tell us who did this to you, bruv," said Number 1 menacingly.

The doctor studied James's chart on a clipboard.

63

"I can't work like this, people. I may have to ask you all to leave."

"Ask away. We ain't going nowhere. He's our blood," said 4.

James's mother glared at the doctor and kissed her teeth. "Who does he think he is?" she asked of no one in particular.

And then the police walked in, a plainclothes and a uniformed officer clutching a file.

"Do that Keyser Soze shit. Don't tell 'em nuffin," said Number 2.

Number 2 had a quick mouth that James could barely tolerate. He shut his eyes and breathed deeply.

James remembered how much he hated the smell of hospitals. The two police officers were standing at his bedside. He opened his eyes, scrutinizing each of their faces and feeling a growing sense of alarm. Something terrible had happened. The memory of being on the roof was already fading, like a dream from last week. Bodies, loud voices and shadows pulling him up, the pain shooting down his back and in his throat, the flashing lights and slow rumble of the ambulance, someone with black eyes screaming in his face; choking on his own puke and blood.

"Where's Ash?" he asked.

Nobody spoke for what seemed like a long while.

"Detective Inspector Whittaker. Have we met before?" asked the plainclothes officer. He was gaunt and wore an unruly beard, speckled with gray.

"No, that was me," said 2, holding his hands up like a cowboy in surrender.

It was an easy mistake. If James looked like any of his brothers it was Number 2. The inspector spun round and acknowledged the Morrison brothers. They all laughed.

"If by Ash you are referring to Ashvin Al Hassan Mohamed, he's dead. I'm hoping you can help us with our inquiries."

The inspector had turned his gaze back to James. His eyes were like shattered blue glass.

"Please leave me alone." James tried to turn his back but his throat felt like it would rip into two. That was when he remembered what they had done and then he couldn't stop the flow of tears.

"I'm afraid I'm going to insist that you all leave. Right now," said the doctor, growing anxious. "That includes you, Inspector. This young man needs some rest."

The doctor's words were like a tent. James entered inside and for a moment he zipped everything out.

Inspector Whittaker narrowed his eyes at the doctor and then leaned closer to James. The look he sent said *I'm not done with you yet.*

When they had all left James glanced up at the IV tubes above his head.

"What are you feeding me?"

"Excuse me?"

"The drip, what's in the drip?"

"Oh, just some pain medication and glucose," the doctor replied. "How are we doing?"

"My neck is killing me," said James. "When can I go?"

The doctor looked at his clipboard. "You shouldn't be feeling any pain in your neck because of sensory loss."

"I don't know what to tell you . . . it hurts like hell."

"You've just had six stitches in your upper lip. You have an abraded band from the right parieto-occipital region distal to the ear by two inches extending below the jaw above your thyroid cartilage. The skin on your neck was worn away and you still have rope embedded on the right side of the trachea. Your esophagus is bruised. The left wing of the hyoid bone is fractured and displaced upward—this is all caused by the sudden motion of the body falling and then being suspended, it's extremely common in hangings. You've been lucky, there was no real injury to your spinal cord."

"What's all that mean in English?"

"It means you're not going home. Not for some time yet. You're dehydrated and suffering from shock though you have a normal pulse, blood pressure and respiration. I'm not sure, but you might have an infection. We're still waiting for results. Not to worry though, we'll have you right as rain in next to no time." The doctor sighed and smiled.

It took some effort but James didn't smile back. All of a sudden "right as rain" didn't make sense to him. He tried to work it out. How could rain be right? He started to feel angry and he had to

65

force himself to let it go. James looked above his head to the left at the empty fruit bowl. The cards had been removed but the envelope with his name on it and the Lucozade were still there. He looked around blankly and his heart began to race, his breath shut off and then he vomited.


The second time James opened his eyes, there was a freshly scrubbed man in his forties with thin cheekbones and funny blond hair—styled like Peter Pan or Tom Cruise—sitting in front of him smiling awkwardly. James closed his eyes again and then reopened them to see if the man was really there. The man smiled as though he realized what James was thinking but he said nothing, just sat there with his legs crossed, smiling. James stared at him for some time. And he stared back. At some point his smile became a half-smile and then he was just sitting there staring. It was discomforting, like stepping out from the warmth into the biting wind.

"You some type of police, or what?" asked James.

"It speaks," the man shouted, clapping his hands together. "I'm glad we got over our standoff. Am I with the police? Oh God, no. Do I look like a policeman? You must be kidding, right?"

There he was smiling in James's face again. He was fashionably bearded and smelled of Listerine and aftershave. Dressed in black down to his smart loafers, he was like the spokesperson for the ultramodern white man. But there was something off. His straight-backed posture, his hair and his skin tone reminded James of an Oompa-Loompa.

"If you're not with the police, you need to leave."

"I don't want us to get off on the wrong foot here, so let me tell you who I am. I am from the Department of Health. I am a psychotherapist and a suicidologist. I have been assigned to your case because I've worked with a member of your family."

"A member of my family? Who?"

"Your eldest brother. I worked with him for six months."

"No you didn't." James couldn't hide his surprise.

"I promise you. For obvious reasons I can't go into specific details but I had to evaluate him before he was moved from Brixton

66

to the category C prison in Stafford. I was assigned to him for six months. I get a lot of work from the Prison Service."

James sighed, thinking about the distance that had grown between him and his brothers.

"My job is to take an evaluation and make an assessment. Then I'll make a report on your mental state of health determining whether you are a threat to yourself or to the wider community. Based on my report, a committee will decide whether you can leave the hospital or not and whether you will be able to return home. What I need to do is to ask you a few questions—it should only take about ten minutes. I'll ask a few standard questions and you just say whatever you feel. However, you must give an answer to each question. Shall we begin?"

His speech sounded rehearsed, almost as if he was recounting an anecdote. James just stared at him blankly. He was thinking about his brother 5, wondering what was going on in his mind.

"Do you mean you could decide to have me sectioned and put in a madhouse just like that?"

"There are a whole myriad of rules and the Mental Health Act Commission reviews all decisions that are appealed."

"So, it's not up to you?"

"Well, not exactly. I don't make up the questions. The governing body sets the questions. So it's up to you and your answers. I tell everyone the same thing, it's very important they take me seriously. We can't have mentally ill people wandering the streets putting innocent lives and themselves at risk."

"And if you say I failed your test? How long would I be put away?"

"Until the doctors saw fit to place you back into society."

James looked at him for a moment. "Define mental illness." He was becoming afraid.

"Mental illness is not defined by the Mental Health Act of 1983. People like myself define the type of mental disorder. These types of disorder are schizophrenia, major depression, bipolar disorder and personality disorder."

James thought of a GQ article he'd seen—"Ten Ways to Spot a New Man"—and then he couldn't help thinking of the therapist having his arse waxed. He smiled.

"Care to share?" asked the therapist.

"I found something funny. That don't make me crazy," said James.

"I didn't say it did. Why so hostile?"

"Here we go. Have you already made up your mind?"

"Have you already made up *your* mind?"

There was a long pause.

James thought of his brother's friend, Dayo, who had robbed a jeweler's when he was twenty. When he was arrested, he panicked and shat himself after being repeatedly kicked in the stomach by three policemen in the back of their van. The police said he was crazy and had him sectioned because he was ashamed and tried to clean up his shit with his hands. He'd been locked away for eleven years. They let him out now and again for supervised visits. James had seen him on one such visit. He was sitting in the kitchen while Dayo spoke to 3 and 5. Dayo told them how, when he had seen his eldest daughter a few years earlier, he had called out to her and she'd run away from him out of fear. He wasn't thinking and ran after her and his day release was revoked for another two years. James had always admired Dayo, wanted to grow up to be like him—a footballer, one of the best in the manor. He'd played for Newham. He'd passed the youth trials for West Ham and even had a picture on his mantel of him sitting with Trevor Brooking that the estate youths were all jealous of. When his daughter ran off like that Dayo stopped fighting; no more appeals, no more day-release applications. He gave up. He'd never get out. If that could happen to Dayo, it could happen to anyone.

The man unzipping his bag broke the long silence. He took out a writing pad.

"May I begin?" he asked in a firmer tone, and continued straight away as though James had said yes.

"First of all, you are not alone, and let me remind you that there is nothing more important than your life. Nothing. My name is Trevor Carrick and I am very pleased to be here."

He extended his right hand and when James did not extend his, he gave a strained smile.

"Look, I've been working with suicidal people and people with mental health issues for nearly twenty years, and I've been firmly dedicated to their rights and support. The first thing I want you to know is that virtually every person I've worked with who attempted suicide and survived, was glad that they lived. So the emotions that cause suicidal feelings pass. Things get better; the sun does come out. Let me extend that hope to you."

Trevor Carrick paused for a moment.

"What is it?" he asked.

"Why are you speaking like that?"

"Like what?"

"I don't know like what. You sound funny."

"I can assure you none of this is meant to be funny, young man."

Trevor Carrick adjusted himself in his seat and then he continued.

"How do you feel today about what has happened?"

"T'riffic."

"Are you avoiding the subject?"

"No."

"Can you tell me what you imagine other people's feelings and reactions are to your suicide attempt?"

"They're upset, I guess."

"Do you understand the consequences of your attempt to commit suicide?"

"I was supposed to die." James sighed. "Look, I don't want to waste your time. I don't know how I feel."

"Can you try?"

Trevor looked at James like he wanted him to speak so James did.

"I always feel like something bad is going to happen. I can't get over it," he said.

"We call that feeling anxious. It's normal but once it hits a certain tipping point, it can become a problem."

"Yeah, well, I feel anxious all the time for no reason."

"What desires, feelings and wishes do you have today based on what you have experienced?"

"I'm a bit hungry. I wanna go home."

"Can you distinguish between inner and outer reality at this moment in time?"

"As opposed to what other time?"

"Let me rephrase. Do you know the difference between pretend mode and real mode?"

"Yes."

"Can you tell me how you go through your emotional processes?"

"Emotional processes?"

"Okay," said Trevor and he crossed and uncrossed his legs. "My grooming rites can take up to three hours, shaving, brushing my teeth, moisturizing, applying mousse to my hair, putting on clothes and taking them off again until they feel right. Emotional processes."

"Okay." James thought for a long moment. "When I get a McDonald's burger I always take the top bun off and check the position of the gherkins. I like them dead in the center. What does that mean?"

Trevor shrugged. "Fine. It is what it is. Your mother tells me you're an avid reader and you love to draw. Is that right?"

"Yes."

"Who is your favorite author?"

"I don't have a favorite. Books get better and better." At home James had a pile of books, stacked neatly next to his futon.

"I brought you a pencil and some paper. Would you like to draw something for me?"

He dug into his bag. James caught a glimpse of a crisp white towel, a paperback and a magazine with Matt Damon on the cover.

Trevor handed him a pencil and a large sheet of white paper. James didn't even raise his head. He sketched a noose and a slip knot and returned the paper. Trevor's expression did not change. He dug deeper into his bag for another pencil and he used it to draw six stickmen around James's picture of the noose. He wrote the names of James's brothers and his mother beside each of the stick figures.

"How does your picture make you feel now?" he asked.

"Why would you do that?" James asked. "You're trying to bait me up."

"No, not at all. Without those people, your picture is incomplete. If you want to kill yourself you have to consider other people and the consequences. What you leave behind is pretty much a disaster."

James shook his head. "When I was up on that roof, I thought of my family at my funeral. It was the thought that gave me the courage to jump."

"Why did you jump *and* use the ropes?"

"What sort of question is that? We tried to kill ourselves."

"Why not one or the other? You would have probably died if you'd jumped. Why the rope?"

"We argued about it. Ash wanted to jump. I thought we should send a message."

"What do you think the message was?"

"Like the lynchings in America. To me everything kind of feels the same. There aren't any violent mobs, but . . . it was meant to be a symbol."

"Can you explain what you mean by that?"

James couldn't explain.

"Do you feel a lack of human connection? Don't you know people care about you?"

"Yes."

"Yes what?"

"Yes, I know people care."

"What is the meaning or purpose of your life?"

James was silent for a moment.

"To finish school, get a good job, get a hot wife, get a car and be happy"

"Good answer," Trevor said. "Now tell me, what do you want most?"

"What do you mean?"

"What do you think would make you happy?"

"I've always wanted to own a bookshop." He paused and studied his hands intently as if waiting for the next sound. "There's an empty shop in Forest Gate with a place in the back where I can paint." He began to cry.

Trevor remained silent for a moment. "Tell me why you're crying."

"Because it's such a small thing to ask, but I know I'll never get it, no way, no how."

Trevor scribbled in his notebook. "Do I remind you of anyone?" he asked without looking up.

71

"Yes," James said. "You look a bit like whassisname, that gay guy off the telly."

"Let me rephrase. The way I'm speaking to you, does it remind you of the way anyone else has spoken to you in your past? Like your father perhaps?"

James took a deep breath. "No."

"How often do you think of your father?"

"Hardly ever."

"Do you miss him?"

"Nope."

"How connected do you feel to what is going on around the world?"

"Such as?"

"Such as the war on terror, say."

"I don't have any views on the war on terror except that Bush is a complete wanker. I don't think we should have gone to Iraq. The thing is, and I have thought about this a lot, no one really cares about what people like me think. No matter what I do I'm never going to matter."

"You shouldn't think like that, you're only seventeen. Give yourself a break. You're in a crisis, it will pass. You have your whole life in front of you. You have to be patient, work hard like everybody else."

"It won't pass. Do you know that Nigerian boy who got stabbed in the leg on his way home from the library and died? He was ten. The boys that did it, the Preddie brothers, they moved from Peckham onto our estate just before they got arrested. Most of their gang, the Young Peckham Boys, live around here now. There are seven gangs I know of in my area. Some all black, some mixed. It all comes down to post codes—except with the RTS, they're from everywhere."

"RTS?"

"Rough Tough Somalis. When boys say hello to me on the street I say hello back but I worry because I keep forgetting who is who and who owns what. That guy Nassirudeen Osawe who got killed at the bus stop on Upper Street in broad daylight the other day by the Shakespeare gang. His sister goes to my school and those guys who did it are at my house with my brothers almost every day. They all know my brothers. I may only be seventeen but I have lived with this shit every day. What I'm feeling won't pass. This doesn't go away."

"I hear what you're saying, but do you think killing yourself is a solution? You can't take all this on, James. You have to put it in a drawer somewhere in the back of your mind like the rest of us. Try not to worry about that stuff for a while."

James couldn't explain any more. He couldn't understand why he was even trying. His throat burned.

"What book are you reading at the moment?"

"I'm not. I gave up with the books."

"Why? I thought you loved them."

"I do."

"Did you read that one about Arsenal?"

"Hornby? Course I did."

"What about Malcolm?"

"Malcolm? You mean Malcolm X? You want me to read Malcolm X in the mess I'm in? No. I read Malcolm when I was like eight. It was the one book all my brothers read, like the Bible."

"Okay, so who do you like to read?"

"Baldwin."

"*Giovanni's Room?*"

"I haven't read that. I've read *The Fire Next Time. Beale Street* and that other one—*Another Country*. I've read that shit like a zillion times."

"I liked *Another Country,* too."

"You read that?"

"Yes, I read all the gay fiction I can lay my hands on."

"*Another Country* is not gay."

"Maybe you need to read it again. You do know about James Baldwin?" Trevor crossed his legs and smiled, waved his arm dismissively.

"Know what?"

Trevor glanced up but than lowered his head to avoid James's eyes and his mouth tightened involuntarily. "Sorry, forget it. Your mother says you also like to write."

"I used to, until they took one of my notebooks and started making fun of me. Then I stopped."

"Who did?"

"Two of my brothers."

"Do you like football?"

"I'm from east London. That's what we do."

"What team do you support?"

"Arsenal."

"Oh, you're a Gooner. So, you see, we do have some things in common. They won 5–nil on Saturday. How does that make you feel?"

"T'riffic. Who scored?"

"Not sure."

Gooner my arse, James thought.

"Why did you choose that particular tower?"

"You mean to jump? I didn't choose. It was Ashvin's idea. He'd heard that lots of people were doing it from there. Because they're disgusting, they're ugly."

"They're thinking of knocking them down," said Trevor.

"They been thinking about a lot of things around here, but let me tell you, they ain't gonna do shit."

"How do you feel about being rescued from the roof?"

"T'riffic."

"Do you want to tell me why you tried to kill yourself?"

"Because I know who I want to be and I keep getting forced into being someone else."

"What do you mean by that?"

James lifted the plaster holding the IV tube in his arm and tried to scratch around the needle. He breathed deeply.

"Think of every tired cliché you've ever heard about black men. I'm trying desperately hard not to be that. I don't want to become a stereotype. Everyone thinks they know me but they don't. I don't suppose it matters to you. Everything I think has already been thought," said James. "Everything I feel has already been felt. Everything I want to do has been done. It's like I don't matter. People who don't even know me are already tired of me. I'm only ever going to be what I don't want to be."

"You keep saying that. What do you mean?"

James wanted Trevor to take him seriously. "I was on the train last week," he said, "and I got into a fight. I sat down opposite a black guy. He looked a few years older than me. He had on baggy jeans, big Timberland boots and a T-shirt three sizes too big. He was just looking at me. Out of the blue he asked me what I was looking at. 'Nothing,' was all I said. We spent the next three or four stops staring each other down. Like, *really* staring each other down. I didn't want to look at him but I didn't want him to think I was backing down or scared, even though I was. I was really scared but I wanted to be strong. You know? I wanted to let him know I wasn't afraid of him being up in my face the way he was. By the sixth or seventh stop I gave up. I looked away but he just wouldn't stop staring. 'What?' I finally asked him at the ninth stop. He didn't answer but he got up when I did and followed me off the train. After we got through the ticket barrier he called me a faggot, said something about the tightness of my jeans. I told him his old man and the whole line of men in his family were faggots and that his mother had sucked my dick."

"And?"

"And he slapped me, which is supposed to be a big dis."

"What do you mean?"

"My brother 4 bitch-slaps people when he knows they can't fight him."

"Oh. Right. So what happened next?"

"We fought. The only reason I fought him was because 4 said that real tough guys don't talk. When they want to fight they fight. And this guy was all talk. Plus, he followed me off at my stop. With a real tough guy, it would have kicked off on the train. It didn't last long, a bunch of people pulled us apart. I had marks on my neck from his fingernails. It was nothing really, but for about a week, every time I saw the marks in the mirror I felt the shame of fighting with another black guy. I was pushed into doing what I would never want to. The thought stalked me, this idea of being forced into things that I don't want to do. That's the story of my life and of the lives of everyone I know. We get pushed around. In the end, we become what we never imagined we would. I don't want to live like that, not ever. I know nobody gives a shit. Who would?"

Trevor was silent for a while. He looked at James intently and then he wrote something else down.

75

"Were you reading Baldwin at the time?"

"What time?"

"On the train, the fight?"

"No."

"What's so bad about being called a faggot?"

"Nothing," James said quickly, "I guess."

"One last question, if you don't mind. If you could be anywhere right now, where would it be?"

"Far away from here on a hill surrounded by tall trees and a lake and some grass."

"Do you mean marijuana?" Trevor held up his clipboard poised to make note.

"I don't smoke weed. I mean grass like in a garden."

Trevor looked at James and he smiled. "Do you ever leave your estate?"

James sighed and closed his eyes. Sometimes, he went to the City at lunchtime. He would buy a frothy coffee and sit in the window of Starbucks or eat a pub lunch in the Seven Stars, that 400-year-old pub behind the Royal Courts of Justice. He liked watching the robed barristers and white men in suits, trying to see where he might fit in one day. Once he saw a tall and angular dark-skinned black man, in his late thirties, wearing a pen lodged in the breast pocket of a navy blue suit with a clean white shirt with initials fancily sewn into his cuffs. At first he just walked by, and they merely eyed each other. Than he stopped, and turned back to face James, moved his *Financial Times* from under his left armpit to his right. Then he looked at his wristwatch, a Rolex Oyster Perpetual, the same as 4 bought 3 for his last birthday. James thought he was just showing off at first. But then he watched the movements of the man's body, his anxious eyes; the way he would hesitate and begin again; seeming scared, like he knew he was one false move away from the street. James didn't want to live like that. But he didn't say any of this to Trevor.

Trevor closed his notebook dramatically. "There, that's it. We're all done," he said.

He sounded like every doctor who had ever stuck a needle in James's arm. Trevor reopened his black pad and then looked at James.

"You will be pleased to know that I won't recommend you being sectioned. You'll most likely be advised to see a therapist and to take some anti-anxiety medication. Nobody can force you to do anything you don't want to, but please leave the option open. Some people believe they can simply use willpower to control their suicidal feelings. The problem with that is there is probably a chemical imbalance in the brain. And that needs to be treated with medicine. So, let me ask you this, James: if you had a broken leg, would you get treatment or would you just keep walking on it, writhing in pain, trying to convince yourself that you just needed willpower to overcome the pain? No," he said after a teacher-like pause, "you would get treatment, and you would do so immediately. You wouldn't even think twice about it. Your situation is similar. If you are diagnosed with clinical depression, or something, then there is a physical cause for your condition. And you need to get it sorted out. It is not just emotion. The brain, after all, is an organ. And sometimes it needs treatment." Trevor stood, zipped up his bag and then placed a business card near the fruit bowl and put his hand on James's shoulder. James shrugged it off.

"You know, sometimes you sound like a robot. You do this a lot, right?"

Trevor smiled. This time, James thought it might be genuine. "I'll bear that in mind. Remember, I'm here for you. You can talk to me any time. But you have to meet me halfway. I can only do so much and I think accepting my limits is an important aspect of what I do. I want you to do something for me that's very, very important. Make a commitment to staying alive. Can you promise me that?"

"I promise." James said just to speed up Trevor's departure.

Trevor patted James arm lightly. "You see, you are more connected than you realize. One final thing. Relax. That's right. Take some deep breaths and do something that you enjoy. Take a candlelit bath, burn an effigy of P. Diddy. I don't know. Go for a walk in the park with a beautiful friend. Listen to some nice music."

Trevor, with his peevish tone and his *GQ* manner, suddenly repulsed James.

"You know what I mean?" Trevor said. "Just take it easy. And engage in these activities that relax you on a regular basis. And let me tell you, James, today is the first day of the rest of your life. You are on your way. On your way to a better life."

He slung his bag over his shoulder and left. James watched him for as long as he could see him and he mulled over everything that had gone wrong in his life. He looked at Trevor's business card. He had not been handed a real business card before, from a white man. Then, James reached over and picked up the letter.

# SEVEN

# MEINA AND JAMES

After reading her letter, James expected Meina to visit at some point. But he had not expected that she would look so like her brother. When she walked into the room, he was standing with his back to the door, looking out of the window, watching out for her. He was still attached to an IV and wore what looked like an oversized blue bib. The sound of her footsteps at the door startled him and he swiveled round too quickly, almost collapsing to the ground. Her eyes were tawny, like her brother's, but set wider apart, giving her face an almost feline appearance—the look he saw was fleeting, it was gone from her face as soon as she smiled but it was a look that would stick in his memory. There was no mistaking the pain.

James had seen her from his window the day before, sitting on a bench in the hospital gardens, under a row of oak trees and a cloud-filled sky. She wore a long raincoat and a wig she had bought for ten pounds at Afroworld on Kingsland High Street in Dalston. It was the type of Afro idealized in the sixties, natural, light and never subdued. Meina wore it defiantly; that day she had been dreaming of being someone else, a strong rebellious sister, out of the reach of pain. Her hands were dug deep into her pockets and she sat with head bent low, staring at her shoes. Around her fellow visitors, doctors, nurses, paramedics and auxiliary workers bustled through the gardens. But, as Meina sat facing the building, nervously trying to steel herself in preparation for her imminent meeting with James, she felt alone, far removed from the people passing her.

She remembered her brother's visits to the homes of her ex-husbands. Ashvin was the reason she had kept on being divorced.

Once, pretending to be a blind beggar, he had sat in the white heat outside one house for almost a week. That was the longest it ever took for any of the husbands to return her to her aunt's house. *Waddaddo*, blind beggars, were believed to have the power of deflecting misfortune by conjuring protective spells or by adding the Qur'an *baraka* (blessings) to a family's personal amulets. Their predictions were always costly. Meina looked out from the confines of a gloomy room that smelled of unwashed laundry, early one Sunday morning. She could not believe her eyes when she saw Ashvin walking toward her new home. He wore metal cuffs on his wrists, and a silver wrapper that had belonged to their father which he had covered with banana leaves, yam vines and what looked like oil.

Meina was with her fourth husband, a thin rodent-faced old man with spiky hair and quick hands—Asad or Ayad, she could no longer remember his name. Like most of the ex-husbands, he was brutal in his adherence to his beliefs and lived in a world of camel clops on desert sand and raised women's voices around the communal water well. This was Bargal, a remote village far in the south where villagers were known to threaten to behead those who did not pray five times a day. The husband had four maddening children—all girls with flashing eyes—who he instructed to bang on the floor with a broom whenever they wanted their father's new bride to fetch something. It was a *mundal*, an old mud house with crumbling walls and a small herd of camels in the dusty, termite-mound-studded yard. The room Meina was kept in was dirty with small windows that let in little light. Ashvin sat opposite the entrance on a low stool, sweating in the ninety-degree heat. The villagers murmured nervously as they passed by. No one dared approach; most just stared inquisitively from their front doors.

Meina had no idea how he had come up with the scheme. It was genius, but she was troubled—if he succeeded, it would only encourage their aunt and her husband to arrange more marriages, to make more money from selling her off. He was a clever, resourceful fourteen-year-old. Their father had told them that blind beggars were considered specialists who "fought" jinns in ceremonies resembling exorcisms. Meina had seen Ashvin's "ceremony" three times before. He would take the head of a dead snake from his pocket and a boiled egg. Passing the egg through the head of the snake, he would break open the shell, eat the egg and spread the bloodied remains around the entrance to the *mundal*. Sometimes, he would light a fire and lightly touch the head or the eyelids of the snake, muttering all the while.

For the first few days, Asad/Ayad hovered at the entrance to the house, his hands clasped behind his back. But, by the Friday of that week, he had lost his resolve. He was a man in total distress, stammering and stuttering. "Oh, blind beggar," he pleaded, "I am the owner of this home. Why me?"

"The eggshells mean sickness," said Ashvin, stretching his neck to look up so that his eyes bore into the old man.

Meina watched from the window as her brother crossed his eyes and spoke up in a raspy, strangled voice—as though he could not bear to confide his secret.

"Do you have a new woman in your house? A young girl?" The husband nodded nervously. Ashvin, looking down and crushing bloodied eggshells between his palms, shook his head, "She is cursed. She will bring sickness to your camels. To the whole village. No doctor will have the cure."

Meina was sure he would be discovered because of the sound of his voice. His accent was rough and throaty-sounding, easily identifiable as belonging to someone from the city, as opposed to the slower, more melodious voices of people who lived in remote villages. But he was never caught out, and when the news of his warning spread, a sense of panic buzzed around the sleepy village. The neighbors demanded the husband leave or send his new bride away.


The sight of Meina on the hospital bench had haunted James. She was eighteen, a grown woman. What did she want from him? But she too was nervous and did not say much that first day. She studied the stitches on his lip and the scar on his neck—a vivid, jagged, raw, red ring. She stood at the door, wide-eyed, with dimples and half-full lips that looked as if they might burst if kissed. Although they had never spoken, James had seen her

81

around Forest Gate, at the bus stop. She had always seemed reserved, unapproachable. In the past they had only nodded acknowledgement once or twice, and now, finding themselves alone, neither one knew what to do.

"My brother wrote a lot in his notebooks," Meina said, finally, still standing. With a small gesture James offered her a seat. He made his way back to his bed but in his haste he stumbled, almost falling over. Each of his steps seemed to require all his effort. James slowly settled on his bed and Meina sat studying him. She realized at once that he had indeed meant to kill himself—Ashvin had not been part of some prank. She saw sadness in him, a melancholy that seemed familiar. "He wrote a lot about you," she said.

"Your voice is different," James said.

"You mean from Ash? My brother is dead. Remember?"

Although Meina's English was almost flawless, unlike her brother's, she slurred her consonants as a French speaker would, not like someone from East Africa where the inflection was speedy, harsh and guttural. Their mother had been harder on her, the daughter, about the correct pronunciation of English words. She said it would act as a protective cloak wherever Meina went in her life.

James said nothing. He sat on the bed and let out a deep, anguished sigh, covering his mouth with his hands; a vein above the wide laceration on his neck stood out, livid and pulsating.

Meina felt her heart pounding and the anger she had been holding in threatened to explode. It was only as she studied the marks on his neck that she really believed that James had not tricked Ashvin into killing himself alone. She watched him ease himself up onto the bed, lying on his side on top of disheveled bed sheets. The look in his eyes was so intense Meina almost forgot how young he was. He looked burdened and ill at ease; perhaps even afraid.

"You okay?"

"Yes. Thanks," he replied.

"Ash wrote that you never lie. Is that true?"

James nodded, seeming confused. "Yes. I mean, no. I don't lie."

Meina ran a hand through her hair and pursed her lips to stop them trembling. "I want to know about the boy he wrote about. The Ethiopian boy in the newspapers. Nalma. I need to know if you knew."

"If I knew what?'

"Did you and Ashvin kill him?" It had sounded better when she practiced in front of the mirror at home.

"Yes, we did."

Meina folded her arms and took a long, hard look at James. He had closed his eyes, turning his head slightly away from her. Tears welled up, but she blinked them back. She moved to stand nearer the bed and tentatively held out her hand, as if seeking comfort.

"To have had a brother like mine was a blessing." That was all she said. And then she left.


The weather was much cooler the next time she showed up; it had rained heavily that morning. Meina waited in the cafe by the cardiology unit until she was sure all his other visitors had gone.

"So," she asked, "did you read my letter?"

"Yeah, I did."

James searched her face for a sign that she was joking. He found none.

"And what do you say?"

"Yes."


He was discharged from the hospital two days later. For hours, he walked past her estate, up and down, looking behind him to see if there was anyone watching. He sat alone in the park until it began to rain, lightly at first, then heavily, then just a slow drizzle. Finally, he made up his mind. As he approached her building, he counted eight boys huddled together on a wall halfway down the street. It was dark and James could not make out who they were. As he drew closer, the boys stopped speaking and turned to face him.

A tall boy in a black parka with fur around the collar slowly came forward, his hand in his coat pocket. James turned to his right and saw another half a dozen boys standing in the shadows with hats or hoods covering their eyes, faces dimly lit from the joints they passed each other. Three more of them sat on the bonnet of a car parked along the street and yet another stood by himself on a gravel path near the entrance to the estate, keeping a lookout. James knew they were all tooled up. The night was cold and still; a woman in a red crocheted hat clicked her heels as she walked by. She carried a red-and-white plastic bag, the air behind her heavy with the smell of KFC. James could just make out the glow of television screens in a few of the rows of identical arched windows. Another boy put a joint to his mouth and lit it, sucking twice until the flame on the tip extinguished and became a dizzying orange spot and then he blew out the match with a blast of smoke.

"Yo! Heads up." He seemed to be speaking out to the dark.

"Didn't you see the wall tags, my yout'?" This time James couldn't tell who had spoken. He remembered the wall daubed with graffiti that he had passed at the entrance but he hadn't taken any notice.

"It's a fucking liberty," came another voice, angry and threatening. James felt his pulse race. He jerked back as someone smashed glass, a bottle, behind him. And then, more boys approached from out of the shadows. Two more came out of the back seat of a Ford with a broken windscreen, one of them wearing a ski mask. The car was clamped and had a local council removal sticker on the passenger window. James wondered how he had missed it. The driver stayed put, hunched over the steering wheel tapping a number into a phone. Wishing he had gone straight home, James looked up the blind street from where he had come and then ahead at the bright lights at Meina's window. Conscious of the many eyes watching his every move, he straightened and struggled to stand firm like a man. His legs trembled, there was a ringing in his ears and he could taste vomit at the back of his throat. He remembered 4 had told him to hit the biggest man if he was ever confronted by a gang. "Strike fast. Strike first." But James could never tell whether 4 was joking or not.

*Hit the biggest.*

His eyes burned and he clenched his fists. All the boys looked big and he had no interest in fighting even the smallest. James sighed, overwhelmed by the weight of the unwritten, unbreakable rules that his brothers had tried to teach him. This is how it was on the estates; you didn't get a second chance to flourish or to say sorry. This is how it would be forever—a life sentence. His breathing slowed. He stared at a slab of broken pavement and wondered why he could never measure up. It was like being in a dream—he couldn't fight and he couldn't run. He looked up at the somber sky and then he conceded. I'm fucked, he thought.

"You took a wrong turn, bruv, you can't come dan here." The boy with the parka looked at James with a quizzical expression. He took out a knife, unfolded it. The street light caught the long silver blade as he wiped it across the thigh of his jeans.

Just then, a woman parted her curtains and leaned out into the street. She was white, ashen-faced, and James thought she looked pregnant. "Terry? You out there? Your dinner's getting cold." The voice was a notch louder than necessary.

"Fuck off, Mum," said a mixed-race boy in a red-and-white pair of Adidas Top Tens. He shook his head slowly with his mouth open wide, dropped his arms to his sides and then looked at the floor.

"Oi, Slater, Mummy said dinner's getting cold," mimicked a voice and there was soft laughter.

"You lot can fuck off 'n' all," said Terry. He shook his head again, flipped open his phone, pushed at the buttons with his thumb. "Fuck all this," he said, "I'm going over to my girl's house. Fucking hate coming round here." He smashed the bottle he carried, turned his back on his friends. "Hello, it's me. You got food in your house?" he said into the phone and walked up the street alone.

The woman did not look surprised when she closed her curtain.

James used the distraction to pick up his pace. He felt spreading waves of fear in his knees first and then all the way up his spine. His body reminded him he was still too weak to run, so he prepared himself as best he could to take a beating or to get knifed. He used both his hands to wipe the sweat from his face and when he passed a phone box he raised his chin to the light so they could be sure to see his face. He kept turning to look as closely as he

could at each of their faces but he couldn't see much because of
the dim street lights. When he finally reached Meina's flat, his
hands were shaking. She had put her front-door key in the envelope with her letter but there was no way he was going to use it.
He rang the bell and almost immediately changed his mind and
was turning to walk away when she opened the door. For a long
moment, they stood looking at each other, then he stepped inside
and Meina watched him lean his back against the wall, his hands
shaking and his chest heaving. He jumped when he heard a sound.
She tried to take his hand but he withdrew it.

"Come in," Meina said, gently tugging at his arm. "I've made
you something to eat." She turned and led him through the flat.

Something happened in that moment. As James walked through
the hall everything behind him turned into a blur. Later he told
her that it was the first time in a long while that he had felt safe.
He let go of a deep breath—as though he had sucked in all the
air in the world.

Meina's was a smaller version of the flat James shared with
his mother and brothers. The same as all state-sponsored flats:
all new fixtures and paper-thin walls, hidden radiators, low ceilings and carpet throughout except in the kitchen where there was
always linoleum.

"It smells nice," he said. He had removed his shoes but seemed
unsure about stepping on the rug in the center of the room.

"It's a cinnamon and apple plug-in air-freshener thing. I turned
it on full blast to drown out the smell of my lamb."

"You have a lamb?"

"No. I *cooked* lamb, silly." Meina laughed, still nervous but
visibly relaxing.

James's hand went up to the scar on his neck; he tried to clear
his throat.

"Are you tired?" she asked.

"A little."

Meina searched his face, wondering if bad intent would show.
She felt a stirring of anticipation, of danger. She had thought it
would feel different being with a man, on her own terms and with
no one else around. Where she came from, not all women observed
purdah, but she had often thought that she might as well have.

Being with James felt wrong, forbidden—as though anything could happen. Being alone with a man not related to her was a disgrace; at home she would have been considered loose, out of control—if something had happened they would have said she'd asked for it since she had invited him into her home. Meina wanted to act like a typical British eighteen-year-old, but she did not know how. She was far from home, but felt as though she had brought all the old rules with her. In Somalia, there were so many rules to protect tradition. But none to protect them from the armed gangs on every street.

They sat on the couch and ate together, watching a DVD. It was a love story with an all-white cast. Meina didn't say anything about her letter and neither did James. Although he shifted uncomfortably in his seat and looked embarrassed during the sex scenes in the movie, he felt like an adult sitting with her, alone in the flat. Although she saw him casting surreptitious glances, Meina pretended not to notice him watching the slender curves of her neck and her arms. Embarrassed when she looked up and caught his eye, James turned to look at a picture on the bookshelf. It was of Meina, her parents and Ashvin, who looked about six years old.

"Where was that picture taken?" he asked.

Meina reclined into her seat on the couch, tilted her head and sighed. "In our garden in Baidoa. Ashvin and my father had just returned from a fishing trip." Her voice was slightly strained. "I know that must sound weird, going on a fishing trip in the middle of a war, but it's not like fishing here in England. In Somalia, we fish when there is nothing else to eat. Mostly we were trapped in our homes, because the guns and tanks ruled the streets. But we still tried not to worry constantly about war or whether we'd ever have a government again. That's the strange thing about the place, people trying to live normal lives. Mostly we needed permission to go out from 'someone who knew someone' who was a member of an armed gang. But not my father. He said he'd never give in to bullies. He said he would always go where he pleased. But my mother would arrange things for us in secret."

Meina gave a tentative smile as she got up. Her eyes flitted over the picture, then she drew the curtains and positioned her back against the wall.

James was still staring at the picture. He couldn't remember Ashvin having such a wide grin. He looked so innocent and happy. Time had diminished that smile, stilled his spirit.

"For a moment, I forgot Ashvin was dead," he said.

Meina moved back to her seat. "There is nothing you can do to bring him back."

In the tense silence, Meina thought of the way life presented whole new storylines without permission. James tried to suppress the urge to cry but a tear trickled out and she saw. He used his palm to wipe his eyes.

"It will be all right," she said.

He didn't respond. He just sat back and faced the screen, unblinking, pretending to be lost in the film.

"Your lamb was good," he said. "I haven't tasted it cooked like that before."

"Should I run you a bath?" Meina regretted the words as soon as they left her mouth. It was something her mother always asked her father after he ate.

"No. It's okay," he answered but he couldn't meet her eyes.

Meina had showed him to her brother's room, but when he got into the bed, under the sheets, James was too anxious to fall asleep. Through the window the moon looked depressed, stuck between heaven and earth. Its somber, almost tentative light spilled down listlessly. The room smelled of Ashvin. For a while, James listened to the couple next door arguing, their voices easily penetrating the thin dividing wall. Eavesdropping on the intimate conversation was interesting at first but after an hour of their cursing he was ready to go and kick down their door.

He woke long before dawn, soaked in his own sweat and overwhelmed with the feeling that he had failed. He had let Ashvin down. He had wanted to die at the time but now, after getting so close, he wasn't so sure what he wanted. The shame he felt shut out everything else. He tried to pray but ended in frustrated tears because he didn't believe in the things he was saying. Meina heard his sobs from her room and got up, knocking gently on his door. But James quietened, remembering where he was.

When he got up in the morning he could hear Meina in the kitchen and smelled coffee. With a forced energy, borne of despair, he lifted half of his body out of bed but his head wouldn't follow. His neck burned, every bit of him was too heavy and his eyes felt as if they had been cemented shut during the night. It was like the worst type of hangover. Meina had left him a towel in the bathroom and he washed and dressed before joining her.

"How was your night?" she said.

"Pretty shitty."

"Pretty shitty?"

"I couldn't sleep."

"Me neither."

James stretched his arms up, "I'd better get home in time for breakfast. I'll pack all my stuff then I'll come back." He turned to her, uncertain. "That is, if you still want me to stay here."

"Can I come with you?" she asked.

James was caught off guard. To answer quickly would have revealed his excitement. He turned to look out of the window but when he allowed himself a small smile Meina caught it. He shrugged. "If you want."

They stepped out of the house holding hands. Meina looked at James, wondering if he had any idea how much such a casual gesture meant to her. The boys gathered at the corner all turned to stare.

"Let's cross," Meina said nervously, trying to pick up the pace. James followed.

Some of the boys also crossed and walked toward them. A tall, light-skinned boy who must have been in his early twenties, with a square face and bulging arm muscles, spoke first, his eyes shining.

"Are you one of them Morrison brothers?" Half his hair was in dreads and he wore an old-fashioned black goose-down gilet with a fur hood. He smiled, showing off discolored teeth.

"Yes." James nodded, and kept hold of Meina's hand.

"Respect." The boy offered James a rough fist, covered with cuts.

James didn't acknowledge the greeting—his brothers had taught him never to look like he was begging for friends.

"My name's Ratchet." The young man lowered his hand, seeming not to notice the snub. "So what, you livin' up these ends now?" he continued.

James exchanged his wily stare for Ratchet's strong one.

"Yeah, maybe." Meina could tell James was nervous; she squeezed his hand but he continued to stare at Ratchet.

Ratchet turned to his friends. "See, I told you." He beckoned to one of the boys; as he came close, James recognized him. He had lost all the menace of the night before. He stood next to Ratchet, raising his head sheepishly.

"One of my boys spoke out of turn to your missus, and another one pulled a knife. They didn't know. No disrespect." Ratchet's tone was severe.

"It's cool," said James. "It's your manor." He gave a gentle nod toward the boy, but he would not meet James's eye.

"He says he didn't know. My boys are normally clear-headed. I don't know what's got into them recently—they been dragging their feet. I got to get 'em something to do. If your family need anything doing, let me know." Ratchet tensed his lips as though he wanted to say something else, but then thought better of it. He raised his right hand again and balled it into a fist twice the size of James's. This time James touched Ratchet's fist solemnly with his own.

"Respect," Ratchet said and thumped his heart three times. "I've got a car. I can drop you off somewheres."

"No, we're good. But thanks."

Meina was surprised by the encounter. She had not realized that the streets of London were carved out into territories just as they had been at home. But here it was not by clans but by class, education, wealth and, she guessed, strength. Each group had its own rules, its own village mentality. She imagined the same wars taking place among the poor all over the world. War has a gender, she thought, and it's male.

"I'm not sure I understand what just happened," she said to James as they walked out of the estate.

"It's complicated," he said, looking down at the ground and letting go of her hand.

"Are you in a gang?"

"No."

"So who are the Morrison Brothers?"

"Well, my brothers. It's hard to describe—it's like a family

90

business. They're my brothers but I'm not like them, they're different." He stopped and turned to face her. "They're drug dealers. You need to know that. And they're ruthless. They don't really care who they hurt. But they don't mean it . . . I mean, they don't mean it all the time."

Meina put her hand on his shoulder. "I'll be fine," she said, "this isn't about me."

"Am I going on?" asked James.

"No. Not at all."

They smiled at one another and then Meina slowed, walking just behind James. He didn't turn to look at her as he spoke. "They don't sell drugs themselves any more," he said, "they use young people, shottas, kids who they think have nothing to lose. They're not really tough; it's like a front they use to keep control. I'm not making sense, am I? What I mean is, they're all trying to act tough, be like my dad. Or at least what they've been told he was like. He got shot for selling drugs. Everyone knows. But when you meet them just try to remember, I am not like them, okay?"

James spoke almost as if to himself—as though airing thoughts that had been on his mind for a while. Finally, he turned to look at Meina. At first she thought he was just looking to see if she was there or still listening. But, for a moment, he frowned and she saw something else and thought perhaps he was checking for understanding or trust. Her pulse quickened and she blushed, pursing her lips in concentration and nodding confirmation. He walked ahead and she followed. At that point, she would have followed him anywhere. They walked at an easy pace through the churchyard toward the Romford road. Voices from traders on Stratford Broadway echoed around offering King Edward potatoes and Granny Smith apples and the air was a confusion of the mingling smells of McDonald's, Pizza Hut and KFC. Groups of teenagers were hanging about, shouting to each other above the din of afternoon traffic. Meina noticed a few people looking at them from the corners of their eyes and twice heard someone say James's name as they passed. James, in silence, maintained a steady pace, eyes scanning some distant thing. To Meina, every-thing in London had always looked oversized: the church spire, the supermarket windows, the gigantic doors to the bank and office buildings, the buses. It was damp, the graying clouds and the creeping stillness promising rain. James led them off the main road and on to a quiet backstreet. There was a strong odor of hot piss and alcohol and the only sounds were a gentle swishing from the rubbing of fabric on James's jacket and the thud of their steps on the concrete. A girl walked by, fifteen years old at the most and pushing a baby in a three-wheeled pram. She stopped, recognizing James.

"S'up, James," she said, immediately mesmerized by James's scar. "What you doing out?" Her hair was slicked down on her face and spots of blue hair gel were visible on her temple.

"S'up, Tammy," said James. Meina had hesitated but he pulled her along and didn't stop walking.

"Who's she?" Meina asked.

James shook his head. "She tells people we're related because my dad used to sleep with her mum. This place never lets you go, even if you don't wanna belong."

"But are you well protected? Like a warlord?" she asked.

"Warlord? Not really." James was thoughtful. "I always think about what will happen when I meet one of their enemies, someone who doesn't show respect. You can't imagine what it's like to walk around like an open target your whole life."

"Yes, I can."

As they walked toward the train station, Meina watched James, thinking about men and war and the satisfaction of fighting. James hadn't gloated over Ratchet's apology, the way the boys had been fearful of his brothers. James didn't look seventeen. He was not much taller than Meina and his features were a sculpted, pure-charcoal black. He had a gentle presence, a tenderness that reminded Meina of her father. She thought of her parents, the love they had shared. As a girl she had prayed for a love like theirs. But after their murder she understood that love was just a game for the gods. It was an unattainable dream, like African unity or world peace. The night before she had lain in bed listening to James crying, wanting to hold and protect him. Her mind drifted. What would it be like to have sex with him? He was young—a baby—but she could feel part of herself already connected to him. It wasn't lust. Not really. It was something else. Up until then Meina had had a built-in disgust for British men, their style of dress, their untidy hair, their vulgarity. James was different. She wanted to know him and have him know her.

"Meina? Why are you staring at me like that? What is it? What's wrong?" James looked uneasy.

"Nothing. My tummy hurts," she lied.

She walked with him, trying not to step on the green weeds stretching out from between the pavement cracks. When they reached the Mandela estate, James stopped in front of a large red rectangular door with a silver intercom where the handle should have been. The Morrison flat was up on the first floor nestled between two pensioners who had disliked the boys since 5 was in his teens when he played hip hop so loudly it shook their windows and rattled their cutlery. There was a sign on the door that read *Warning: no ticket, no laundry.* One of his brothers had put it up to remind customers that they did not give credit.

James inhaled deeply. He didn't want to go in. He turned to Meina.

"Look. My brothers . . . they're a bit, well . . . you have to kind of brace yourself, is what I'm trying to say." He exhaled and pressed the bell.

"Who be dis?"

James sighed and leaned against the door. "It's me."

"Where's your key?"

"I just wanted to warn you, I'm with someone," said James.

"Who?"

"She's cool. Open the door."

There was a loud buzz as heavy bolts were automatically released.

Their building was three stories of sixteen flats and maisonettes overflowing with smells from different corners of the world. Each flat had a reinforced front door with two or four windows depending on the number of bedrooms. The main entrance, with the intercom, opened onto a communal garden where dogfights were held on the last Friday of every month. The garden was a small patch of disheartened grass generally full of dog shit, soiled nappies, unemptied bins and mail-order clothes on the shared washing line.

The Morrisons had owned number 28 for over twenty years. James's father, Bunny, had bought it under a rent-to-buy scheme dreamed up by Margaret Thatcher, in the days before the poll tax or the community charge. He had paid for it in three cash instalments. It was during the recession in the early eighties when everyone had to smoke weed. Bunny said his weed was so good that when Bob Marley played at the Speakeasy club in Hackney in 1973, his people would only deal with Bunny.

"James is here," a voice in the distance came from the first-floor landing. James tried to lift his head up but winced as the pain shot through his neck muscles and reverberated along his spine. Then, his mother's face peered over the balcony.

"Thank God you're safe. Hurry up, we've been waiting."

James closed his eyes, inhaled the foul winds from the tenements and slowly, reluctantly, re-entered his world.


The maisonette was cluttered and haphazard, with bold colors, red, white and black. It didn't look like an ex-council flat inside, but it was. If there was a style it was hoardist—newly painted maximalist narc-deco with heavy wine-colored curtains. There were four bedrooms upstairs and a tiny kitchen off the living room. The space was dominated by big expensive furniture but lacked spirit. Old wine boxes were filled with stacks of empty CDs, there were six massive flat-screen TVs, hundreds of DVDs and piles of *Vibe* and *Essence* magazines. The only sign of warmth in the room was James's futon, one of those cotton-covered things that came with a free matching storage ottoman. James kept all his favorite things in the ottoman box, like a sea captain's chest, beside his bed. His mother had threatened to buy him a proper bed but he had refused, he loved sleeping on the old futon; with its stains, its worn and faded blue upholstery, its lumpy dips and ripples, its smell of sameness, it stood in marked contrast with the lushness of the rest of the room.

James and Meina entered the living room. Light fought to get in through the curtains covering the long window that took up much of the left wall. The room smelled of oatmeal. James's mother had cooked Quaker Oats with extra sugar, just the way he liked. James paused, took a slow look at his brothers and grimaced. One of the brothers, skinny with smiling eyes, was slumped over his elbows at the table with a green blanket over his shoulders. He was either high or drunk—or perhaps both. Another brother, this one with features remarkably similar to James's, sat at the same table playing cards by himself. Only one brother, neatly dressed in black shirt and jeans, stood up as James and Meina entered the room. His skin was clear, several shades lighter than James's. He was good-looking and could have passed for a professional footballer. Another brother fumbled with a mobile phone before slapping it shut. "Who's the honey?" he smiled, removing a toothpick from his teeth and wiping his mouth with a napkin. He was bigger than the other brothers—with well-toned muscles—and wore a blue knitted Kangol. One brother did not look up at all. He sat at the head of the table reading the *Voice*. He was thin and drawn with graying hair and sad, anxious-looking eyes. James and Meina kept still in the open doorway, overcome by an oven-cleaner smell. 2 switched on the television and turned it up—that's what they used as background noise whenever they were about to discuss "business." Meina got the feeling she had walked into a sitcom. She was fascinated. While the news droned on, her heart leaped from fear to embarrassment as she worked out what she would say and waited for her initial feeling of awkwardness to pass. 5 folded the paper then looked up at James.

"You've become a minor celebrity," he said. "You've made the *Voice*. It says here that in London over the last three months more than fifty black boys under eighteen have committed suicide. You survived though. You've had five different requests for interviews and the BBC want you to take part in a *Newsnight* debate."

His brothers laughed but James looked panicked and confused. He told Meina later that he was remembering being chased through Victoria Park in Bow by a black Alsatian with yellow eyes. He had managed to run to his brother 5 who was arguing with his then girlfriend by the swings. His brother beat the owner—an Irishman—so badly that he ended up on a life-support machine for three weeks. Then 5 took the dog and it got killed in a dogfight that won him £500—a monkey.

"Don't tell me," said James. "It's bad for business." He walked slowly to the pine dining table, pulled an extra seat from the back of the room and offered it to Meina.

Once she was seated, he stood behind her chair and announced, with curious formality, "Everyone, this is Meina. She's my guest." The word "guest" came out harshly, as though he was begging everyone to mind their manners. Meina heard one of the brothers suck on his teeth loudly.

The brother who looked most like James raised himself off his chair and farted loudly. "Whoa. That was a ripper," he laughed.

"Oh, bad guts! That stinks. You're an animal," said the brother in the black shirt, covering his nose and wafting the air around his face. "And in front of James's *guest*."

The brothers laughed again. James glared at the culprit.

"What you looking at me like that for?" his brother asked, shrugging his shoulders. "If you hold in your farts they can kill you. Besides, it wasn't me. It was the mice—they're getting proper lively around here." Meina was confused, glancing around the room for signs of mice, but James reached out and touched her arm, shaking his head.

"What's wrong?" asked James's mother and she reached to pull him close, moaning softly as she looked at the scars on his neck. James pulled away and went to the kitchen, coming back with eight bowls and taking a seat between his mother and Meina. Although only forty-eight, she had already lost most of her hair and two front teeth. Her remaining teeth were bad, chipped in places and discolored. Meina watched as she tried to scoop oatmeal porridge into the first bowl. It had a bad smell, like molding potato, and her hands shook as she struggled to get any in the dish.

"I'm fine, I'm fine. It'll only take me a couple of seconds," she said.

No one seemed to be listening. Perhaps she knew everyone was watching her, pretending not to notice all the effort it took her to do something so simple. She spilled a spoonful. "Would you like some oats?" She gave Meina a hard stare, daring her to refuse.

"Oh, yes please."

"One scoop or two?"

She was spilling it over the table. Meina looked at James.

"Two," he said. The he leaned in and whispered to Meina, pointing across the table at his brothers, "He's Number 1, that's Number 2, he's Number 3, Number 4 and that's my oldest brother, 5." Meina nodded, still mesmerized by the mother's unfruitful efforts. Eventually she managed to scoop enough into the bowls but there was a terrible mess. She stood and looked around the room. She walked slowly—much too slowly for someone her age. She took several steps, holding onto the edge of the table, and then turned and went back to her seat. Meina had always thought of addicts as the lowest form of humanity, but here was this woman, a mother, still trying to feed her boys. It was confusing. She had resisted the strong urge to get up and help her serve, worried that she would be overstepping some boundary. She forced herself to keep still and sighed when she realized she had been holding her breath. Did they expect her to eat the sludge that had been slopped into her bowl? She looked at James, his head down, staring at his own bowl. They all ate the cold porridge.

"So, why'd you do it?" asked 2.

They had obviously been discussing James before he arrived with Meina. What had they missed? Where had they gone wrong? And what could they do to make James better?

They all stared at him. Waiting. Their expressions were different but all lacking in warmth. 3 appeared quietly by James's left side and patted his shoulder.

"No jokes this morning?" asked James.

"What you did is definitely not good for business," 3 replied. "It makes the family look bad."

"The fuck is wrong with you?" said 4. "You don't even shave yet and already you want to kill yourself. S'cuse my French, Mum. I know we agreed we wouldn't, but what the hell is wrong with him? How you let some traumatized African boy make you put a rope around your neck and jump from a roof?"

Meina felt her gut clench. She wanted to say something but she was afraid—4 was by far the meanest-looking of James's brothers.

"If he told you to jump off a bridge wouldya do it?" said 2, mimicking their mother's voice. There was heavy laughter— suddenly it felt like the hottest day of the year and Meina could feel her face flush. James had the good sense not to speak; he sat still in his chair, his hand reaching up to rub the scars on his neck. He glanced at his mother with a look that was both contemptuous and pleading. Her shoulders sagged in an ill-fitting, fluff-covered jumper. What did she think of him?

"So, what you wanna do?" asked 5.

James shrugged, not looking up.

"If you still wanna die, let me do it, idiot," offered 4.

James lowered his head even closer to the table and let out a sob. For a moment nobody spoke.

"Okay, okay. What can we do to help make things better?" asked 5. He sounded sincere.

"Let me be," James said, almost in a whisper.

"He is coming to live with me." Meina took a deep breath and forced herself to look at the brothers, her chin raised up. "I'm the sister of the 'traumatized African.' We only came here to collect his things." For a moment, a ring of silence thinned the air until nothing remained except the throb of hearts.

"Lookie here, you must have lost your mind, coming in here talking all that shit. You ain't taking my son any place, African," said James's mother. She had risen unsteadily to her feet and spat the last word out. The venom in Mrs. Morrison's voice shocked Meina.

James spoke slowly through his tears as he scanned his brothers' faces. "I can't stay here. I'm moving in with Meina and that's that." There were soft chuckles from two of the brothers. James bowed his head and rubbed his forehead with his hands, sighing then gritting his teeth as if in pain. His mother handed him a tissue, her voice suddenly gentle. "Don't cry in front of your girl-friend, son."

"Where do you live?" asked 3.

"On Lumumba."

"That's only 'round the corner," said 2.

Numbers 1 and 2 looked at each other. "Ratchet's boys," they said together and smiled.

"Ratchet?" asked 3.

"Remember Genesis's little brother?" said 2.

"Pissants. Why would we remember him?" asked 4.

"That where you stayed last night?" 5 asked James. "Did anyone see you?"

"Yes. I met Ratchet and his friends."

"Shit. Now the whole neighborhood know," said 4.

Meina sat still, her eyes darting from one brother to the other as she followed the conversation.

"Look, I don't want anything from you guys," said James looking at no one in particular. "I just need a break. I've spent my whole life living in your shadow, but I can take care of myself."

"Then you should learn how to behave," snapped 4. "Let him go." He waved his arm. "Ungrateful piece of shit. You watch how fast his skinny arse comes running when a bunch of those fuckers kick in his little girlfriend's front door and start waving pistols in his face."

There was a long silence and then 5 spoke.

"3, help your brother pack. 4, you drive him to the flat and help him unpack. Make sure the whole neighborhood sees you doing it."

"I need some money," said James. 5 raised his eyebrows at him and James slid down in his seat. If he had a tail it would have curled between his legs and up around his head.

"You got some nuts on you, boy," said 5, in almost velvet tones. "You hate what it is we do, but now you want our money?"

There was more laughter.

When 5 spoke everyone heard. He wasn't quite a bully but it was close. They all watched him walk over to James's futon, un-zip one of the cushions and count off notes from a thick wad hidden there. "Here. Two grand. Don't spend it all at once." He turned to Meina. "And you . . . don't even think of telling anyone what you just saw."

James's mother pulled on Meina's arm. "Listen, sweetheart, I need to take your number," she said.

"I don't have a phone."

"Well, get one," said 5, throwing some money at Meina.

"I don't need your money."

"Don't get pissy, sis," said 4. "We're not interested in your love life, but anything happen to our little brother here and I'm going to hold you personally responsible." He turned to James. "And let me tell you something else for free, little brother. You think you found yourself a pretty girlfriend? Well, don't get carried away. She may be pushing all the right buttons now but these black girls are fucking crazies. They're the devil's work. Believe me, I'm only telling you this because I love you. Forget drugs, forget guns, and forget about the white man. You get the wrong black chick and she'll snatch your soul and then she'll start to fuck you up—"

"And when you're lying in the road with blood coming out your ears, she still won't be satisfied," interrupted 5.

They all laughed in that wolflike way they did, like a pack. Meina looked at their mother, hoping for support. But Mrs. Morrison just shrugged. "We're serious," Number 3 said. "It's time to use your head. Don't make her any promises and stand your ground. Black women are like Brazil nuts, you can't tell a bad one until you've cracked it and taken a bite."

"And wear a rubber at all times," added 2.

James listened to his brothers as one might a passing airplane on a beautiful day. It sounded like they were preparing him for war.

"Doesn't Danny W's babymother live on Lumumba?" asked 3.

"That's right, I used to bone her. Terry Stevenson, she lives at number 44." It was the first time Number 1 had spoken.

"Yeah, I remember her. She was hot," said 2.

1 and 2 laughed hysterically.

"She wasn't hot," said 3.

"I'm not saying she was hot to look at," said 1. "But I think we would all agree she had body for days."

"I give you that," said 2 looking at 3.

"All right, I concur," said 3 after a long moment. "She was fit."

"Somebody call Danny and tell him the coup," said 5.

"You know Danny's gonna want work," said 3.

"So is Ratchet," said 2.

"I'll give a little something to Danny W. He's cool. But didn't I see Ratchet on *Top of the Pops* or something?"

"Not *Top of the Pops*. It was one of those other music shows.

He went in the charts at number 11 or some shit. He's into that grime or grindi or whatever the fuck. He got an 18,000-pound advance by Black Dawg, bought a 7,000-pound Rolex, some trainers and a piece of shit SUV with 33-inch rims that were more expensive than his ride," laughed 1.

"Jesus. Grindigrime? Is that what they're calling being a twat these days?"

"I told you. Pissants," said 4.

5 sighed loudly. "3, go talk to Ratchet. Throw him something. Not real work—just let him do something so he thinks he's on the firm."

"Something like what?" asked 3.

"Use your imagination," said 5 and Number 3 smiled.


The SUV pulled into the center of Lumumba estate, tinted windows vibrating with the sound of Fifty Cent. The driver's door clicked open and James's brother 4 jumped out, a white Kangol perched at a ridiculous angle on his massive bald head. 2 and 3 also jumped out, opened the boot and wrestled out two suitcases full of James's things. James and Meina sat in the back seat trying not to notice the twitching curtains. James's face was solemn, flushed with embarrassment. They had hardly spoken since leaving his flat.

"Are you angry with me?" he asked.

"I don't have AIDS."

"I know you don't."

"Why does your brother 5 look like that?" Meina had to shout above the din in the car.

"Like what?"

"Sad."

"He's been that way since he got back from prison. He sleeps with a loaded gun beside him and most nights he sweats his sheets and screams out. I asked him what it was like once and after he chewed my head off he said going to prison had cost him his soul."

Just before they'd left, 5 had called James out of the maisonette. By then, the rain had started. Meina was waiting for James, holding the front door. She saw 5 hand James a sheet of A4 paper with a list of numbers on it.

"Put this somewhere safe," he said. "If you need anything take it, all you need to do is to let one of us know. These are your family privileges, your inheritance. I know what you're going through but I have to be honest with you, not everyone spoke up for you. They think you're too young and way too irresponsible but I think you're old enough now. And listen, if your mother asks you anything about this money, say nothing. You hear me?"

The resolve in his brother's voice brought tears to James's eyes. He began scratching at his neck. 5 leaned closer to him, lowering his voice, "If you want to leave, you're free to leave, but you understand what you're doing, right, James? You're leaving us."

James could not look at him. Despite what he said about their drug dealing, he did have respect for his brothers. Meina watched and winced as James rubbed the scar on his throat. She could see he wanted to cry, but he was holding it in to prove something to his big brother. It was painful to watch.

"Come here," said 5, drawing James into a tight embrace. "I know how you feel, James. If you've got to go, you've got to go. But try to make sense of your life. I made a lot of mistakes, but in the space of five years I've accumulated over thirty bank accounts. There's just under sixty thousand pounds in each one. Why just under sixty?" He pulled back and looked at James, waiting for an answer.

James wiped his eyes and puffed out his chest.

"Just under sixty thousand because that's the limit an individual is allowed in this country without risking the financial authorities being contacted behind their backs." James sounded like an actor reciting lines.

5 smiled. "And what else?"

"Swiss bank accounts are overrated."

Then there was a silence. When James saw his brother's tears he was shocked, he lowered his eyes in embarrassment.

"I never dreamed this is what I'd become. Sometimes I can't look at myself in the mirror. Sometimes when I think about what your brothers and me are I feel sick. Drugs corrupt lives. How did I let our mother get addicted to crack? I blame myself. I started all this, they just followed my lead. It's not just the money, James; it's the power, the feeling of being in absolute control of your own fate. It shouldn't have been like this, but the alternatives for people like me are laughable. It's gotta be different for you, James, you hear me?" 5 grabbed his brother's shoulders. "Look at me." James tried to wriggle free, he struggled and finally managed to push his brother away. 5 pulled a tissue from his back pocket and blew his nose and then laughed.

"I don't want you to be stupid," said 5. "One day you're gonna be in control of all we've worked for." Suddenly, without warning, 5 raised his hand and struck James hard on the left side of his face.

"Look at me." His voice was menacing. "What did I just say?"

"You said you don't want me to be stupid," said James, holding his stinging cheek.

5 stared at him for a moment and then pulled out a box of jimis. "You have to be careful with these African girls. AIDS is big out there. Always wear your t'ings. You hear me? Don't bring AIDS into our family; you've caused enough trouble already."

James looked at 5 with hatred burning in his eyes. He turned, glancing at Meina, realizing that she had heard. "I can't believe you just said that," he said to his brother. "You really are dumb sometimes, d'you know that?"

# EIGHT

# MEINA

DURING THOSE FIRST DAYS we were happy not to see anyone else. We stayed together, out of step with the rest of the world. Each day was a struggle and each night a battle with terrible dreams. Sometimes, I would hear him sobbing in the early hours but I didn't dare ask questions over breakfast in the morning. I know James heard my own tears—but he didn't say anything. Instead, we just provided each other with reassurance. There were awkward moments such as the time he caught me smelling my breath in my hands, or once when I forgot myself and stepped out of the bathroom looking for a towel, my hair was soaking wet, and he saw my tits.

In the light of day, we did as much as possible to act as if our wounds had healed.

James hardly ever went outside the flat. He only had to visit the doctor once a week and he didn't go to school. We ate and shopped together, I would compile the shopping list and he would push the trolley around Morrisons. We watched pirate DVDs that James bought from the Chinese man who stood outside the Forest Gate Pizza Hut on Friday nights. We discovered we shared a love of painting, and bought cheap canvases from Woolworths in Stratford and spent weekends on the canal in Camden where we would picnic, talk and he would paint the Senegalese boys who sold shit weed and I painted the market stalls and the canal boats. James said he hated London—but he knew it so well. I was fascinated by the things and places he showed me. He could get tasty Jamaican or Nigerian food in Dalston; Senegalese in Stratford; the best Chinese food ever in Leytonstone and delicious Turkish kebabs near the college in Walthamstow. Once, when I complained

I had never had fish and chips, James took me to a place behind Neal Street in Covent Garden that made me understand what all the fuss was about.

Our brief escape from reality ended suddenly one Sunday night with a loud knock on the door. It startled us; we stared at each other as though someone knocking on the door wasn't the most natural thing in the world.

"I'll get it," I said.

"No, wait, let me check the window first . . . Shit."

It was Detective Inspector Whittaker, the policeman who had visited James in the hospital. There was a police van and an unmarked car outside. Whittaker entered our living room uninvited, wearing a neat double-breasted suit. He walked around slowly and poked his head into each room.

"How bitter another's bread is, thou shalt know by tasting it; and how hard to the feet another's stairs are, up and down to go," he recited, ignoring us both.

"What do you want?" asked James. "My brothers don't live here."

I moved toward James. We stood side by side, facing the inspector.

"Aahhh, Bisto." Whittaker tilted his head to the side, smiling. He stared at James for a moment.

"I'd like to speak to you in connection with my investigations into the death of Nalma Kamal. We have a neighbor who witnessed a fight and a serious sexual assault—this young man was beaten within an inch of his life, raped and shot point-blank. We think someone, a boy, saw the whole thing. Unfortunately for you, James, you fit the description."

My heart was in my mouth.

"If you could prove it was me, you'd be taking me in," said James.

"We're still making inquiries. We're waiting for results on residue found on the gun." He scrutinized James's face for a reaction. "Everything in good time," said Whittaker. "You aren't a suspect but I have a strong suspicion you were there. Is there anything you want to say? I'll find out the truth in the end."

I stretched out a finger and touched James's hand. I couldn't stop my heavy breathing. We should have anticipated this and worked out what to say. I felt James's hand tremble.

"You can't just walk around our house," he said, watching the inspector do exactly that.

"*Our* house." The inspector smiled at us mockingly and walked on through the living room and then stuck his head into Ashvin's bedroom. "Where does the family start? It starts with a young man falling in love with a girl—no superior alternative has yet been found." He turned to James. "That's Churchill, young man. You know Churchill?"

"What do you want?" I asked.

Whittaker spoke while still looking into Ashvin's room. It almost seemed he was being careful not to enter.

"I don't have any proof yet but I have been doing this a long time." His voice was grave. "James Morrison, I'd like to know where you were on June 6. It should be easy enough to remember since it was your best friend's birthday, a day you spent together, is that right?"

"Yeah. So what?" said James.

"How did you boys choose to celebrate?"

James smiled. I could see him contemplating telling Whittaker the truth. He felt he had nothing to lose.

Trying my best to maintain some equilibrium, I placed a hand on James's shoulder. "They spent it here with me," I said.

Inspector Whittaker was slightly thrown. I'd answered very quickly.

"I baked a chocolate cake and I rented a movie from Stratford Blockbusters. It was *Black Hawk Down*—my brother's favorite."

"Can you prove it?" asked the inspector.

"I have a membership card."

"I'll need to take your membership number." He turned to James. "So you were here?"

James looked at me and sighed. "Yes," he said.

The inspector seemed to be able to feel James's ambivalence. "Is this true? You watched a film?"

James nodded. "Yes."

"And this *Black Hawk Down*—can you remind me what it's about?"

"A failed US mission in Somalia. We debated the accuracy of the film for most of the night."

"I'm not asking you, miss." His face reddened as he spoke, and then turned back to James. "Who's in it? Anyone I might know?"

"Who's in it? I dunno, why don't you go rent it and find out?"

I closed my eyes for a second. I wished James hadn't said that.

"Who's in it?" The inspector put his face close to James's.

I felt James's body stiffen as he tried to keep his composure.

"The only person I can remember is Ewan McGregor. He drank a lot of coffee in the movie. Must have given him real bad coffee breath." James made a "you've got bad breath" expression but I saw the anger spreading across the inspector's face scared him.

"Think you're smart? Well, I get a hard-on for little boys like you and I'm what they call a patient Freudian. People always slip, and when they do, I'm right there." He clapped his hands together loudly.

"Look, I haven't done anything wrong. I'm not scared of you," said James quietly, but the inspector was already letting himself out.

I closed the front door and I watched James's chest heave as I made my way over to the couch. "Come. Sit down with me," I said and gently tugged his arm. He stiffened and his eyes hardened.

"Nobody understands what I'm feeling. Nobody wants to know except when they think I've done something wrong. I'm sick of this shit. Of living in this neighborhood, being humiliated all the time, treated like some animal by everybody."

He looked so injured and vulnerable. It was as if a great weight had fallen and was pressing on him.

"I'm going out," he said.

"Where?" I asked.

"I don't know. To be by myself."

"I'm coming with you," I said.

I hadn't thought out what I'd just said. All I wanted was to chase away the trouble I saw on his face, the way I wished I had been given the chance to do with Ashvin. I wasn't sure what I would do or say if James ignored me and walked out. All I knew was that I wanted a chance to make a new life and I couldn't allow him to run away with my hopes. I put my arm on his shoulder hoping that by now he understood the things that were going on in my mind: I was tired of being on my own without a family, full of fear, tired of things not going my way. I blushed when I tasted my tears. I cried even more as he clawed in his pocket digging out a crumpled tissue and frantically dabbing at my eyes.

I wanted to hug him but I didn't.

"We were doing okay, weren't we? You don't need to run," I said. "Everything you want is here. You can talk to me. Tell me what's wrong. I can help you if you tell me what you want." I stood and led James into my bedroom. I walked over to the window and closed it. I turned to him. "I want to know what really happened on my brother's birthday. Tell me the truth."

He looked at me for a moment and then he sat down on the bed and told me. While he spoke I listened, impassive, not saying anything or moving at all for that matter. Halfway through James's story, I began to sob. But I kept myself still, facing the weak orange light of the street lamp beyond the window.

# NINE

# JAMES

IT WAS THE MORNING of Ashvin's birthday. We started out by going to see Sheikh Ali. I thought we were only going for a laugh. You must have seen him in Stratford, outside the mall handing out his business cards. He says he can advise and fix things. He is majorly busy; we had to make an appointment to see him a couple of days before. We went to his flat on Lansdowne Road. Near the house the police raided for terrorists and then shot that guy by mistake, starting that whole fuss in the papers. The flat was creepy. It was like a small storefront with an iron crucifix welded to the fence post. Above the roll-down steel gate on his door was a sign that said "Eternal Sacred Order of the Cherubim and Seraphim Church." There were about two dozen people in the front room, Pentecostals or something. Africans. They were rocking back and forth, reading psalms and singing hymns. It was some kind of weirdo church. Apparently they were paying Sheikh Ali rent for two of his rooms, so we had to walk through them to get to the room at the back. Thinking about it, we should have known the sheikh was a fraud—Christians and Muslims don't mix like that. Anyway, we had to wait for what seemed like ages. There was a pastor wearing a white robe and a purple collar.

"Raise your hand if you need a miracle this month. We have to remain here all night long to pray for all our sins," he shouted. More and more people in these funny three-cornered white hats and robes arrived carrying picnic coolers and bags of food. It was like a service; some of the men pounded out rhythms on African drums. The ceiling tiles were all stained brown and shit. Two women stood barefoot, swaying softly. Their eyes looked funny and they were singing, "Jesus watches over me," all out of tune, like. The pastor started reading through passages from the Book of Revelation, and then the gathering crowd took turns shouting "testify," and asking the Lord for protection from sickness, from unemployment, from the kidnapping of their children. It was fucked up. We watched for a while. Ash didn't say anything. And then the sheikh led us into his private room.

It was cramped with all these really primitive furnishings and no seats except his, this massive wicker chair with bamboo carvings on it, and all around were these scary pictures.

"The fuck?" I said.

Ash laughed. "Relax. They're Nigerian gods."

He pointed out Shango and Obatala and Oshun. There were all these statues and mirrors with strange designs. Sheikh Ali wore this ragged white tunic and lifted his hands above our heads and started saying stuff that Ashvin thought was Arabic. He made us sit on this thick pile rug. We were laughing at first but he got all serious, like. He had a really deep voice and his beard was all patchy. I thought I was going to shit in my pants, I swear. He burned some stuff inside this glass contraption that was about twelve inches long and he made us smoke it. We started feeling sleepy as we watched him compiling numbers in this chart he had on the wall and then he was pulling out this book and then pulling out another. "I've almost finished," he said.

Ashvin and me looked at each other—we both felt weird.

"Don't fall asleep," I said. "And if I do, don't fucking leave me here."

"I won't leave you, but you don't leave me," Ash said and then we couldn't stop laughing. We laughed so much I started to cry because I couldn't stop and I was afraid of whatever it was we'd smoked.


*I opened my eyes and I was in a place that I knew was home to millions of people, the sky was liquid gold. There were people everywhere, criss-crossing the sands and scrubs on camelback— pilgrims performing the haj and merchants selling perfume, beads, essential oils and henna. I was in a market. A herbalist called me to his stall and told me about a poisonous desert plant that could*

*be eaten in emergencies. He said I could eat the leaves if I boiled*
*them. He said I would grow to love the taste and he said I should*
*search for it. He made me a powerful charm to wear that took*
*the shape of a small snake. It had alternating crystals and five*
*blue beads. When I turned it to look underneath, I saw it had the*
*word* Ogun *carved in red and it stung my eyes. The herbalist*
*warned that I should never remove the charm. Then he left.*

*A cockerel crowed somewhere and I sensed evil in the herbalist*
*and his words. I turned and continued to walk away from the*
*market to the highway where I would get on a bus, where I would*
*be free.*

*It was not yet dawn, but the bus stop was overflowing when I*
*arrived. It was where, at a rotary, six streets met helter-skelter.*
*People shouted and shoved. I smelled the aromas of saffron, black*
*cardamom spice, meat and incense; I looked at a box of old fruit,*
*thought of festering mold and ripening, life and death. I didn't*
*know where to focus my eyes until I heard the shrill voice of a*
*woman sitting near a basket of carp. She was naked. I had seen*
*her somewhere before. I concentrated on her severe face, and then*
*I remembered. She was my schoolteacher, Miss Bukolov from*
*Belarus.*

*I watched Miss Bukolov closely. She had a gun, a Baikal pistol.*
*When she pointed it at me I noticed she had tiny flecks of blue*
*lint in her hair.*

*"If you ever wank over me again I will shoot you in the head."*
*"I'm sorry, don't shoot," I said and I started to cry.*
*She laughed and spoke to herself. I listened carefully to her*
*voice until I was sure it was in fact her.*

*"Look at my head and tell me which is bigger," she said. "What*
*I carry in front of my head or what I carry behind it?"*
*I saw a bus and jumped on it and I felt relieved when it started*
*to pull away.*

*"Hey, you, James," shouted Miss Bukolov. "You have grown into*
*a fine-looking man but you forget the good manners I taught you."*
*When I turned she was sitting in the seat directly behind me*
*pointing the gun. "I hate you," she said.*

*"Miss Bukolov," I said, "I'm sorry, I won't ever wank again."*
*She leaned back in her seat, still pointing the gun at me.*

"Come closer," she said.

I stood up and leaned toward her. I stopped leaning over to her when I could feel the warmth of her mouth on the hairs on the back of my neck.

"Please," I said.

"Look at my head and tell me which is bigger, what I carry in front of my head or what I carry behind it?"

I couldn't tell what she meant. I looked at her face, at the shape of her head.

It had a slight bulge at the back.

"Miss Bukolov, the one behind is bigger."

She burst out laughing. "Thank you, thank you, thank you."

She asked the driver to stop and she jumped off the bus. I watched her crawling away on her hands and knees. The bus driver began to laugh, too, loudly; I thought my ears would burst.

"James, you little wanker, I am magic and I can turn you into a trog," he said and then he started laughing again.

When the bus driver turned to face me, I had to look twice, but I recognized him. It was Mr. Shilton, my biology teacher.

"Trog!" I said and my heart raced.

"I hate you," he said.

"Me or all of us?" I asked.

"Every one of you," he said and he laughed.

"So, who is my brother's keeper?"

"Your brother's what?" he said, and he laughed uncontrollably. "I hate all of you. Everyone does. There are no men among you, no leaders. You're all lying in filthy beds with envy and malice, squabbling on pavements and in one-pound chicken shops, talking loudly, saying nothing. Your women hate you, your mothers don't believe in you, you'll never get jobs because nobody trusts you. Your children don't respect you and they paint their bodies with meaningless words and symbols. Your brothers think you're a wimp because you don't have a gun. Your fathers run out on you, no religion claims you, the echoes of your ancestors have been drowned out by rhyming treachery and all the world governments think you're a joke. I am your teacher and I hate you and don't you ever call me Trog." He let go of the steering wheel and gave me a hard push.

*"Who is your leader?" he asked.*

*"I don't have one," I said and I started to cry again when Trog thumped me on the nose.*

*"Sir, what are you doing? Let me off, I wanna get off."*

*"Listen to me, kid, you've got no chance, stay on the bus, enjoy yourself."*

*The bus stopped and I ran and kept running.*

Ash and I woke up sweating. Sheikh Ali was still collating numbers on this wall chart thing.

"Why do you both fill your minds with so many negative thoughts?" he asked. "Let them go before they consume you."

Sheikh Ali said he had had a vision of death, that we were both smeared with blood. That was when your brother went crazy. He looked so much taller when he stood over Sheikh Ali, his face screwed up in anger.

"What did you give me?" Ash said.

"You some sort of nonce?" I said.

"Sit down. Keep your voices down," said the sheikh.

"What did you give me?" Ashvin gritted his teeth.

"Ashvin, what's going on?" I had never seen him like that before. He punched Sheikh Ali squarely on the top of his head.

"Let us out," he said and he grabbed the glass thing and hurled it against the wall. There were splinters of glass everywhere and for a second the room froze. Sheikh Ali was rooted to the spot. He looked Ashvin straight in the eye and then started thumping the walls, blind with rage.

"How dare you?" he screamed, waving his arms frantically, trying to gather the bits and pieces together. It was intense. The sheikh was cursing with the anguished expression on his face growing more and more acute. He pulled at his hair and looked at Ashvin and then he didn't seem to know what to do—he just stood there motionless, without saying anything. Then he screamed: "That belonged to my father. Damn you. You are damned."

Ashvin laughed. "Damned? Is that all? I thought you were supposed to tell me something I didn't know already."

We ran off. When we got out of the flat it was already dark.

We had been in there the whole day, which was weird because it didn't feel that way. We got on the number 25 bus, both reeking of this incense stuff. Ashvin was acting weird. He brought out this little bottle of vodka and a small tin of Vaseline. He didn't drink from the bottle, he just gargled.

"What are you doing? I thought you didn't drink."

"It numbs the pain," he said.

He brought out a packet of razor blades, rubbed them with Vaseline, and started putting them in his mouth. He put four in his mouth. Don't ask me how. One under his tongue, one on the roof of his mouth and one in both his cheeks.

"The fuck, Ash. What you doing?"

He took another mouthful of alcohol and spat blood behind his seat. Nobody saw. When he opened his mouth, he had four blades positioned neatly inside.

"What's that for?"

"The Vaseline makes them easier to spit out. It's a Somali gangster thing. Women use it as protection against rape."

I shook my head. "That's some crazy Third World ghetto shit."

Ash laughed.

We got off in Forest Gate, outside the Nkrumah estate, and we were just hanging out—we went to the Internet cafe and I ate the chicken and chips we got for a pound. I wasn't really thinking anything of it at first, but then Nalma Kamal pulled up in his blue Fiat Punto. He parked, slammed the car door when he got out and gave a slight nod of acknowledgement. I felt a plum-sized ball in my throat. It felt like being tied inside a plastic bag. Your brother knew exactly what he was doing, like he had it all planned.

Nalma was tall, big. His neck was like a bull's. He was wearing baggy jeans and Timberland boots.

"Whass gwaning?" he said. He patted the sides of his hair, and rubbed at the two or three hairs that he'd twisted into a pointy beard on his chin. Then he stiffened and readied himself for what he probably imagined could be the worst. I knew a little bit about Nalma. He'd lived in Africa in varying states of terror for most of his childhood. He too had seen many things that others might not see in a lifetime. His family was from Ethiopia, and everyone said he'd seen his father killed in their backyard when Ethiopia went to war with Eritrea or some shit. He'd lost contact with his mother and his sister when the family went into exile. He got asylum into Britain in 2001. Before he got his own place on Nkrumah, he lived in a hostel in Walthamstow and joined the Scare Dem Crew about two years ago.

He wasn't afraid. The three of us just stood there looking at each other. They were both smiling. I wanted to run.

"Two against one, yeah?" said Nalma. "How you gonna come to my manor and jump me? Didn't anyone tell you how I roll?" He spoke as if he was doing all he could to make himself angry.

Slowly, as if he had arrived at a painful and difficult decision, he used his right hand to pull his gun from under his white shirt. He pointed it at me. He didn't look like he was afraid to shoot me.

"Wait," I said.

"Oh, so you wanna talk now? But I thought you was supposed to be a bad man."

"No. Wait," I said. But I didn't know what else to say.

Nalma just laughed.

Your brother raised his hands and said, "I just want a fair fight. Just me and you, no knives, no guns."

To this day, I wonder why Nalma put his gun down. He just stood there for a while looking into your brother's eyes, thinking his own thoughts. Ash's stare was like smoldering embers. And then Nalma lowered the gun, tucked it into the waistband of his jeans. He smiled, but I could see he was nervous. It was really weird. After that, we all got into his Punto as though we were three friends and Ashvin directed him to drive west to a spot in Forest Gate where the old Percy Ingle's cake factory is, behind the dark fields, you know, where all the empty garages are?

As he drove, Nalma kept looking at me in the rear-view mirror, and when he pulled up he rested his head against the glass and closed his eyes for a moment like he understood what was going to happen. He was breathing heavily, and there was sweat at his temples. I think he was praying. When he was done he turned the ignition off and we got out.

Before I knew it they rushed at each other, they pounded each other, dodging and ducking each other's heavy blows. Soon they were both on the ground, clinging to each other, then exchanging punches to the face, to the head and to the chest the whole time. They stopped for only an instant, and then they smashed into each other again. I couldn't tell who was winning at first, but then Nalma got on top. The gun fell from his waistband. That was when Ash started spitting razor blades. I had never seen shit like that before. Nalma staggered backwards as the first blade sliced near his eye. The second, third and fourth didn't miss. It was disgusting. Ash started shouting at me.

"Get the gun. Get the gun."

I kicked it and it slid over to near Ash's thigh.

Ash picked up the gun as Nalma was bent over trying to support himself with the palms of his hands. Ash did this crazy wrestling move and tripped him over. There was this loud thud as Ashvin smashed the butt of Nalma's gun into his nose. "How do you like it?" he said and he smashed it over and over again. It was terrifying. And then, Ash laughed. It was a strange laugh, unfamiliar. We were inseparable; we sat next to each other in class— not talking much but always together. Outside school we talked about everything: what was on television, the state of the world. Sometimes we'd be together and we wouldn't feel the need to exchange words at all but I wouldn't be bored. Ashvin was always intense, but in that moment I got really scared because I'd never heard him laugh like that before. Nalma collapsed to the ground and thrashed about. He stopped moving for a moment but I knew he was still okay at that point because he was breathing heavily and spitting out teeth and stuff. But then Ashvin turned him around, slammed a knee into his ribs and started tugging at his belt. Nalma was screaming, and his screams got louder when he saw the amount of blood there was on his hands. I couldn't understand why Ash was crying, but tears streamed down his face. I was behind them. I edged closer to be sure of what I was seeing. Ash pulled Nalma's jeans and underwear off, and I thought Nalma was in for a whipping. He was trying frantically to work his body against Ashvin's grasp, but a sudden blow made him lurch to the side and then his legs buckled. Then, your brother dropped his own trousers as if he was going to piss but he spat on his hand and started to rub his dick. Ash grabbed Nalma's shoulder, pulled him up. Nalma tried to kick him but the rest of his body was limp. Ash grabbed his neck from behind with his left arm and smashed the point of his right elbow into Nalma's back. Then he crooked his own back and straightened his dick and then he squeezed it in, penetrating him.

"What are you doing?" I moved toward him. I was going to drag him away. But he didn't answer. Whatever it was I saw in Ash, Nalma sensed it, too. He tilted his head slightly to look at me and I saw terror start in his eyes and then run across his face. He couldn't move because Ashvin held him firmly around his waist. Nalma, gritting his teeth and grimacing with pain, had no energy left, his mouth gaped in shock. For an instant he gathered strength from somewhere and shook Ash off, but Ash smashed an elbow into the side of his face. Nalma was ready to drop, but he kept trying to spin round, to shoot his right hand up to reach Ashvin's forearm but Ash bent his other arm behind his back and held his neck down so he couldn't reach. Nalma's desperate screams echoed and then became muffled. His breathing labored, the fight in him crawled away. Then he submitted. His head smashed into the ground and stayed there. I was glad when he turned his face away from me because I didn't want to see the cuts around his eyes. There was nothing I could do. I squinted down the street. Behind them in the distance shone the pulsing lights of Forest Gate. Panic spread through me. I was there but I also felt separated. I felt a sense of shame. It was all so animalistic and brutal. My blood was pounding and I was frightened and also sort of excited by my own fear or adrenaline or whatever.

Ashvin grabbed Nalma's hands and put them behind his back; he dragged his legs apart and pulled him up into a doggy position, still forcing him to look down. Ash spat in his palm again, somehow got himself erect and then, bending Nalma forward, he fucked him again, slowly inch by inch. His eyes were half closed. Nalma tried to move but Ash kept squeezing his neck and telling him to keep his eyes fixed on the ground. If Nalma tried to get up, Ashvin bent his knees by force. I'll never forget the way Ashvin looked when he penetrated Nalma, the way he started off moving his hips really slowly, unsteadily, but then he got really rough. With each thrust I heard a sickeningly dull thud and a smack as Ashvin's stomach connected with Nalma's buttocks. Both their angry cries split the night. Ashvin was crying and breathing hard at the same time. Blood trickled down the back of Nalma's legs. I looked up at the stars in the dead sky. They didn't twinkle. Nothing moved. The air was pungent with blood and feces. My heart felt out of sync, beating in a way I had never felt it beat before. Ashvin had one hand on Nalma's hip, the other he used to press down on his neck. Nalma was yelping, clawing at the ground like a dog. Ashvin was ramming him, he tore him and scratched him and beat him until Nalma was totally limp. When he was done, he whispered something into Nalma's ear. He didn't think I heard him but I did. I could see the moon between the trees and I just wanted to run, to get away. But I just sat there and I was ashamed because I was hard.

He said, "Your countrymen gave me a gift and now it is my birthday and I give it to you."

Nalma was alive when we left him but just after we reached the garages I thought I heard a gunshot; the roar of the traffic hid it so I couldn't be sure.

We didn't pull the trigger but it was our fault.

# TEN

# MEINA

JAMES STOPPED TALKING AND sat there staring at the bedroom wall, rubbing his palms across his thighs. I walked over to the chest of drawers, opened the top drawer and pulled out a small tub of pills. I handed them to James.

"What are these?"

"They are antiretroviral drugs for HIV. I found them in Ash's room. He never told me. But I saw a letter from the hospital when an immigration officer at Heathrow Airport was interviewing us. My guardian had to show his supporting paperwork—bank statements, proof of address and confirmation letters from our schools—just before our new passports were stamped 'Permission to enter.'"

"What did the letter say?"

"Nothing much. It had his name on it and I saw 'HIV-positive.' Mr. Bloom gave me a strange look at the time—he knew I saw—and when I glanced at Ash he froze and the flesh on his cheeks was trembling. I wanted to say something but I didn't. I was angry with Ash at first for not telling me and then I felt guilty."

I stood behind James and placed both my hands on his shoulders. He turned and gently kissed the nape of my neck.

I touched his cheek and felt the pulse beneath his jaw.

"Why do you touch me like that?" he asked.

"Like what?"

"Like I'm a child."

I removed my hands quickly. "My guardian is coming here tomorrow. I'm going to let him know what happened with Nalma, he may be able to help."

James frowned. "Who is your guardian?"

"His name is Mr. Bloom."

"I don't think you should tell anyone."

"Don't worry." I sat down and crossed my legs. "He'll be able to tell us what to do."

"I mean, who is he to you? Ash never said anything about him."

"He was a friend of my father's. You'll meet him tomorrow," I said. "You're worried about Whittaker. I can tell."

"No. I don't care about him or about anything any more."

The wind whispered against the window. Everything in the room felt sad. I thought of the time Ash and I spent with Mr. Bloom. He lived in a vast condominium with a powerful electricity generator that was built to ensure the power supply never went out with the rest of Somalia. The building had twenty-four-hour armed security and was surrounded by Western-style shops. It was in the southern port town of Kismayo, a supposed safe zone. There were checkpoints everywhere, and despite the service offered by the Special Protection Unit, aid workers, UNICEF workers, journalists and NGOs were targeted indiscriminately in the area, kidnapped or shot. People lived in constant fear of ambush, car bombs and remote-control landmines. But it felt safe to Ash and me. That was the first time we lived with Mr. Bloom. I stayed there happily for four months but Ashvin hardly ever came out of his room. I didn't know what was going on at the time. I was too busy reading Mr. Bloom's books, eating cheeseburgers and strawberry jam and Chinese food to notice. I now know it was when Ash was first diagnosed with HIV. Since the death of our parents, Ash had stopped saying what he was thinking, but Mr. Bloom has told me since that Ashvin hated going to the hospital. Once I asked him why he was so resentful toward Mr. Bloom.

"Baba told me to be wary of white men. Bloom tries to be so nice. I'm confused," he said. I think the real reason was because Bloom was the only person who knew he was infected. For me, things seemed fine until our aunt started showing up on Saturday evenings. I remember the first time it happened.

"They need a home where they truly belong, a traditional upbringing. I'm ready to play my part." She spoke in a soft, caring voice and I believed her because I wanted to.

She had Mr. Bloom wrapped all the way round her finger by then.

"Of course," said Mr. Bloom. He thought it was the right thing to do. "But since I have already put in my application for permanent guardianship, I want to continue to provide financial support, to ensure the process will still go through, in case they check."

My aunt adjusted her headdress and tried to appear calm, but she didn't. I should have known then. I shiver when I think about how badly I misjudged her—I had no idea what she had planned. Ashvin never liked her. He watched her carefully whenever she was around. "I don't trust that woman," he said.


I was surprised when James kissed me. I had been married six times but before that night I had never had consensual sex. I had talked with other girls—my real friends in Somalia—about their fears of abduction, and nurses came to my school regularly for special "stop the silence" classes and polio vaccinations. They would talk to teenage girls about the myth that sex with virgins was a cure for male HIV infection, preventing transmission of disease from mother to child, coercive sex; they warned us off seeking the attention of men, to have regular tests and they gave us proper sanitary pads. These classes were always about fear, so I wasn't at all prepared for the magic I felt when James's lips touched mine. I had no comprehension of the true power of a man—I ached for him. I felt I had waited all my life for his kiss. It was as though I was a weightless being carried along a river, and yet I was afraid. I gently touched the stitches on his lip with my finger.

"They'll dissolve soon. It's where I bit myself."

I winced. His thick, woolly hair was softer than I had imagined.

"Sorry, TMI."

"TMI?" I asked.

"Too much information."

I smiled and he leaned in toward me, gently pushing his tongue between my lips. It was like opening my eyes and being able to see for the first time. I hoped I wouldn't wake up tomorrow and find it was all a dream. His breath was light, his lips like silk. I wasn't sure I was doing it right. I closed my eyes when I saw he had closed his and only opened them once, for a second, when our teeth clashed. I felt reassured when he ran his hand over my face with care, on my head, through my hair, down, down, until he gripped my lower back. I gasped when I touched his neck and for a moment I pulled away. My hand was wet.

"James, you're bleeding. Did I hurt you?"

"It keeps doing that. Sorry," he said.

"I'm sorry."

I kissed him. Then I felt him touching my lower back under my shirt where my skin was hot and damp.

I wanted to stop him. I must have tensed my body.

"Meina, are you okay?"

I was confused. He wasn't meant to sound so warm. I was trembling. It was like electricity was passing through me. I looked at the window. It was a bright night but I couldn't see the moon. I thought I should stop. But I needed to prove something to myself.

"Do you want to?" I asked.

He opened his eyes.

"What's wrong?" I thought perhaps I had embarrassed him.

"Do *you* want to?"

I moved his hand from my back and placed it on the front of my panties, letting him feel my heat. I felt him trembling as he fumbled with the elastic on the inside of my left thigh. I was wet. I opened my eyes to see him looking at my face.

"Meina, is it okay?" he said.

"Yes."

He widened my legs.

"God," I said when I felt his finger inside me. I had no idea I could be happily led to the undignified places he took me. He opened me up and together we made love.

When I fell asleep, James made his way to the other bedroom in the dark. I woke again at one o'clock and found it difficult to go back to sleep. I wrapped the blanket around the bottom of my feet. I wondered if he lay awake like me, listening for sounds all around in the dark, groping for a reason to get up.

# ELEVEN

# MEINA

THAT NIGHT WAS FILLED with vivid memories of my father. I always had an image of him conducting his interviews in an expensive room in a huge white castle. I went with him once to a place called the Alibi in Baidoa. He made me wait opposite the entrance but I went and peeked inside through a crack in the wooden door at the back. The front door faced the corner of the main street, across from a deli and discount store in a part of town that was then unfamiliar to me. Both sides of the Alibi building had signs bearing the bar's name in peeling yellow paint accompanied by a faded blue elephant logo with the shape of the African continent in bold. The building's three stories looked noticeably worn, with chipped blue-and-green paint and barred or boarded-up windows. The chalkboard outside touted the air conditioning, but there was no mention of the bare, peeling mud-colored walls, layers of grime everywhere or the bar stools that were held together by duct tape.

The Alibi was about 250 kilometers from the war zone in Mogadishu. I had heard my father and some of his teacher friends say it was the only decent secret bar left in Baidoa. Ashvin asked him about it once and my father said it was where big business was done. There were no paved roads or street names and the rains had created ravines with crumbly sides; the entire area was virtually impassable. The first time my father met him, Mr. Bloom's driver got stuck in the sandy chasms.

In the center of the main room stood two dilapidated picnic tables; they used two wooden stands for a bar. With the exception of the counters and the picnic tables the room was bare. A wet sludgy substance covered the floor, a mixture of beer and dirt and who knows what else.

There were broken beer bottles on the floor, too, and empty plastic cups swelled in the corners and around the tables. My father said the beer was like battery acid but the Alibi served this special hot buttered rum that tasted like heaven. It was made by mixing butter, rum and goat's milk, whipped in house with four different spices and brown sugar, stirred forty or fifty times and taste-tested by the regulars. Many of the regulars were drunk and danced on the tables. In another front room, local guys lined up at the bar to holler over the soccer game on a small, mounted black-and-white TV, while others cheered on the often highly competitive pool games. A harshly lit, graffiti-marred back room provided extra seating and a Top Forty reggae list played loudly on a strange homemade jukebox.

It was the most unlikely friendship. Mr. Bloom represented everything my father despised about Westerners in Africa. My father, well, he was black. Mr. Bloom had not had a black male friend before. He had worked with many, even chased a football around the park with a couple. But friendship? Never.

My father was a handsome man who commanded the respect of the beautiful. He blushed easily and, although he laughed without exception at all of Mr. Bloom's jokes, he was very intelligent. After eight years abroad, he had returned to Somalia in 1974. He was only twenty-five years old and eager to begin building a professional life, to play a part in developing a modern Somalia. My father never lost his ambition. He worked closely with the Somali experts in Scandinavia (where he met Mashood, my mother) and for the Norwegian Ministry of Foreign Affairs. During his four years in the UK he worked at the Department of Economics and International Development at the University of Bath before he returned to Somalia where he built his reputation at the University of Mogadishu. What Mr. Bloom liked most about my father was his candor, the way he never tried to impress. He didn't pretend he was anything other than what he was and that, according to Bloom, made the relationship honest.

Their friendship was cemented the night they finally got round to doing the interview in my father's study at the back of our house. Mr. Bloom loved being in our home. It was clean, with haphazard shelving and furniture covered in sailcloth. It was decorated with ceramic bowls and locally sculptured vessels. There were cushioned nooks for reading, decorative bundles and twigs and sticks and odd baskets filled with bits of cut firewood. Our house was always brimming with people with familial or professional bonds: poets, writers, academics and children running around and shooting marbles on the veranda. My father's friends, who drank seriously despite the alcohol ban, seemed to enjoy Mr. Bloom's presence. Soon, he was at our house more than his own.

Our house looked across a river that was still and blue. But there was always fighting in the area. People kept light to a minimum out of fear of the roaming militia; ash from the fighting covered the streets and many buildings, but from inside our home, the war seemed like flashes of distant lightning.

# TWELVE

# MEINA

MY FATHER'S STUDY WAS a small igloo stuffed with books, lit by a cluster of candles and had a single block of wood for a desk. There were two overturned Coca-Cola crates for chairs. The only sign of the modern times was his minidisk player that had "Property of the New York Times" stamped across the face. I remember sitting with Ashvin outside the study that night, listening to our father asking questions. My father didn't encourage us exactly, but he knew we were there. By that time, the two men were more like family than friends. The interview went on long after Ashvin and I had gone to sleep, until dawn. My father's two thousand scathing words appeared in the international pages of the *New York Times*, my mother showed it to me. I didn't understand it very much. It was something about the issue of skyrocketing food and fuel prices in Somalia which he linked to China's expansion and its influence on world trade; the way the West used green politics to slow down the pace of economies in the Third World; the way the West had been ravaging the world with impunity since the beginning of the Industrial Revolution.

Two weeks after the publication of my father's article, he was invited to speak in Mogadishu at a protest rally over high food prices. He took Ash and me with him, despite our mother's disapproval. It was peaceful to begin with; the crowd cheered his speech. Then something happened and people started hurling rocks at cars, shops and buses. Some people were wounded, others began looting the restaurants and shops, and fighting broke out in Baraka market. As people thundered past, I fell and lost a sandal. I felt an odd sensation, it was as if my leg muscles had turned to water and my heart thudded out of control. I thought I would be lost to the clamor of feet and the swirling clouds. I felt foolish when Ashvin found me. He raised an eyebrow when I mumbled something ridiculous about retrieving my sandal. He held my hand tightly as he led me back to my father. He was a small boy and had to keep turning his back to zigzag through the throng. "Don't let go," he said frowning with concentration, his head bent down. If I close my eyes, I can still smell the sweat from all the rushing bodies and feel the chaos all around. But everything became still when my father, the sunlight behind him, hugged us and told us to remain close as we walked back to safety.

Soon after that the Ethiopian men came wearing uniforms supplied by the Transitional Government and murdered my mother and father. It rained early the next morning. I could see the trees outside bending in the high wind. I called Mr. Bloom for help and sat waiting with Ashvin for a long time beside the open window. It felt like all the promises that had ever been made had been broken.

It wasn't the first time the soldiers had been to our house. Three of them had come once before. They wanted to warn us of the danger we were in because of what they had overheard their officers saying. My father had to give them protection money. It was one of the few times I ever heard my parents arguing. My mother said the soldiers' visit would become routine. She begged him to sell up and buy a house in another village but my father refused. "Abandon my house? All I'm doing is telling the truth. I left my country once before, I'm tired of running. This is *my* house." When my father got something in his mind that was that. Their raised voices didn't bother me until I realized how frightened my mother was—she sat up at night staring out of the window, listening to the distant sound of gunfire around Baidoa. I watched her one night for a while, not wanting to disturb her thoughts. She had a habit of gently rubbing the right palm of her hand against the back of her left. Looking back, it didn't seem like she was expecting anybody. She looked more like she was preparing for the worst. The next morning, my mother cooked a large breakfast and seemed herself again. We ate together and laughed and my father took Ashvin fishing while my mother read aloud from one of her books,

*Mariama Ba*, I think. Shortly after that—perhaps a week—both of my parents were dead.

I remember it was late morning by the time I called Mr. Bloom. Ash didn't want me to. I tried my best to speak clearly and calmly over the telephone. He had worked all night and was preparing to enjoy a newlyweds' party with his then girlfriend, Sossina. He came to our house alone through the back. We were washing our parents' feet when he arrived. Nobody spoke. Mr. Bloom let out a deep sigh. He closed his eyes, tilted his head and stood there, one hand holding the gun, the other clutching his ponytail, teetering on the edge of saying something, but he seemed to have swallowed his words. Ashvin glanced at him and then sat by the window. I remember Mr. Bloom wore a gray T-shirt that was wet in patches with sweat. When I first noticed him he looked like he was holding up the wall with his back. I saw him lower his gun and take my father's hand, check his pulse. My father was covered in blood, his throat had been cut and he had been shot several times. I remember Mr. Bloom tried to wipe blood from my father's mouth and nose. He didn't see me see him do it; he made the sign of the cross and he kissed my father. That was when I knew he was my father's true friend. Nobody else I called came, at least not when it mattered—that's the point about the black/white thing. Mostly it's character that counts. You never really know people until something happens in life. Nobody teaches you that. Ashvin did not cry, he looked weak and feverish. He only spoke once. "Why do you think this has happened? To us?" I had nothing to say and Ash just sat in silence, looking out of the window.

# THIRTEEN

# MEINA

IT WAS COLD THE next morning. When James came into the living room I stopped talking. He asked me if I wouldn't mind turning up the central heating.

I stood and gave him a hug. He felt warm.

"I cooked breakfast," I said.

Immediately, I could tell, by the way he looked at Mr. Bloom, that James was going to be hostile. Mr. Bloom wore a black sweater over an expensive white shirt. His dark rheumy eyes were set deep in his leathery face and he had long silver hair, which was thinning. He swirled his coffee for a moment, stared at James the way he might look at a dog, not hatefully, but as if at a completely different species—as though he was telling James he could never walk or talk in the same way as him. I don't know what he was looking at him like that for. I watched James try to square up to him. Mr. Bloom smiled, as if he was laughing at him.

James told me later he thought Bloom was a "proper wanker."

"I'm Larry Bloom." He half stood and extended his right hand. James shook his hand and sat in the chair facing him.

"How are you feeling?"

"How are *you* feeling?" James said.

He didn't want him to think they were friends.

"I'm Meina's guardian," Mr. Bloom said. "Forgive me, I don't mean to pry, but I've heard so much about you. You were very close to Ashvin, I know, and you must have been under a lot of stress to do what you did. Those feelings don't just go away like that." He snapped his fingers. "Believe me. Go easy on yourself. I know you think you can take care of yourself but everyone needs help sometimes, even old white men like me." Mr. Bloom stopped speaking when he saw the icy expression on James's face.

I made a show of glancing out the window. "It's raining outside," I said.

They continued to watch each other.

"Look," Mr. Bloom said, "the only reason I'm here is to make sure Armeina is all right. I know this may be somewhat awkward but she told me what you told her yesterday, and I think the best thing is for you to get away for a bit. At least until things quiet down. We were thinking about where you could go. We haven't come up with anywhere suitable yet." He spoke with a casual authority.

"I'm not going anywhere," James said.

There was silence. I heard a trickle of water from the shower. James had probably not turned it off properly.

"You a policeman or what?"

"James," I said, "what's wrong?"

"No, it's all right," said Mr. Bloom. "Let him speak. I'd feel a bit strange, too, if I woke up to find a complete stranger in my home."

"So are you a policeman?" James asked again.

"In a manner of speaking I guess you could say that, but lucky for you, James, I'm on your side." Mr. Bloom smiled unconvincingly, and then he walked across the room and began to fumble in his well-traveled leather satchel. He pulled out a blue Manila folder just as I gave James a hot plate of scrambled eggs, beans and sausages. I could tell James was hungry, but I knew he wouldn't eat if Mr. Bloom stared at him the way he had been doing.

Mr. Bloom unclasped the file clip and then he slid away his plate and put the folder on the table. The cover read:

Morrisons—Operation Facilitate
1, 2, 3, 4 and 5
28 Kimberley Way
(Mandela Estate)
Special Enforcement Unit

Mr. Bloom began to leaf through the pages. "This is a copy of the police file on your family. It's as long as your arm. Frankly, and I have already told Meina, I don't like the idea of you living with her. But as long as you keep her happy, I am prepared to see how things go . . ." He looked up from the file for a moment to see James's reaction. Saw none.

"I think we understand each other," said Mr. Bloom. "I don't think they can connect you to the murder of Nalma, but that won't stop them harassing you because of your family. I need to speak with—" he turned another sheet, searching for a name— "Inspector Whittaker to sort this situation out as best I can. If you went away, you'd be doing me a favor."

"My brothers are the dealers, Mr. Bloom. Not me."

James looked up at me and I blushed.

I was wearing a wrapper over my nightdress. One of the straps slipped off my shoulder and James gave me a smile and I felt open for living in that moment, wide awake as though anything could happen. It was like the way I felt whenever I woke up too early, when I got to see the most brilliant sunlight spreading evenly over the world.

James finally started eating his food. There was no juice left in the fridge so I gave him a Diet Coke.

Mr. Bloom looked at my bare shoulder, and then followed my gaze over to James.

"Do you have any other family you could look up?" he asked.

"I have a half-sister. But we've haven't seen each other in years. She lives in Cornwall with her mother but she sends me birthday cards so I do have her address."

"Very good," Bloom said, "perfect. You should go there while I sort this out."

"I told you, I'm not going anywhere. Besides, I've done nothing wrong," protested James.

"No one is saying you've done anything wrong. Sometimes it's just a good way of allowing things to blow over. You'll love Cornwall. Where does your sister live?"

"In Cornwall."

"*Where* in Cornwall?"

I could tell James felt betrayed. I thought of how I could make it up to him. I walked over to the window. Something was brewing in the air, behind the rushing gray clouds, like an electric storm.

Raindrops glistened on the leaves and petals of the flowers in the front garden of the pensioner who lived opposite. Birds extended their wings against the force of the wind and mocked the stray cat in the safe distance far below. I watched the cat looking up expectantly at the birds from the base of the oak tree, lured by all his hunter senses—sight, sound, smell. Even the tree bent down to tease him. The cat remained stubbornly patient.

"If you do decide to go to Cornwall I want to come," I said.

"I don't think that would be a good idea, Meina," said Mr. Bloom.

I could feel the thoughts going through James's mind. He didn't have any friends. He didn't like his family. He was worried that his morbid feelings would reawaken. He decided it would be good to get away but in truth he was scared to because, like me, he knew he couldn't run from his own self. He had to start getting to know people, start to share new experiences, if he was going to make a case for life, a fresh start.

"How do you get to Cornwall?" he asked.

# FOURTEEN

# NUMBER 5

THERE WAS A LOUD rapping at the window, the unmistakable jingle of keys. James had gone to pick up the remainder of his belongings, leaving Meina alone in the flat. The unexpected noise frightened her and, dazed, she stood up with surprise. She thought it was Ashvin. The tapping took up again, echoing around the flat. When she stretched her neck and peeked out the window she could make out a tall, distinguished figure standing at the door—it took her just a moment to recognize James's brother, 5. He tapped his keys against the glass impatiently.

"Yo! Yo, sis! Open up, it's me. It's me, the outlaw Jesse James . . . 5," he said. He was the last person she expected to see.

Meina crossed the hallway, pushing her hair out of her face. She bent over and looked through the spyhole. "James isn't here. He went to get some stuff at your flat."

5 smiled, baring all his teeth. "For Cornwall, I know. I just left him. But I want to speak to you. Open the door, sis."

Meina unlocked the door and 5, authoritative, breezed in. He considered her a moment, smiled. "Que pasa, baby?" he said.

Meina could only watch.

5 exuded street-manliness, rugged strength outside the law, but there was something charming about him, the way he winked and smiled when he spoke. Meina thought there was something graceful about him, too, although she couldn't quite put her finger on it. As he passed her, 5 looked bored as if he were thinking of something else to do, or some other place to be. He rubbed his hands together as he surveyed the room. His arms looked bulky in his thick beige woolly cardigan; it had large red buttons and

a smiley Japanese face embroidered in red on the back. Meina shivered. She couldn't think what to say.

"Put the kettle on, sis. Coffee. White. Two." He stopped pacing and flopped down on the sofa, picking up the remote control for the television. "In your own time, I got plenty."

He didn't look like a dealer or a murderer. He was not particularly mean-looking, no flash jewelry, just baggy jeans with gold wings painted on both back pockets. But he made the air fizzle with unpredictability. Meina felt uneasy. She wasn't afraid, not exactly, but had the strong feeling he could make her afraid. He didn't look like someone who knew how to take no for an answer. Like a warlord.

"Look," said 5, "I've had a hard time dealing with the idea of my little brother leaving home. I'm the oldest. I have to decide what is best for my family whether I like it or not. I thought, as we're neighbors, I'd just show my face, so people round here know the score, nah mean, sis? Now, how about that coffee?" He turned, stretching out on the couch and dangling his feet over the armrest.

Meina sighed and, reluctantly, went to put the kettle on.

"Nice place, sis," he shouted to her in the kitchen. "Tip-top."

When Meina returned with his coffee, 5 was flicking through one of her gossip magazines.

"How can you read this bollocks? These people need a dose of the real world." He threw the magazine back on the pile. "You shouldn't read all that dieting shit."

"I'm a grown woman."

5 looked at her for a moment, laughed. "You sound like James."

"What's this about?" Meina asked. She felt her mouth going dry, crossed her arms over her chest and felt her heart pounding.

"Relax, sis, sit down." He slurped his coffee. "Oohh, perfecto. Got any bickies? You'll never keep a Morrison without McVitie's Digestives, I'll tell you that from kickoff."

"I don't mean to be rude, but I'm getting ready to leave," said Meina.

He ignored her. "So, you're African, right? Somalian, yeah?"

Meina gritted her teeth. "Somali, yes, and I don't have AIDS if that's what you came here to ask me."

"Look, I'm sorry about that. It was a stupid thing to say."

"What's my being African got to do with anything? Both my parents went to school, to college, and I *was* happy sometimes in Somalia . . . for your information." Meina straightened her back and rolled her eyes.

"Whoa. Okay, I get it. I was just asking." He sighed. "Look, all of this has been a bit of a head rush for me. It's tragic what happened. I'm sorry about your brother," he said. "We all are. James means a lot to me, believe it or not. Could we just start again?" He offered his right hand and grinned; amazingly it was infectious. "Peace?" he said.

Meina shook his hand. It was soft and warm like a child's but his grip was firm.

"I'm sorry," said 5.

"'S fine," said Meina.

"So, you guys are going away to lie low?"

"No. We're just taking a break. A change of scenery." Meina was surprised at how much like Mr. Bloom she sounded.

"A change of scenery? That's exactly what James just said." He paused, looking at her tits. "You could do modeling, you know."

It was so blatant. Meina looked at him, stunned. She gave him what she thought was her hardest, most solemn expression, but there was still a moment before 5 chuckled, waved his arms and averted his eyes. He rubbed his hands together and blew on them as if he was cold.

"So what's the dealio with you and my little brother?" he asked.

"We're going to live together."

"Why?" He lowered his head, narrowed his eyes at Meina.

*Why?* She shrugged. "Why?"

"Yeah. Why? You look like you could get any man you want. Why do you want to live with my little brother?"

"I don't know. I don't want to live by myself. I think together we might stand a chance." Meina regretted the words as soon as they left her mouth. They seemed to hang in the air like net curtains caressed by a gust of wind. She expected him to burst out laughing but instead he smiled calmly.

"Furry muff. But what happens when you get bored?"

"I'm not going to get bored. What's this about?"

"James is a good kid. If you're loyal to him, take care of him, he could be all right for you. You guys could make a nice little family, like the Waltons. Except you wouldn't have to take no shit."

*The Waltons?*

"You were spoiled as a child, I can tell." He smiled. "You were, weren't you?"

Meina thought of her father, of bouncing on his knee while Ashvin stretched his arms waiting for his turn. "You are my first son, but she is my first daughter." And he would kiss her on the nose.

"So, you do have a smile," said 5.

Meina didn't respond. She stood motionless, realizing she was becoming less uneasy. A police siren claimed the silence as she rubbed her left palm against the back of her right hand.

"What do you know about my family? Be honest. Go on, say the first thing that comes to your mind," said 5.

"You're drug dealers."

5 was silent for a moment. There was menace in his gaze and then he chuckled. "What d'you know about being a dealer?" He turned to look out of the window. He was glassy-eyed when he took another gulp of coffee. That was when Meina noticed his eyes were bloodshot, as though he needed sleep. He wasn't aggressive toward her but she could tell he was getting more and more restless. 5 couldn't keep his eyes focused on one thing for any length of time. One minute he'd stand up and seem happy, smiling warmly, but then halfway through a sentence, he would sit down quickly and say nothing. Meina couldn't keep up with anything he said after a while because he jumped from one subject to the next as though he couldn't concentrate. And if she interrupted him or tried to say anything he became irritated. But at the same time he seemed calm. It reminded Meina of what it was like living with Ashvin when he first started acting out of character, with the mood swings. Sometimes, Ash would stand up and sit down five or six times, and then feel guilty about damaging the sofa. He couldn't make any decisions. He would put his jacket on only to take it off again. Whenever Meina asked him about his strange behavior he would get angry, deny anything was wrong, storm off.

She wouldn't see him again for days. Sometimes he would act like that, like 5, for weeks. Meina remembered being afraid of her own brother. She suddenly felt angry at Ash. If he'd spoken to her she was sure she could have helped him, but, she felt, he didn't trust her enough to talk to her.

Meina watched as 5 stood up straight and then bent over and grabbed his ankles. Then he started to stretch his arms out. Then he held on tightly to his waist. She thought he was going to start exercising, doing star jumps or something, but he didn't. He stretched his arms and just grabbed at his ankles a few more times until he began to sweat.

"You okay?" Meina spoke gently.

"I'm just loosening up," he said, "don't wanna get fat, like."

Again, for a second, Meina saw Ashvin in James's brother. He looked nothing like Ash but when he sat down and started talking fast, almost to himself, arched forward in a rather childish manner, 5 called Ash to Meina's mind. She didn't think 5 would hurt her, but she definitely felt a bit uneasy when he started pacing the room, going on and on. They didn't discuss much at all; in fact, despite hanging on his every word, Meina wouldn't remember anything he said. Where her brother seemed morbidly depressed and enveloped in gloomy thoughts, 5 had a particular hardness about him, something sinister. His words betrayed a bitterness that he seemed to have allowed to fester. Perhaps it was from years spent in prison or living in this neighborhood. Meina used to wonder the same thing about the boys at home, those who became soldiers when they were very young. Those who, in time, would be capable of doing anything.

# FIFTEEN

# JAMES

I DON'T KNOW WHAT 5 said to Meina, but she burst into tears and almost squeezed the life out of me when I got back to her flat. She was trembling but wouldn't tell me what was wrong. It took me over an hour to calm her.

I couldn't tell you the reason I decided to go to Cornwall; it just felt like a good idea at the time. It was still raining when we left. Meina and I were going to make our way alone, Mr. Bloom would meet us down there in a couple of days. We waited half an hour for a cab and we had to meet the driver at the top of the road because he refused to drive into the estate.

"Those boys are bad boys," he said, pointing to Ratchet and his crew. He had a strong Pakistani accent. "Three times, they rob me. I report police, they do nothing. Lazy bad boys. I come here with nothing. I get job. Every morning I wake up at dawn. Look at time. You are my first job. Fifty pound I pay controller. I not complain. Have to work. I have wife. Three children. Send money home in Pakistan. Those boys they don't like work. No school. No job. Bad boys. Lazy."

"Leyton station," I said, catching his eye in the rear-view mirror.

We passed rows of shops; some closed down, some shiny and new. Phone shops, a KFC, a kebab shop, a one-pound shop, Primark, a pizzeria and three Internet shops. There were lots of people selling stuff, mostly stolen goods, download pirates. The rows of houses were two-story, Victorian, over a hundred years old. Everything was dangerous and loud—scheming opportunism everywhere.

My eye caught one of the proper vendors—he had been here a long while—a Chinese man with a gold tooth selling mangoes and fresh vegetables from a crate that said "N. Korea" in bright red letters. As always, the tire place across the street had men hanging around wearing oily sports gear. For them, today was no different; three men under a tarpaulin roof, barrel chests, denim jeans and steel-toe-capped boots. The pavement was strewn with stacks of rubber for sale. I stared at a man in oil-spattered gray tracksuit bottoms working under a battered BMW 323i with a G-Unit sticker on the bumper. When I wound the window down I felt the stinking morning breath of east London rush against my cheeks, I saw the looming vastness, heard the pssst-pssst sound of blasted air. Over there a wide expanse of trees and labyrinthine streets; decaying pavements for miles pockmarked with decades of neglect. Over here a poster of a double-decker bus in the window of a chip shop that read "London remembers 2005."

I sat with my legs pressed against Meina's. She linked one of my arms with hers. The news was being read by a sleepy male voice on the radio. There had been rioting and a running street battle in Birmingham. Asians had been in violent clashes with blacks over the alleged rape of a young Jamaican girl inside an Asian-owned hair salon. During the fighting, an eighteen-year-old black man had been stabbed to death by a group of armed Asian men. He was on his way to work. I wasn't sure whether to laugh at the story or cry. Meina squeezed my arm as though she could tell what I was thinking. There was another report on hurricane Noel that was about to hit the Bahamas. The driver kept watching me through the rear-view and switched over to Radio 1.

"Who do you think names all the hurricanes?" asked Meina.

I shrugged. "Can you see the way he keeps looking at me? He thinks I'm gonna rob him." I sighed heavily and tears welled in my eyes. Meina clasped her hand in mine and smiled. "Don't worry about me," I said.

"But I do." And then: "Can you promise me you'll try to have some fun?"

I didn't answer. I was trying to remember the name of the black kid on Merseyside who got murdered with the ax in his head by that footballer's brother. What was his name? Barton.

"I'm okay," I said when she forced me to acknowledge her gaze.

"Don't lie," she said. "You're just like my brother. It's not your fight."

"I'm sorry, Meina," I said, letting go of her hand, "but you're wrong."


We took the train to Liverpool Street station and changed for the Metropolitan line to Paddington where we bought tickets to Penzance. The ticket salesman told us the next train left at 1:06. We walked around for a bit, bought munchies, books and magazines from WH Smith and shared a coffee (double mocha macchiato with whipped cream). We were tired by the time we got on the train. It was fairly quiet, so we got one of those four seats with a table to ourselves. Meina worried that we would be asked to move but I told her it was cool. Eventually, the train started to move. We packed our bags in the overhead rack and then, knackered, fell asleep. After twenty minutes, a black man in a blue uniform woke me up asking for tickets.

"You have them right?" I joked.

"No," she said, "I gave them all to you."

I laughed and pulled the four orange tickets out of my pocket, like a magician.

"Ta-da."

The ticket man didn't find it funny. He took the "out" tickets and punched a hole through them with his machine without saying anything.

*Lickle shits.*

Meina pulled out three gossip magazines and a book of short stories she had bought. I unfolded the *Guardian* and tried to hide my book, *Another Country*. She seemed engrossed in an article I could see was all about a TV presenter who was having an affair with another TV presenter. She saw me watching over my paper and laughed.

"You look like a proper *Guardian* reader," she said and then moved over to the seat next to mine. She kissed me. It felt forced, a nervous gesture. I wanted her. Before she could back away I held her wrists and I kissed her back, feeling her strong pulse when I moved my fingertips to her neck. I guess she could feel me getting hard because she flinched. I slid my arms around her waist and for a moment she held me, then she let go and slid back on the seat, flushed with embarrassment. I couldn't quite work her out. Was she my girlfriend or not? Maybe tongue kissing in public was a bit much for her. Could she tell I was embarrassed, too, at my thing sticking up from my jeans? I shielded myself with the newspaper.

"Now I know what type of woman reads all that stuff," I said, pointing to her magazines.

She smiled. But she still didn't look at me.

"How much do you think you can tell about a person by what they read?" she asked.

"Nothing," I said. I slid my Baldwin novel under my *Guardian*.

"Everything," she said. I hoped I wasn't sweating.

"What's going on in the serious papers?"

"Can you believe it?" I said. "After thirteen years, they think they've got the evidence to convict those five white guys who killed Stephen Lawrence . . . Thirteen years, that poor woman."

"What poor woman? Who is Stephen Lawrence?"

I shook my head. "Who is Stephen Lawrence? Are you serious? Don't they test you people when you come into the country?"

"You people? What do you mean by that?" She tried to kick me under the table.

"Stephen Lawrence is our Emmitt Till. My brothers used to bang on about it all the time. I remember 5 said his death made it all clear. He said Stephen Lawrence was the black boy who showed the world that the black man in the UK had no bollocks, was dead, had no value. He said we stood by, we watched, we did nothing."

Meina just stared at me blankly.

"Don't look at me like that. What are you looking at me like that for?"

"You look funny when you're angry."

"I'm not angry, just thinking."

"Really?" She laughed and raised her eyebrows. "So, what else does the paper say?"

"Not much . . . Some celebrity has adopted a black boy. From Senegal . . . that makes me sick."

"Why?"

"What do you mean, why? It's part of that Western fantasy to own all things exotic. These are black boys we're talking about who'll grow into black men. Not Louis Vuitton bags."

"Being adopted is the best thing that could happen to these children. It's a blessing," she said.

Exasperated, I folded away my paper. "I've probably read more gossip stuff in this than all those magazines put together. What about you? What's going on in your celebrity world?"

"Nothing much. There are a few pictures of some royals. What do you think about them?"

"I bet you can guess," I said. "I had time for Diana but they killed her because she was with an African."

Meina gave me her "what are you on about?" look. I waved her off dismissively and tried to cross my legs. "Meina, can I ask you something?"

"What?"

"Will you go out with me?"

"Go where?"

"I mean, you know, be my girl?"

"So you'll be staying with me?" she said and I felt myself blush. I lowered my eyes. "For a while, God willing."

She laughed nervously.

"I'm sorry I kissed you like that before," I said.

"Don't worry about it." She turned her face to look out of the window. "It looks so peaceful."

I pressed my head against the glass. I have lived in London all my life and I had never seen anything like it; it looked vast, unending. "It's true what people say about us Londoners and the M25—that no one ventures beyond it," I said, but I'm not sure she understood what I meant.

Later, a woman in her late twenties got on and sat in our carriage. She wore a T-shirt under her coat with a Basquiat image on it and cooed softly into a mobile phone but I couldn't hear what she was saying. I fell asleep. When I woke up she had gone and two businessmen in dark suits and colorful striped ties sat in her place. One, with chubby red cheeks and clear green eyes, read the *Financial Times*. The other, with dark circles under his eyes and hair that he kept pushing behind his ears, was snoring loudly one minute, and reading a book by Andy McNab the next. Every now and then, the men spoke to each other in the same flat tone. I must have been staring because one of them looked up at me like I had my nuts out, as though they were in his face. Suddenly, a woman in her fifties with a long black scarf—patterned with licorice allsorts—wrapped several times around her neck entered the carriage carrying a large silver case; it looked like some sort of instrument. She sat and placed the case upright between her legs. As I watched her stroke the loose wispy hairs that had escaped her bun I noticed the sticker on her case—"Beware the cello player." I tried to imagine the sound of a cello. I couldn't. For a second I wished for a world where it was okay to ask strangers for favors.

"Meina? Can I ask you something else?"

"What?"

"Do you blame me for what happened to Ashvin? Be honest."

"No." She stared at me, then asked: "Have you done *Anna Karenina* at school yet?"

"Who's she? I haven't touched her," I joked.

"No, silly, it's a book. She's a character who commits suicide."

"I go to Forest Gate Boys, babe. Nobody knows *Anna Karenina*. I don't think I've had the same teacher in any subject for more than six months."

"Anyway, Anna Karenina kills herself. Not because she is trapped but as a form of revenge on someone. I wondered if Ashvin was trying to hurt me."

"Don't do that to yourself, Meina. Ash just couldn't see another way 'round it. What God, the world, the universe had done to him. He tried to move on. He tried." I reached out to touch her hand.

"I did blame you at first," she said. "But now I understand his death is a test that I have to survive. I believed in him because he promised me things would be all right. You know, we didn't speak much, the two of us. Sometimes, we could spend a whole day in the same room without saying a word. I miss him."

She leaned in closer to me and touched my face. We kissed.

We both dozed during the long journey, but fortunately we were awake as the Great Western train took us close to the cliff edge and we saw green hills, the harbors, the impressive churches and old buildings as we went through the main stations in Cornwall: Liskeard, St. Austell, Truro and Carbis Bay. The train slowed and we arrived at Penzance soon after five. We didn't have to wait long for a taxi. It was a green Mercedes. The driver was a white man in his forties with an old-school moustache that turned down at the ends. As he drove slowly through the small fishing ports along the Cornish coastline it felt as though we had stepped into a different time. There were farmhouses with signs that read "Closed for the season." Great white birds with black beaks stretched their wings and floated through the low-hanging clouds.

"Are you nervous?" Meina asked.

"About what?"

"Seeing your sister."

"Not really. She's not really my sister, is she? She's my half-sister. We don't even know each other."

"Half-sister? We have no such words at home. Your sister is always your sister and your brother your brother. What's her name?"

"Belinda. She has my grandmother's name."

"When did you last see her?"

"At my father's funeral. It was kind of awkward because our mothers weren't even mildly polite to each other, but I remember we were sitting at the same table. I have a picture of us some-where eating cake. We looked alike. I don't know how true it is but I think she was on his lap when he was shot."

"What did he die of?"

"He was shot."

By the time we arrived at the accommodation, Mr. Bloom had arranged for us, just outside Hayle, night was falling. The bed and breakfast was an old stone farmhouse surrounded by vines, ferns and roses. We rang the bell at the front door and a thickset woman with droopy eyes, mousy-brown hair and a veil of freckles on her face opened it. She looked distracted.

"I'm Pearl. Please come in," she said.

The hall was more like a living room—large with soft wall lights. It was simple and unpretentious, but there was a musky smell about it, like a damp towel, as though the windows had been shut all summer. The paint on the walls and doors was flaking and there were random objects everywhere: jars, bottles, brass animals, colorful feathers.

"Only two bags?" said Pearl as she tried to pull them from me.

"I can manage, thanks," I said, but she took them anyway.

"You have a lovely place," said Meina.

"I have the world's best collection of objects with absolutely no value," said Pearl. She gestured up at the storm lanterns hung in rows around the walls. "I put those up to help guests to find their way back on dark nights." She headed for the stairs. "Follow me. Try not to disturb my husband. He had a stroke but he doesn't miss much."

Meina and I both turned to our left, and only then did we notice the man wrapped in a heavy blanket, sitting in a wheelchair in the far corner of the room behind a dining table. The table, dressed with blue gingham fabric, had been decked with a bottle of red wine and berries in a basket. The man leaned forward, nodding his head involuntarily. He had a napkin tucked around his neck and a head of wavy black hair.

"Mr. Bloom said separate rooms. Is that right?"

It sounded like a question, but it wasn't. She was already on her way up the stairs as she spoke.

"We have six guest rooms, nothing fancy, mind. Three small rooms on the first floor and three rooms on the second. I'll put you both on the top."

The wide stairs were imposing. I had to hold on to the iron railings to keep from making them creak so much. There were several doors on the second floor, very close to each other and painted different shades of blue. Pearl smiled as she handed me the keys.

"Rooms four and five," she said. "No fighting."

Meina peeked her head through to look at the rooms before handing me the key to number 5. As far as I could tell, the rooms were exactly the same, simple with blue walls and a view out to the sea. The beds set in a niche in the far wall were painted white and had been laid with cushions and patterned eiderdowns.

After I had washed I got straight into bed—it had been a long journey and the food I'd eaten on the train had upset my stomach. Lying down felt like being inside a boat. I couldn't sleep so I got up and stared out at the view through the window. The sky was dark except for the silver-blue light from the crescent moon reflected on the sea, which altered with every shift of the waves. I felt humbled by the vastness of everything around me. It all looked so vivid, yet so still. It was as if there was a message in the sky from God. I didn't know what it said, but it felt like everything had a reason for life here. All my senses were suddenly amplified. When I looked out of that window all my doubts, all the pressure, all the dangerous thoughts shattered into thousands of pieces and disappeared into the sky. I turned to see Meina standing at my door, her thumb between the pages of a book. She had been watching me.

"Breathtaking, isn't it?" she said, coming to stand next to me. "It's the first place I've been here that reminds me of home."

"Really?"

"If my country were peaceful this is how beautiful it could be. This looks like Mogadishu used to, near Buujimo Shineemo, the old cinema that used to be surrounded by brightly colored buildings put up near the market by the Italians. Now there are sandbags everywhere, where Ethiopian soldiers with camouflage on their backs and flip-flops on their feet hide in the shadows with heavy guns. People in robes crossing at intersections back and forth. Everybody scurrying around because death can come from anywhere."

"What's wrong?" I could see her cheeks glistening.

"Nothing," she said.

"No, come on. What is it?"

"It's nothing, honestly, I'm fine."

I remained silent for a moment, chewing on her lie.

"What were you reading?" I asked.

"It's a book of short stories, I told you already," she said.

"I meant which one?"

"It's called 'Bright and Morning Star' by Richard Wright. Do you know him?"

"Yes, but I haven't read that. What's it about?"

"I'm not finished yet but so far it's about a mother worrying about her son who is out trying to organize a Communist meeting."

"Will you read it to me?"

"I don't know, James. It's very sad."

"You have to stop doing that."

"What?"

"You keep worrying that I can't handle stuff. I can."

"You tried to commit suicide. Why are you kidding yourself into thinking you're all right?"

"Kidding myself?"

"You're acting as though nothing happened, but it did. Something did happen. I lost my brother."

I kept silent. I'd known all along that she still blamed me.

"Will you read it to me or not?"

She did. We lay on my bed and she read in a quiet voice. It was one of those stories you read and you never forgot, one that made you feel for your ancestors, one that made all your own troubles pale in comparison.

"I'm going to try to write a short story like that one day," she said when she had finished.

"I think you will. Can you recite poems like Ash?" I asked.

"No."

"Yes you can. He told me you could quote loads. He used to recite his favorite poem sometimes when we were together. He said it was by Langston Hughes. I know some of it by heart. 'Suffer Poor Negro—'"

"That's by David Diop. It's in a collection of poems edited by Langston Hughes." Meina laughed. "My brother was so dumb. And it wasn't his favorite poem. His favorite was . . . I don't remember all of it or who wrote it but our father liked it very much. It went something like":

> You are a man, my son.
> You are a man tonight.
> They are all here:
> Those of your first moon
> Those you call fathers,
> Look, look at them well;
> They alone are the guardians of the earth
> Of the earth that drank your blood.

Her chin began quivering. The room was quiet save for a gentle tap on the window of naked tree branches blown by the wind. She sniffed her runny nose and then turned and wept into my pillow.

"Big girls don't cry," I said patting her back. I didn't know what else to do. "If you stop crying I'll buy you a . . . pretty dress."

She sat up and looked out at the moon. Something like a smile parted her lips.

"You promise?"

"Promise what?"

"To buy me a dress, silly," she said pushing her palm against my chest.

"Of course," I said. "A real expensive one like Victoria Beckham from the magazines." I pulled her toward me.

Something happened between us on that first evening in Cornwall. Something sudden and carnal and frantic that left my heart pounding in a blissful state where I was unsure whether I was dreaming or dead or alive. Afterwards we lay naked, side by side, holding hands. She stayed with me, and this time I held her tightly. She buried her head under my chin, on my neck, as the wind broke through the cracks and the sea crashed violently against the shore.

When I opened my eyes an hour later, I felt bad for lying on her arm. But I was glad she hadn't let go of me.

"Are you still tired?" I asked.

She didn't answer.

"I'm starving," I said.

"I could eat, too."

"Shall we go to my sister's?"

"Right now?" she said surfacing from under the heavy sheet.

"Yes, I want to get it over with."

"Come on, then," she said, rubbing her eyes. "Let's go."


The night was peaceful. I took a long look at a stocky man standing under the glow emitted from a street lamp. He was in a baseball cap and jogging bottoms. Just as I got nervous he began jogging down the street and I noticed the gleaming eyes of a black-and-white dog strolling beside him. Most of the streets sloped down to the center of the town, but we walked in the opposite direction for almost twenty minutes past huddles of granite cottages and cobbled courtyards with the warm sea breeze wafting over us like an embrace. We had a full view of the green hills over which the moon poured a bold light.

"It looks like a stage," I said.

Meina tilted her head. "It's beautiful," she said. Then, after a while, "Are you sure this is it?"

"Trevescan Place, number 14. This is it."

The moment I knocked on the door, I was sure it was a mistake.

"Let's go," I said, but it was too late.

"Bell? I've told you a hundred times. Where's your key?"

I knew she was only forty-five but she looked older. She was tall and scruffy-looking, only just this side of fat. She smiled when she saw us.

"Oh, sorry," she said, "I thought you were my Belinda. You must be here for the sleepover. It's not here this week, it's in the cave on Hell's Mouth. Just follow the signs on the road until you see their lights in the cave."

"What's so funny?" Meina asked when we left.

"That was the white woman who my father was seeing on the side. I could hear my mother's angry voice when I saw her. 'That bitch. She ain't even pretty. Just a regular, cheap, white ho.'"

We walked for another ten minutes, following pink balloons and arrows, with our arms around one another mostly for support. We stopped walking once. I buried my head in Meina's hair and kissed her neck. She drew me in and pressed her lips against mine. I couldn't stop myself.

"Doesn't it feel great out here?" I said.

"Yes, but what if we got stranded?"

"Then we'd spend all night in those hills," I said and laughed.

"What's up with you?"

"I don't know. I feel like I could take all my clothes off and run wild for miles."

"Yeah? Well, don't," she said and she kissed me again.

I heard voices echoing before I saw the cave. It was at a fork in the road between two cliff edges. Lights had been wired to a car battery and roughly arranged at the mouth of the cave, stretched across the wall on netting. We could see that bodies took up most of the space inside, six of them dressed in dark colors, all in their teens. It looked like a medieval cybercafe and smelled strongly of fish and chips.

There was a radio playing. The presenter sounded like he was climaxing when he announced he would be playing the new Britney Spears. There were two boys and four girls huddled around a calabash. One of them, an Indian-looking girl with a long forehead, read aloud: "'On this occasion, however, the spirit of suicide Rekla Merchant had not come merely to mock.'"

All six of them started when we entered.

"I'm James. I'm looking for Belinda."

"My God!" a girl's voice shrieked from inside the cave. "It's my brother."

The girl who spoke had a voice that could have belonged to a boy. Her mouth opened and closed and her tongue touched her lips but at first no more words came out.

"You're my brother," she said eventually, standing in front of me.

There wasn't any denying it. Those were Morrison eyes; that was a Morrison mouth, a Morrison nose. Not only had she stolen my father and my grandmother's name, she'd stolen my father's looks, too. She even had his thick eyebrows.

She was tall and had a slight chip in her front tooth. She looked a lot like me, but for the lightness of her skin and the wild, matted hair that fell way past her shoulders. Except for her shocking-pink nail polish everything else she wore was black. She put her hands to her head, as if trying to tidy her hair, but it was useless. It was only when she hugged me that I realized I was shaking. Then, she turned to the others. "It's all right. They're on the level," she said. Then she turned back to Meina and gave her a welcoming hug, too. "These are my friends: Ritchie, Judith, Kimi, Diane and Kat." The gang all gave waves and small nods. "Where's that bottle of wine?"

They cheered noisily like a band of thieves.

"How did you get here? Where are you staying?"

"At a place called the Mermaid," I said.

A lean, scrawny boy with tight blond curls handed her a bottle.

"That's the fussy dressmaker woman's place, right?" he said. "We got banned from there last year."

There was another rowdy cheer and chinks from the clash of cups, glasses and beer bottles.

# SIXTEEN

# JAMES

PAT AND BELINDA HAD lived in the house on Trevescan Place since they'd left London. It was one of several cottages on a slope, opposite a row of fruit trees backing onto the coast. Meina sat with me, holding my hand. Bell sat alongside her mother in the living room at a small black dining table. The wood floors were covered in part by a colorful rug. It was a large but cozy room with four small windows facing the east. There was a large painting I recognized as Equiano the African on the chimney wall above an open log fire. A framed picture of my father, smiling, with his arms wrapped lovingly around Pat and Belinda sat on the marble fireplace. The picture troubled me, I didn't like looking at my own father and feeling like a stranger.

After banging around in the kitchen for half an hour, Pat had presented an impromptu dinner of leftovers: cream of mushroom soup, some chicken with herb-seasoned white rice and green beans. It was hard to imagine my father with this woman.

Life was complicated, I thought. Not just the living but dealing with the realities and the instinct for order that other people have, that I didn't always grasp.

"I know I'm a stranger to you," said Pat, "but I loved your father very much. You look like him, you know. I'm glad you've come. It means a lot to me and Bell."

My mother had told me that my father only went out with Pat because of the size of her tits. I had to struggle constantly to keep my eyes from her unruly bosom; it moved when she spoke and she kept adjusting her bra. I watched her shift her heavy frame to make herself a cup of green tea. She said she worked in a pub (Thursday was her only day off)—in her too-tight denim skirt and revealing striped top, she looked like she ought to. She rubbed her chubby hands together, speaking to me in a low, measured voice.

"Your father was a strong man." She paused, and looked cautiously at all of us to be sure she wasn't being mocked. "He wanted out of Forest Gate. He stopped drinking, you know, tried to clean up, but he died before he got a chance to move. Things were tough for Bell and me when we arrived down here but it worked out in the end. It always does, you know, James. People manage. We have to."

I lowered my head and kept still for a long while. A gusty wind blew and I could hear the sound of waves.

Pat walked calmly to the kitchen sink, and I watched as she wiped her hands on a dishcloth, and then put on a CD. It was a gospel-style voice singing with what sounded like a recording of a seventies soul band. I was surprised at her choice of music. Belinda must have caught my expression.

"Gross, right?" she said when she saw me watching her mother nod her head to the rhythm. Belinda had my father's jawline. She was strangely cold to her mother. It took me a while to notice but Belinda seemed to get more agitated every time her mother spoke. She would huff, shift uncomfortably in her seat or roll her eyes.

I felt awkward with Pat and Belinda eyeing the ligature scars on my neck. It was still raw in places but the edges seemed to have turned blue. It made my skin feel sore and looked almost transparent. I didn't want anyone to feel uncomfortable on my account so I spoke up.

"I know you know what happened. Meina's brother, Ashvin, was my best friend. He died."

Pat looked alarmed and raised her hand to her mouth.

Belinda muttered, "How awful," under her breath and then for what seemed like ages there was silence.

"How's Bertha?" asked Pat, trying to change the subject.

It had been a long time since I had heard anybody use my mother's name.

"She's addicted to crack," I answered.

"Oh." Pat tried hard to mask her surprise.

"And . . . er . . . how are your brothers?"

"Had they started dealing before you left?" I asked.

First she went pale. Then her skin flushed with color. "Yes, I think so," she said.

"Well, they're the same more or less then." I was starting to get angry at this casual meaningless questioning, everything that was unsaid, but we all managed to smile through.

Meina looked at Belinda. "So," she said awkwardly, "those guys in the cave. Are they your best friends?"

Finally, Pat sighed and looked straight at me. "You know, I always liked your mother," she said.

"What?" said Belinda. "Was that before or after you started screwing her man?"

"May I have another drink?" Meina asked.

"You were friends before, right? You and my mum?" I insisted, welcoming the guilt I finally saw on Pat's face.

Meina narrowed her eyes and straightened her back, focusing on Bell. I turned to Bell and for a moment I studied the shape of her face, her eyes and the shock of hair.

"Yes . . . I loved your father . . . Unforgivable things happen," said Pat. "Your mother was a friend. Of course, I haven't seen her since the funeral—she wanted to argue with me even then, but anyone who knows me will tell you I'm not the quarreling sort."

Belinda tutted. "That's so lame. So what sort *are* you, Mother?"

Pat pursed her lips as if to stop her angry words. "When you get to my age you'll know nothing stands in the way of true love. Anyway, it's good to see you, James. And Meina, I'm sorry for your loss." She stood and put her hand on my shoulder, crouched and kissed Meina on both cheeks. Then she picked up her book and put a bit of paper in it to mark her page, sighing. "Sometimes, Bell, you can be so . . . so uncivilized," she said. "I'm going to bed."

There was a resounding silence. I could see Meina felt embarrassed. I said nothing.

"Mum, I was just kidding," shouted Belinda. But Pat was already gone.

Belinda poured herself another drink, held her glass up to the light so she could look underneath it. "God, it feels good to have a drink without feeling guilty about it." Her eyes widened and she grinned at herself as she raised the glass. "To the return of the prodigal brother. Is that the right word?" she said chuckling.

Meina and I exchanged glances.

"Please, you guys, don't look like that. You have no idea. I saw my father shot. I was there. Then to move out here, the middle of nowhere. The few black kids around don't want to talk to me; white kids don't want to talk to me. It's all her fault." She sighed. "I used to drink every day. I tried to sleep with every white boy in my class. I wanted to sleep with every one of them in the school."

Meina looked horrified. "Why d'you do that?" she asked.

"You don't understand. I was hated in that school. For no reason. I couldn't understand why they hated me so much. Nigger this 'n' nigger that . . . when I left London I didn't even think I was black. I mean, I lived with a white woman who loved R&B but that was as far as it went. I didn't fully absorb the fact that I was black until I got here. Then I realized it was so obvious to the rest of the world. Everybody seemed fascinated with the color of my skin. There was no one to teach me what it meant to be black. I didn't understand why they hated me. What did I do?" She looked at her glass, took a gulp of the brown liquid and smiled prettily. "So you're my brother?" She touched my cheek. "I've always wondered stuff about you."

"Stuff like what?" I said.

"A bunch of little stuff." She laughed and for an instant she resembled her mother.

"What's your favorite cereal?" she said.

"Crunchy Nut Cornflakes."

"Erykah Badu or Alicia Keys?"

I screwed up my face and my lips trembled when I smiled so I turned away from her. "To listen to or get busy with?"

"Both."

"Definitely get busy with Alicia Keys, but I prefer Erykah's voice."

Bell started a funny-sounding rendition of "Call Tyrone" (*I think you better caaall Ty-rone*).

"Like . . . have you had sex?"

I blushed. "Well . . . yes, lots of times." I saw Bell smile at Meina.

"So, who have you had sex with?"

"With lots of different girls."

"If you could spend a night with any celebrity who would it be?"

"Jurnee Smollett."

"That little girl from *Eve's Bayou*?"

"She ain't little any more."

We both laughed. It was like we were proving black credentials.

"Charlie Brown or Bart Simpson?"

"Charlie Brown."

"Stevie or Prince?"

"Stevie."

"*Reservoir Dogs* or *Usual Suspects*?"

"*Reservoir Dogs* . . . no, I mean *Usual Suspects*."

"Naomi or Tyra?"

"Naomi, any day, every day. I have a picture of her."

"Will Smith or Denzel?"

"Neither."

"If you had to pick?"

"Neither."

"What's your favorite drink?"

"Sprite."

"Duh. I mean proper drink?"

"I don't have one."

She touched my cheek again. "My own, real brother." She filled her glass as if to keep her hands busy and this time she asked Meina and me to raise our glasses. We waited for her to make a toast.

"I think you two make a fucking lovely couple," she said. She swallowed a mouthful and burped.

"I've never felt I belonged in Cornwall," said Bell. "I love it and hate it at the same time. I feel like I'm a London girl inside."

"I hate London. It feels so much better out here," I said.

"It does feel nice," Meina said, looking out toward the night sky.

"But London is where it's all happening," said Bell. "You have Brixton Academy and Wembley, all the best gigs. You have grime music, all the best clubs, DJs and radio stations. Not that I care, but you've even got Buckingham Palace. I can't wait until I get some money together and figure out what to do with myself when I get back."

I had never been to Buckingham Palace, Brixton Academy or Wembley Stadium and I hated grime. It was the first time I had been identified with those things by an outsider. It felt confusing.

"I'd seriously think about that if I were you," I said. "London just feels so crazy right now. When you're there, you don't feel as much a part of it as when you aren't. I don't feel, like, any of those places belong to me."

"What do you mean, crazy?"

"I mean it's rough. I know this sounds cheesy but London doesn't take prisoners and when it goes down nobody could give a shit."

"Rough how?"

"Rough, rough . . . I met a guy the other day who I hadn't seen since he got put away for shooting his sister. He said the 'safe' accommodation social services had found for him since his release didn't feel safe, and he couldn't bear to go back to the estate where his family lives. He used to push weights but when I saw him he was skinny. He said he'd lost two stone during his time inside. And he looked twelve years old except for his eyes, which had that old-man look that some people carry about, like they've seen too much."

"Shot his sister?" Meina said.

"Yeah, shot her in the face. He was only thirteen at the time. His mother buried her boyfriend's gun in the back garden. She got two years for possession and for not giving up the name of her boyfriend. Of course everyone knows who he is, some clown from the Nkrumah estate. But the scary thing is everybody has a gun buried in the garden—you have to have a gun or at least know someone with one. Guns are part of the environment, like a final defense."

"What's his name?" asked Bell.

"Keeshon," I said. "He was playing with his lighter and I noticed the tips of his fingers were all black like my mother's, a sure sign he was on crack. I was afraid for him. His mother's boyfriend was afraid he would talk, give the police his name. He started thinking that maybe Keeshon would want to seek revenge. Keeshon told me he didn't want to carry a knife but if he didn't have one he couldn't defend himself. He said he didn't want people to think he was a pussy but he didn't want to kill anyone, and it's too dangerous to talk to the police. I understood him, you know. Whatever happens I remember thinking it would never be the same. He's never going to be the boy I used to kick a ball with over on Wanstead Flats, who dreamed he was gonna be Pelé. All that was over. You know what really gets me is that bad shit happens to every one of us, I mean people like me. I'm always afraid of whatever it is that's lurking out there for me."

"What did he say to you about his sister?" asked Bell.

"I didn't ask but he kept playing with his lighter, like I wasn't even there, and he kept saying how much he loved her. It's all just so fucked up. I mean, what do you think is going to happen to him walking around in that state? He's fucked."

"Is that why you came down here?" asked Bell.

"I didn't want to come. But since I got here it's like being able to breathe freely, like I've wanted to be here all my life, away from all the crap."

"Nothing is going to happen to you," Meina said. "You don't have to think like that. I like London. It doesn't feel dangerous to me in that way. Before my parents were murdered, my father received death threats, and we were in constant fear for our lives because it was impossible to distinguish between the fighters. When I came to England, I was still so afraid whenever I saw a black man in uniform. Many of these men in Africa with their guns, they're lawless, unchecked. We had no one to protect us. Once Ashvin escaped being kidnapped by two men with a gun he met on his way home from school. He denied he was related to my father. Some of the offices and facilities at the university where my father taught were vandalized and burned. Another time, we were shot at on our way to market. Bullets shattered the back windscreen of our car, pierced my mother's headscarf, and our poor driver, Hassan, was killed on the spot."

Sadness crept into the room. I felt caged. My neck ached and itched; I rubbed at it because it was too painful for me to try to scratch. Meina must have sensed my discomfort. She leaned over and kissed my hands. I held my breath, reached out and gently rubbed her back. I closed my eyes and rested my head on her shoulder.

Bell didn't look like she was paying much attention. She poured herself another drink. "All the women should form an army and lock up all the men around the world. Including you, my brother," she said, slurring her words.

"You know 5 was in prison?" I said.

"Why?"

"He beat up some guy, put him in a wheelchair."

Meina shivered and searched for something in my eyes.

"I asked him why he did it. 'I love this country,' he said, 'I just can't stand some of the fuckers who live in it.'"


Later, when it got chilly, Belinda and I went to her bedroom to pull the sheets and blankets from the bed to keep us all warm on the floor under the table. Her room was small. She had a desk by her window with an expensive laptop and printer. There were a few books on some shelves, some Japanese names and three thick volumes by Alexandre Dumas.

"You write?" I asked.

"No. I like to draw—and there's bugger all else to do out here."

We stood together staring at the picture of the two of us eating cake together when we were kids.

"Do you ever visit his grave?" she said.

"I used to go every month. But it's been ages."

"I don't remember where he was buried."

"Just behind Forest Gate, in Manor Park. There's only one cemetery."

"Will you take me sometime?"

"Sure."

She kissed my cheek and leaned against me. "When I was little Dad used to read to me from the books he had bought for you."

I turned my head. Belinda seemed oblivious to how much it hurt me to hear her say that.

Bell carried the sheets and blankets and I took the pillows. Meina and I discarded our shoes and socks and lay either side of Bell. "Let's make it cozy," she said linking her arms and worming her legs between ours. "You guys should come in the spring. I'd like that. We sleep with all the windows down and you can smell fresh flowers and hear the waves. That's when I sleep best."

The three of us slept together, breathing against each other's necks in a heap under the dining table.


I woke late, tangled in a mesh of arms and legs. The day started beautifully; the house was so quiet I woke to the morning calls of seabirds. The sun stung my eyes as it cast a steady beam through the window of the room. Meina said it was by far the best thing about not being in Somalia—the quiet mornings. When I tried to imagine what it was like for her I couldn't. But that morning, when I looked at them both still sleeping, I felt happy. I should have known the day would turn out badly.

At breakfast, Pat scowled at Bell who was wearing a bright red dress with a brown leather jacket. Meina had borrowed clothes from her and wore long black boots and a white sweater dress. She had spent the morning braiding Bell's hair. I told them they looked glamorous, older, like women. Perhaps it was the red lipstick.

We met up with Belinda's on–off boyfriend, Kimi—the boy with the blond curls—who Meina and I had seen briefly the previous night. I felt a bit strange when we met and did that bumping-shoulder bro thing. Kimi kissed Meina on both cheeks. She told me she didn't like the smell he carried of cigarettes. When she asked, I told her I thought Kimi looked different.

"Last night he looked like the nerd who would have a frog in his pocket; today he turns up in vintage Pumas, and a James Baldwin T-shirt. He's all right with me."

I couldn't work out how Kimi got to be with Bell. I didn't think there was anything especially sexy about him but they looked happy. He looked like someone who would be a killer Scrabble player or who knew all the answers to a crossword, like he had lots of cool stuff in his mind.

"I like the way you put yourself together," I told him and I meant it.

"I call him Greenie," said Bell and she kissed Kimi on the mouth. "He always had boogers falling out of his nose at school but he was the only one who was nice to me when I first arrived. He said to me: 'I don't think you're a nigger,' in this cute little voice." Bell laughed and kissed him again.

We went to a place called the Riverside. Despite its name, it was by the roadside in the basement of an office building. It was sparse and laid-back with a sign offering Wi-Fi on a snaking bar top, bare bricks and fake bookshelves here and there. Years of cigarette smoke had given the place a gray pallor; and it was filled with black-and-white shots of Jack the Ripper's London. It felt like one of those modern pubs that try too hard to look traditional, like in the Docklands, all wrong, but Bell said they served the best cheesecake.

Meina sat opposite Bell, huddled with me in a red velvet booth with deep pink cushions under a picture of the Kray twins. Greenie said it was sacrilegious to play dance mixes of Nina Simone and Billie Holiday on a too-loud sound system. The place had a heavy, delicious smell of homemade cake but it was claustrophobic, like we were in a laundry. A butch white girl with green hair cut in a Mohican, skinny black jeans and red DMs came to take our orders. The cakes had poncey names like "Gladiator," "Matrix" and "Heat" and even a chocolate one called "Mean Sweet."

Greenie and I worked our way through a four-layered carrot cake ("Sin City"), and Meina and Bell ate a strawberry cheesecake with two big scoops of cherry Häagen-Dazs—"the Dolly Parton." The sun came out and Greenie suggested we hire bikes from a shop where his mate worked.

"It's only twenty minutes' walk," he said. "You know, Bell, up by Longrock. It's nice out; we can give them a tour."

"No, Greenie," said Bell. "I've been on one of your tours. Let's get the bikes but we should just mess around, nothing boring."

Greenie looked at me and I nodded.

"I haven't been on a bicycle for years," Meina said.

We walked down a narrow, sloping lane with a row of small shops where locals, tourists, students, backpackers and surfers sat at the open tables of restaurants, cafes and pubs. It seemed a lot longer than twenty minutes. Finally, we found ourselves walking along a wide sandy beach where the rocks were slippery and covered with glistening seaweed.

The shop was a low brick building with bikes lined up on the wall outside. Greenie's mate Michael agreed to let us have the bikes as long as we were back before his boss came to close up at six.

"No worries," said Greenie.

"Where you headed?" asked Michael.

"Not sure yet. Probably along the Mount, show them Marazion, Paul and Mousehole. Don't worry, we'll have 'em back on time."

We took off along a dedicated cycle track, down a path above a sandy bay where surfers in wetsuits huddled in a pack waiting for waves. It felt good to be outside, cycling around places where nobody would have heard of my brothers or me. I shut out all sound, everything became absolutely silent and I could hear my heart pounding, felt the blood rushing around my body and the tensing and relaxing of my calf muscles. Suddenly I was pedaling faster and faster. Greenie thought I was trying to race so he lowered his head and pedaled to catch up with me. I couldn't stop myself. I remembered how much I used to love cycling around West Ham Park on Saturday mornings while my father sat on a bench reading about football in the *Sun*.

"Don't go anywhere I can't see you."

"All right, Dad," I'd say and then I'd be off like a rocket.

Later, as the sun cast golden light on the clear water, we walked the bikes to a chip shop Bell and Greenie liked. We ordered plaice and chips and I sat by the window, trying to listen to the sound of the water through the maddening cries of the gulls. A fisherman stood in his boat, working deftly with thick rope in his hands, and clusters of black and brown seaweed floated on the edge of the shore. I rested my head on my arms, looking out at the horizon. I noticed everything. In silence I tried to find something ugly, some flaw in the scene. I had always loved the sunset but it hadn't fully registered as out of the ordinary until then.

"It's breathtaking," I said. I thought of Ashvin and had to fight to stop my tears.

Eventually we took the bikes back and went along the beach again.

"Greenie," I said, "what do you think of James Baldwin?"

Greenie stood, stuck out his chest and pointed to his T-shirt. "James Baldwin is the dog's nuts," he shouted out to the Atlantic and his voice echoed all around the cliff (the dog's nuts . . . dog's nuts . . . nuts).

"But do you know anything about his personal life?" I asked when he'd calmed down.

"You mean about him being queer?"

"Yeah. Don't you feel funny wearing his shirt?"

"Fuck no, this here's my coolest shirt. This one and my Van Morrison. Why? You like Baldwin?"

"I love Baldwin. I mean, he's my favorite but I thought you had to be gay to like him."

Greenie and Bell laughed. I walked away.

Meina caught up with me. "You can like who you want. It really doesn't matter about them being gay or not," she said.

"Yeah? In Leytonstone a guy got stabbed for asking someone for a light in a weird voice."

"So what? You can't live in constant fear of what stupid people think."

She reached out for my hand and we walked back toward the others.

"Do you believe in real love?" I asked.

"I don't know. I'm sure my parents loved each other."

"Have you ever been in love before?"

"Definitely not," said Meina and Bell must have heard.

"How do you think love feels?" she asked.

"You don't know?" said Greenie, puzzled. He shook his head, lit a spliff and after a few puffs he passed it to Bell.

I watched her inhale deeply.

"Greenie," I said, "I like you and all, but don't give that shit to my sister ever again."

My heart thudded. At first I thought Bell was about to start an argument. Greenie looked like he was about to say something but thought better of it. Bell tightened her lips and I saw her search my eyes. She gave me a sort of sullen look, blowing thick smoke into my face and I watched it rise between us like a slow dance. But it seemed as if she recognized something.

"Easy, brother," she said.

"I'm serious," I said.

It was silent for a while.

"In my village, they say love is a pain without remedy," Meina said. "We have annual rituals where virgins paint their eyes, gird their hips with love beads and wear white silk and then they carry the pain of their lovers in ceremonial jars and they go to the river and pour out the pain. Where I come from they say the water trembles because of the pain of love."

It was dusk and all seemed quiet. I watched Meina as the sun glowed on her face. "You're beautiful," I said. I took a deep breath and kissed her hands and throat. I watched a bird float carefree in the darkening sky and realized then that I could search for the rest of my life but might never find what I had in my grasp right then.

When it got dark Greenie tried but failed to get us into the club night at the Turk's Head. I heard Bell telling Meina it was the oldest pub in Penzance. But we couldn't get in because the doorman refused to believe us when we lied and said we were twenty-one.

"I've got whisky at home," said Bell and so we headed back to Trevescan Place.

Mr. Bloom's silver Jag was outside Bell's house when we got back. Pat sat huddled at the dining table with Mr. Bloom and Inspector Whittaker, they both looked tired and drained. They all stood when we entered noisily. I noticed Pat's eyes were red and puffy, her hair was still damp from a shower and she fumbled with the waistband of her yellow bathrobe. I noticed mascara on her sleeves. She stared straight ahead.

I couldn't work out what was wrong. Then, I felt afraid. My palms were sweating. Bad things always happened to people like me, I thought.

"Mum? What is it? What's wrong?" said Bell.

I let go of Meina's hand when Inspector Whittaker took a deep breath. It was like a slow-motion scene in a movie.

"Sit down, please," he said, nodding at me

I sat straightaway. My stomach clenched.

"I'm sorry but I have very sad and difficult information for you today. There has been a tragic accident. Your brothers are dead." He paused, shifting on his feet. "I have been instructed to drive you back to London where your mother is waiting to be with you at this time. When you get back to London if you want to discuss this you may do so with a special police counselor in the family crisis intervention team."

I wasn't sure if I had heard him at first. The good-cop bit didn't suit Whittaker. His speech was rushed and sounded scripted. At first I thought he was joking, but then I wondered why he was looking at me like we were friends.

"Which one?" I asked.

"All of them, James. They're all dead."

"Oh, Jesus," said Bell.

I gasped and cupped my mouth. Then, I laughed and stood up. Meina made the mistake of trying to touch me but I pushed her away. Everything slowed. There was an awful quiet.

"All of them? How?"

Whittaker's voice was low, strained and slightly rhythmical. "Your oldest brother shot them all dead, and then turned the gun on himself in the early hours of this morning. He had apparently stopped taking his antidepressant medication."

"Poor James," said Pat. "You poor, poor dear."

I felt heat rising in my chest, I couldn't breathe. Larry Bloom put his arms around Meina. I recognized the bewildered look spread across her face. "It's true," Bloom said turning to me. "I'm so sorry, truly I am."

"Your mother's asking for you. She wants you back," said the inspector.

"Shit, shit, shit," said Greenie, wringing his hands.

I bowed my head. I couldn't distinguish the voices in my ears. Something inside told me it was true—I'd known all along that something bad was going to happen. Later Meina said she heard me whisper, "God is so cruel, so cold-blooded," but I can't remember saying that. My knees gave way. I stumbled, punched the wall and made a spitting noise that hurt the back of my throat. Then, I screamed.

# SEVENTEEN

# JAMES

THIRTY MINUTES LATER WE were in Mr. Bloom's car. I had always loved driving long distances, but on this journey I stared out of the window not really taking anything in, blind and deaf with a dull ache in my chest. Memories flashed past—small things, like my brothers all dressed up as clowns on my fifth birthday. I was exhausted. Meina told me my neck was bleeding and that I would make myself ill if I didn't stop crying. I told her to leave me alone.

I could feel the veins bursting at my temples and the swelling in my neck growing. I covered my face with my arms.

"It doesn't make any sense," I said. "It's all shit, everything's just shit."

"It'll get better," Meina whispered, "I promise."

I was surprised her touch still had an effect on me. I felt disconnected from everything else. The grief—at one point I thought I would vomit. Grief sucked all the air out of the car. I kept touching my neck, half expecting the wound to burst open. I remembered being up on the roof, wanting to die. Whittaker and Bloom kept exchanging glances. Bloom spoke once. "James," he said, "I know it's difficult but—" My glare broke him off. Inspector Whittaker regarded me nervously and he blushed. I curled up in the back seat close to the door with my back to Meina.

"Don't wake him, whatever you do," said Mr. Bloom a few minutes later when Meina draped a blanket over me. He thought I couldn't hear. She used a corner of the wool to wipe my face. Slowly, my anger dissolved into a whimper and then I must have fallen asleep.

I don't know how long I slept, but the closer we got to east London, the more restless I became and eventually was fully awake again.

Whittaker had put on some music during the journey, the same thing over and over, a demented opera version of a tune I recognized from a Toyota advert or something.

"Enough . . . no more with the screaming bitches," said Mr. Bloom at some point.

"The screaming bitch you are referring to is Adelina Patti, my friend."

Bloom leaned over and switched CDs for Sarah Vaughan singing "It Never Entered My Mind."

"Inspector Whittaker, can I ask you something?" I said.

"Anything," he said, watching me in the rear-view.

There were hundreds of dead bugs on the far edges of the windscreen. The inspector's phone vibrated. It hadn't stopped buzzing the whole way. Everyone wanted him.

"What was the point of setting up Operation Trident?" I asked.

I watched Whittaker in the rearview. He explored my face as his own expression burst with something like surprise. Then he spoke without emotion from the back of his throat as if reciting from some policeman's handbook. "Trident," he said, "is the initiative we set up to investigate murders within the black community in London."

"Yes, Inspector," I said. Everyone knows that. What I want to know is the point at which you guys decided to separate a black life from a white one?"

He gave me a quick glance and shrugged. "It's not as simple as that . . ." he said and Mr. Bloom turned up the music (*Once you warned me that if you scorned me I'd sing the maiden's prayer again*).

"Inspector Whittaker?"

"What?"

"You got a lot of connections in the Met?"

"Some. What do you need?"

"Well, if anything ever happens to me could you maybe make sure Trident don't get the case?"

Mr. Bloom laughed. "You're a cheeky little bugger, aren't you?"

"I don't know what you're laughing for, you worked there, too," said Whittaker.

While Bloom parked the car, Meina, the inspector and I walked to my mother's boyfriend's front door. I had been sitting for so long I could hardly straighten my legs. There were white men everywhere, policemen. One with a pot belly stood guarding the front door. Meina held my hand but I couldn't even look at her. There was nothing left now . . . this time I wouldn't mess it up. It was just the matter of finding the space.

"I'll stay here," said Mr. Bloom.

The temperature had plummeted and the wind cut straight through my jeans. The night air was choking with that curious sickening odor blown up from Beckton. Beckton. Site of the largest sewage works in the UK. The smell up there wasn't exactly like shit but it was something very close. There was also a distinct smell of burning rubber. I saw Meina fixed on an old tire burning in the road.

"That's the kids," I said. "Lookouts. They burn tires when the police are about."

Shadows of thick evergreens broke up the sky, their forms almost humanlike, branches cutting up a strange bluish light from the moon. My boots scuffed across the black pavement, broken glass crunched under my feet.

"How are you doing?" asked Inspector Whittaker when we reached the flat. His skin was pasty. He had changed in a service station. He wore a blue jumper and one of those wax Barbour jackets only civil servants, bankers and off-duty policemen wear. To me, he looked a bit lost outside the comfort of his suit. I could tell he was good at his job, but I thought perhaps he didn't like it. He was frowning.

"I'm all right," I said. I felt weak and I sat on the ground. "Did you actually see their bodies?"

"Yes, son. Regrettably I did. But you won't be able to see them. Not for a long while yet." He looked strained.

The smell of rubber was everywhere. I locked my fingers and put my hands on my head. "How can they all be dead?"

Meina cried when I said that. I could feel she was suffering. Her eyes were on me as she sobbed. Everything slowed down and I couldn't make myself stand up. I just sat there.

"Get up, son. Pull yourself together, you have to be strong for your mother," said Inspector Whittaker. He helped me to my feet.

"I'm fine," I said.

I could tell Whittaker was hesitating about something. An irritating thought that must have been troubling him for a while.

"I want to say something before you go in," he said. "Now would be a good time to put an end to the family business, wouldn't you say? You'll be under an enormous pressure to keep it going but I'm just saying we could call it quits, right here, right now." He looked at me for a moment and sighed. "'A man is strong before he is moral.' I think it was Faulkner who said that. Think about it, James. If you agree, I can close the files. I won't come after you for anything, if you know what I mean?"

It was the first time I had ever thought about myself so directly connected to drug dealing. My hands were trembling, I only realized they were numb when I dug into my pockets. I decided that I liked Whittaker. He knew I was different, I could tell. At last someone who looked at *me*. Someone had finally separated me from everyone else.

"I'm going to have to get back to my office," said Whittaker. He took out his wallet and opened it, shuffled through a stack of bills, credit cards and photographs. "Here's my card." He wrote his mobile number on the back.

"I'm serious, kid. Anything you need." He sighed when he saw my expression. "Look," he said. His fists were clenched. "You don't have to go bad. I have seen this happen a thousand times, families being torn apart like this. You have a choice. Allow yourself time to mourn but don't do anything crazy. You have to play your hand. Don't keep it bottled up inside." His voice was forlorn. He held my wrists, his breath smelled vaguely of the boiled sweet he had been sucking on in the car. I could see the green veins in his neck. "Look at me," he said. "Don't be stupid. Don't get angry at the world." He released my arms slowly. "If there is anything you need, you call me."

*Play your hand* . . . I had heard this before.

"I will," I said and Meina and I watched the inspector walk away. We were outside Skeets's front door. I didn't want to go in.

It was one of those old Parker Morris council flats built in the seventies. Unfortunately for Skeets, his building fell just outside the catchment area of the English Heritage scheme that had recently cleared twelve tower blocks and replaced them with maisonettes under the Forest Gate Olympic Regeneration Programme. His flat was a long-forgotten, run-down sorrowful hole, ideal for a crack den. It had woodchip wallpaper, badly cracked ceilings and greasy chipboard kitchen units barely on their hinges. The bathroom door was busted; it lay on its side in the passage like a wounded dog. There was a smell of disin-fectant—Dettol or something—that failed to hide the pervading smell of sick, and I could see black mold growing in the spaces between the white tiles. Slowly, I looked around the living room, taking it all in.

Skeets sat on the far side. I had no idea who the other people in the room were. They were all watching me. They looked to me as though they were going out of their way to look like crack-heads in their shabby unironed clothes. I heard the sound of  a car starting up outside. Skeets stood abruptly and walked to the window. "Looks like the rozzers have gone. You can all leave now," he said, still checking the window. People started shuffling to their feet and heading to the door. "Oi, wake up, go on," said Skeets to a man I hadn't noticed sitting in the sofa nearest the kitchen whose eyes had remained closed.

After a few seconds, the man shook off his sleep and came slowly to his feet. He bent down, picked up his coat and shuf-fled down the hallway, clutching his belongings to his chest. Skeets watched them all leave but he stayed. As they passed, some of them touched my shoulder, saying how sorry they were, and the hairs on the back of my neck stood up and made me shiver. I looked cautiously behind me as Skeets moved his tall skinny body toward the passage. He pulled his dreadlocks, long and gray, out of his face and I heard him put the security chain across his front door. I didn't like being locked in his house.

It was dark and bleak in the room, crowded with dusty plastic flowers and dirty lace doilies, a room desperately crying out for fresh air. There was a picture of a vexed young Rasta with his arms folded, and a corner sofa big enough to seat five. The single window was shaded by exhausted red velvet curtains. It was like an eye, through which I could see far out into the gloom of east London. The only sound was the drone of an old refrigerator. Skeets switched a light on, turning the window into a mirror so that I saw her standing there behind me. My temples pumped against my skull as I exchanged looks with my mother. We saw all there was to see of each other. She burst into tears and moved to embrace me. "It's you," she cried. I couldn't hug her back.

"I'll wait outside," said Meina, as she backed out of the room.

My mother looked old. The crack had taken something out of her soul a long time ago. I had waited, as all my brothers had, but whatever it was that went missing had never come back. Her eyes were agitated and some of her hair was showing from the sides of her headscarf; her dressing gown had opened to reveal one of her sagging breasts. All her fingertips were black. I saw her catch a glimpse of her reflection in the window, and she walked over and drew the curtains shut. Skeets looked ghostly in the dark. His face was bony and pale and I could only see the whites of his glaring eyes.

My mother came back to me and I felt her body trembling against mine; she smelled of sweat.

"It's a mercy you weren't here." She stepped away from me again, took a deep breath and in the tense silence we tried to avert our eyes from one another.

"I don't remember everything. I was smoking, son. I'm sorry. But I remember the blood. There was blood everywhere. All over my babies. 5 woke up screaming in the night. Not like any time before, this was much, much worse. When I went to give him water he was soaked in sweat, staring out at the moon; it was big and bright. His eyes . . . his eyes looked full of the devil's thoughts. He put his gun to my head, told me to stop using. He swore if I dared touch drugs again he'd come back for me. 'Come back from where?' I asked him. He didn't sound right when he spoke, he sounded like he was already dead." Her hands were shaking as she pulled something from the pocket of her gown. "He gave me this."

She handed me a small white envelope with my name on it. It was a letter from 5. It had already been opened.

"'Go hide, old woman, before I change my mind.' That's what he said to me. It was like he was someone else. The veins were swelling in his neck and he was shaking. I went to my room and crawled under the bed. I heard it all. Five shots; boom, all my babies gone. I don't remember anything after that." She held her head in her hands and wept.

Maybe it was shock. Or shame. Maybe she was still high. I couldn't tell.

"James," she said, "I can't lie to you because you the only family I got. I need to stay high to keep the images of my babies from entering my head. Them police want me to go back there but you can tell 'em from me, I ain't never going back to that house. Not for shit."

I looked at her for a long time, and then at Skeets. I was shivering but it wasn't cold. I felt I would throw up any second. I could see my whole life there in front of me. Day in, day out, in that cramped room in Forest Gate with my mum and Skeets. It was about five o'clock in the morning. No moon. No sun. I could see the raw artificial lights glowing down over Stratford, a vast nightmare of desolation and petty antagonisms. I was crying.

"Hush now, baby," said my mother.

We sat there together, lost in our shared grief. She stroked my face and hair, gently pulled my head toward her chest and then clamped her hands behind my back as she did when I was little.

"Baby, do you know about the money? Where is all our money at?"

I took a deep breath and pulled back. A gentle light beamed in from the window and Skeets looked right at me. Beads of sweat glistened on my forehead and more than anything else I wanted to run.

"What money?" I asked.


"Where shall I take you?" asked Bloom when we returned to the safety of his car. I was crying. "Take it easy, James." His voice was awkward. "Do you want to go back to Meina's?"

"No. Do you think you could take me to my father's grave?"

"Sure. Where?"

"Manor Park. I'll show you the way."

We arrived just as the caretaker, a shriveled old man who, with his spiky gray beard, looked about eighty years old, opened the gates. It was early, but he let us through. Mr. Bloom pulled up by a large monument in the shape of a woman, Mary Magdalene probably. I read the words inscribed: *But O for the touch of a vanished hand and the sound of a voice that is still.*

"Can I use your phone?" I asked.

"Of course," said Bloom.

"I'll need to take it with me. I need to make one call. I won't look at your messages."

"Of course," he repeated. "Stay on it as long as you want."

I slid off my jacket, lowered myself and rested my back against the edge of my father's headstone. I glanced around—some of the weeds were overgrown, obscuring some of the older headstones. I looked up at the sky and for a moment I was still. Then I shook my head, rocked back and forth and read my brother's letter.

James,

I have begun this letter five times and torn it up five times. I keep seeing your face, the face of our father and the faces of our brothers. This will be the last time you hear from me.

I'm sorry for what I have to do but this ain't no way for us to live. Marcus Garvey described us as a mighty race . . . I sure don't feel like I'm a part of it. I hate doing what I do. I hate myself. I've spent a long time trying to please no one but myself. I have no idea who I really am but I know I'm not a poisoner of black kids. I see too much blood when I look in the mirror, black blood everywhere. I can escape the mirror, James, but I can't escape myself.

I have never had the chance to tell you about my son, Ricardo. His mother is Carla. She lives in Piauí, northeast Brazil. I met Carla years ago at that Sunday-night club on the Lea Bridge road. She was one of those girls who wore expensive shit. You know the type, getting mashed on Moet and half an E and dancing all night. Turns out she was only in London two weeks. I liked her from the get-go. We started chatting, swapped numbers and ended up getting close. I even took her to the airport when she left. Somehow we stayed in touch—she sent letters but she never told me she got pregnant, not until he was born. I didn't give a shit at first but it was always in the back of my mind, like. I wondered sometimes about that little boy I had somewhere in Brazil. I met up with her on the last business trip I took. I spent two weeks with them. That was real life, James. It's been ages since I have seen my boy. They mean everything in the world to me but I don't see them because I'm a disaster.

Your girl Meina sort of reminds me of my Carla. You're onto a winner there. She looks like she might be able to boil an egg and read bedtime stories to your kids (not like some of these ghetto chicks). Don't be a screwup like me. (Your dick is the devil—don't listen.) Hold on to her. Make yourself a good family, protect them, be the best that you can be. Don't be stupid.

Always remember me, remember your brothers. You're on your own now. This is not the time to be weak, be strong. Don't let life turn you into a victim.

When you leave for Brazil, be sure to take clothes for my boy (he will be four) and cigarettes for her (Marlboro). Keep an eye on Ricardo; he is the only thing about me that is pure. Their address is:

House Teresina
Rua das barrocas
Santa Rosa, Piauí
Brazil

It's not going to be easy. I don't envy you, James. But you've always been straight as a hard-on. You are black. You are under eighteen. I don't see a place for you, not in the age we live in. I don't even know what to say to you. Still, don't make me catch you down in hell. I have racked my brain to offer you some words of wisdom. I could only come up with this: don't be afraid. This is your home, don't be driven from it. You have to survive.

Remember your brothers: Dahrren, Jerome, Loryn and Kieran.

And me,

Nathan

I read the letter a few times before pulling out my wallet and searching for Trevor Carrick's business card. *Trevor Carrick, Psychotherapist.*

My father's headstone was black marble. I wondered who had chosen the uninspired words: *Gone but not forgotten, ever loved husband and father, at rest.* Probably Nathan.

I looked around at some of the other graves with freshly laid flowers: lilies, tulips, irises. They looked doomed. The sun was soft, shots of light beamed on the marble headstones. I dialed Trevor Carrick's mobile number.

It was answered on the fourth ring.

"Hello, Mr. Carrick. This is James Morrison. I'm hoping you remember who I am. We met—"

"James, I know who you are."

Silence.

"I'm sorry to trouble you. But you said I could call if I needed help. Well . . . my brothers . . . well . . . what did you give me your card for, Mr. Carrick?"

"James, I heard about what happened and I'm sorry."

"That's all right. But, Mr. Carrick, I need some help."

"Anything."

"I don't know what to do."

Silence.

"Are you there? I said I don't know what to do."

"Well," he said, "well . . . you could . . . Look, I'm glad you called. It shows . . ."

I didn't understand Carrick's dithering. I felt like I was being mocked.

"James? . . . James, I'm sorry," said Carrick, "I just don't know what to say."

I looked at the red button on Mr. Bloom's phone and cut the call. I lay at my father's grave, surrounded by trees, with my eyes closed, for a long time. My mind was blank. There was no one else about except for a couple walking hand in hand following a path far ahead. I lay there, waiting for time to start up again.

I sat with my father for over an hour. I had my brother's letter on my lap. I stared up at the gray slowly spreading over the sky and the pigeon shit on the red rooftops on the red-brick houses across the street. There was just stillness. When I walked out of the cemetery, Larry Bloom was sitting in the car waiting patiently listening to Sarah Vaughan with the windows down.

"Where's Meina?" I asked.

"I wasn't sure how long you were going to need. I thought it best to take her home."

"Good. I need to ask you a favor," I said.

# EIGHTEEN

# LARRY BLOOM

I HAD BEEN TO Brazil a few times but never to our destination, Piauí State in the northeast. After a few phone calls to an old friend, Horatio Roberto de Souza, a retired army colonel and security chief, everything was arranged. James hardly spoke a word to me or to Meina during the entire flight. He had been acting as though what had happened was beyond him; pretending that there was nothing wrong. It disturbed me because I had seen this response before in Ashvin and Armeina.

For most of the flight, he kept his arms folded across his chest under his blanket, only rousing once when Meina insisted he eat. I wouldn't have agreed to take him given his suicide attempt, but the therapist thought it was a good way of monitoring his behavior for now. At one point, I caught James's eyes open and I made an attempt at a conversation.

"Did you watch the movie?" I asked.

He gave a deep sigh, looked genuinely pissed off. There was a flash of life in his eyes for a second but his voice was barely a whisper. "No."

"How are you?" I asked.

"T'riffic," he said and then he shut his eyes. I looked at Meina and she just nodded as if to say let him be.

He only spoke once after that, during our descent when he complained to Meina of a sharp pain in his ears.

"It's normal, just swallow," I said.

I hired a Hyundai from a pretty mulatta at the desk. She wore a black cotton frock that was very tight at the top, which her arse stretched at the seams. She had shoulder-length plaits that bobbed when she spoke.

"Most police officers require you to have a notarized color photocopy of your driver's license with all the details translated into Portuguese," she said before I showed her my old Met Police badge and slipped her my email address.

"What type of girl do you take me for?" she demanded. She leaned her hefty chest across her desk and gave me one of those big Brazilian smiles. I made sure she saw me look down at her thick legs.

"That's what I hope to find out," I said.

When she squealed out her laugh, Meina walked away and James laughed as he followed her. If you could call it a laugh, it was more like a cough or a chuckle. It took a while to get used to Meina reaching out every now and then to touch James. It seemed she was no longer the naive little girl I always thought she was. Her withdrawal from me had hit me hard, harder than I expected. My wishful thinking was over, done with, but this made her no less beautiful. I tried to ignore their displays of affection but it was difficult. Perhaps I should have made my play sooner. In the end, I started to like him; I decided James coming along when he did was for the best. There is something charming about him, an unmistakable intelligence, but he was far from friendly: he was colder toward me than a beach pebble in winter, but always polite. Seeing them together, waiting for me by the car, I couldn't help thinking they made a good couple. I think they understood each other.

"Jeesh, she reminded me of someone I knew when I was in the Met," I said when we got in the car.

"Why did you leave the police?" asked James.

"I didn't leave exactly. My employment was terminated." I turned and waved to the girl behind the desk who was looking at us through the glass window.

"Are you sure you could manage a woman like that, Mr. Bloom?" James said as we drove out of the car park.

"I'd stake my reputation on it," I said.

Our journey would take six hours. The air conditioning was weak and when I opened the window I could hear the sea being thrashed by the wind; the cool rushing air felt good against the side of my face. The hot sun made everything seem lavishly bright and full, and made me think of Somalia. Then I thought of Meina's father—he was a good man, a beautiful man, unwavering in his beliefs with stubborn pride for himself and his country. Despite the heat, I shivered. You don't realize how fragile you are until you lose someone, it's the same for all of us.

The modern road from the airport took us along the Poti River, then Frei Serafim with its luxury apartment buildings, banana palms with scorched fronds. The air was sour from the burning turf and the heat brought out the veins in my hands and arms. It must have been up in the nineties. I scanned everything, taking in the details of the surroundings: the flowers, intense red, yellow and purple, in bloom dotted on the sides of the road; a few crumpled old slackers dozing in the shade; gold and ebony faces spewing out of cars and side streets; the scorched stuccoed buildings and their jagged facades; the trees and the hills seemed greener, more vibrant; the sky, flecked with shapely clouds and swooping birds, was a circus of early-summer delights. The whole earth was simmering in front of me and my eyes hurt as I drove. We went past waterfalls and the many lakes surrounding Ilhabela where we stopped to see the colonial church Nossa Senhora d'Ajuda, built in 1803 from rocks, shells and whale oil. Then we continued our way along the coast through stunning views of the shoreline.

I thought I was lost after an hour's drive, when we took the first exit off at a lush, green roundabout and then all signs of the twenty-first century seemed to run out. Suddenly, I felt like I was driving behind the scenes of the set of an old Western: I saw lots of men in hammocks and I saw a sorry looking *faro* band playing in the shade. I tried to imagine the place we were going as we drove on along small dirt roads. We passed farmers, blacks and Indians mostly, planting by hand. By now, I had a permanent sheet of sweat on my face and opened the window, almost suffocating at the rush of musky smelling dirt and sand from the disturbed roads as gusts of wind brushed up clouds of dust from passing cars. Now and then, I thought I could see flashes of light reflecting over the dark slated roofs of the rows of small dwellings slumped across the sandy plains. Occasionally, when they thought I wasn't paying any attention, I saw Meina and James kiss in the back seat. I watched his hands through the rear-view but he didn't do anything untoward. It had been some time since I had seen a couple kiss as though they meant it. Perhaps I hadn't been looking.

We ate dinner at an outdoor restaurant. James hardly spoke during the meal but at least he ate it. Then, without warning, he was crying silently. Meina tried to hold him but he even shrugged her off.

They are a strange breed, black men. Some arrogant and insensitive, some lawless, some too humble and some downright mean. Most seem to think that their harsh circumstances make them different from everybody else. During my time in the Metropolitan Police, I had a lot of dealings with young black boys, always certain in their minds that they had done nothing wrong. I know I had seeds of repugnance inside me then, dark and hateful because there was something about them that I couldn't ever know. Watching them didn't tell me anything; talking to them helped but it was never enough. There was something else. I couldn't put my finger on it but it was there, always putting something out of tune between me and them.

I always thought that essentially people were the same, the past is the past, we all share the same level of existence with an equal chance to get through the bog of life and its pitfalls. Of course my views changed after my time in Somalia, after I met Ashvin and Armeina. For them, things were different. I knew they wouldn't survive if I left them there and it was the same feeling I got looking at James. Mohamed was a simple man, fiercely loyal to old ideals, he had a good standing in his community but in the end he had nothing whatsoever to show for his years of hard work. He told me once: "If you grow up with the stench of something foul, it takes a lot of scrubbing to rid yourself of the smell. It takes a lot of willpower to distinguish yourself from the stink, to remember the stink is not you." James had never reached the level of security with his family that existed with other, normal, families. Violence and drugs had seen to that. I wondered what would become of him: a job he would become dependent upon? A house of his own? A decent wife if he was lucky, and kids he probably couldn't afford.

James dropped his fork and looked up from his plate. "Why

are you staring at me like that?" he said. "You're always looking at me funny. Do you know that?"

I apologized.

It was almost midnight when we finally reached Esperantina, one of the harshest, most deserted villages in the northeast between Fortaleza and São Luís. Our hotel, an old colonial building that used to house the state's first public prison, was down a long one-way road of naked rock, coffee bushes, carnauba palms and hummingbirds. After ringing the reception bell for over ten minutes, we introduced ourselves to the couple who owned the house, a homely looking white woman who may have been pretty once named Maria and her black husband Romao. He moved his arm from his wife's plump waist when he saw me and after our quick handshakes he planted a cigar in the breast pocket of my shirt.

"My small gift to big white man," Romao said smiling.

"You are a crazy," said his wife and he laughed and planted a kiss on her mouth. They were in their mid-seventies and they smiled with something like pride at their grandson, Ignacio, an ungainly but handsome sixteen-year-old. He waddled as he took slow steps up a staircase that was like a sturdy ladder and showed us to our rooms. I kissed Meina goodnight.

"Goodnight, James," I said, turning to open the door to his room. If he was upset with me for putting them in separate rooms he didn't show it.

He nodded. "G'night, Mr. Bloom."

My room was nothing special. It was clean but lacked a woman's touch: no flowers, no sweet fragrance. It was spacious, the walls were bold blue and it had a grand four-poster. I sat down at a dusty writing table, stretched out my legs and lit the cigar Romao had given me. I flicked through the thick leather-bound Bible and then phoned down and asked for a large cup of whatever coffee I could smell brewing. At first, I heard James's footsteps, but then they stopped.

I opened my window and stared out at the deserted street.

"What do you expect me to do now? Where do I go from here?"

It took me a while to work out that it was James I heard shouting. I figured he was having a bad dream. I heard water from the shower running in his room, the toilet flushed and then his footsteps went downstairs. It was just after two in the morning. I went downstairs too and found James sitting at the dining table in a dark living room, drinking from a bottle of Coke. The lights were low.

"That stuff isn't good for you," I said.

He grimaced. "Leave me alone."

He spoke so softly I barely heard him. His eyes were bloodshot and full of tears. I stood beside him, and watched the tears fall against his brown skin, his hair like bramble; he had a musky smell, there was sweat on his temples; he sniffed his nose in a battle with gravity and his dignity. I was about to leave him there alone when I suddenly thought of Ashvin. He had never really taken to me the way Armeina did. I could never reach him, I never really tried.

"Your eyes are red. You must get some sleep."

"Let me be," he said.

"Look, you've been saying that for two days now. I heard you up there pacing the boards, up and down, just now. Armeina's a good kid, she's like . . . she's my daughter. For whatever reason, she's taken to you. If you screw that up it will be one of the many mistakes in your life you'll regret. If you're serious about Armeina then I am going to be a part of your life, so why don't you tell me what's going through your mind?"

He raised an eyebrow. "Your daughter? You're a white man. And like every white man I have ever run across you define me in terms of my relationship to you. Why do you people do that? You think you're doing me a favor by just standing there. Well, you ain't. Maybe *I'm* doing you a favor."

James was much more worldly-wise than he looked. The last thing I wanted was an argument with a bereaved seventeen-year-old.

"I'm sick of you looking down at me. Don't laugh at me." He looked directly into my eyes, indignant.

Maybe he was right. Maybe I had always felt a sense of superiority toward black men. I liked the power I could have over them. As a policeman, I could send them down to where they didn't want to be.

James was a stranger to me but in many ways I felt like I had been trying to know him forever. For an instant, I thought I had turned into one of those phony middle-class lefties, the sort I had hated most of my life, but I reassured myself. What I felt was a normal human emotion; after all, James was just a boy. Perhaps I was confused, I don't know. I held his gaze, wondering if this was what hope felt like.

"I want you to be able to trust me. If I've learned anything over the years it is to have no fear, not even of the worst," I said.

I had never in my life had such a strong desire to reach someone. I gripped his shoulder momentarily as though *I* were the fragile child. He looked at my hand. I removed it and then I placed it back and I held him. He glanced up at me and he said, "Nathan was lonely, and I know what it feels like, to step outside real life. I've been doing it for so long." He started to cry. "I want to feel alive again. I don't know what I'm doing here. I don't know what I'll say. I'm afraid."

"Don't worry," I said, "it will be fine."


In the morning, during a fine peal of bells announcing High Mass, Romao joined us for breakfast. He wore a smart shirt with a gold watch dangling from his white trousers and had a transistor radio propped lovingly on his lap.

Ignacio wore old trainers and cut-off shorts to breakfast, exposing his chubby knees. We ate thin slices of ham and fresh hammock, warm home-baked bread, and fruit smoothies Ignacio called *vitamina* made from guava, passion fruit and peach. I had three cups of *cafezinho* that was served in tiny demitasse cups with sugar-dipped orange peel. James was wearing jeans, his skin golden against his white shirt, but he looked grumpy. He yawned and yawned again and hunched his shoulders over the table in a show of exaggerated boredom. After a short conversation, Meina turned to Romao and said, "James wants to know about the monument with the big head." She laughed at James, her eyes lit up.

Romao looked over at the great monument in the square below, sipped from his cup and then lit the cigar that he had held between his strong, calloused fingers. "Do you believe in God?"

"No," James said with an expression of contempt.

"You are not happy?"

"No," said James.

"I can tell," Romao said. He looked at James and laughed. "It's good. You would not be a black man if you were happy all the time in life. When there is drought you look for rain. Maybe you never find it but you do not stop looking. This is life, my friend."

James stared at Romao oddly for some time, almost with reverence. Romao gave him a patient smile while he undid a button on his damp shirt.

"Very nice," said Romao. "So we are two men of the devil." He poured himself a glass of rum, and filled a short glass for me. We clinked and he took a sip. For a long moment, he watched his cigar burn.

# NINETEEN

# MEINA

IT WAS JUST AFTER three when we arrived. The temperature had swelled well above ninety, like in the African sun. Inside the car, the dashboard smelled as though it might be melting. I reclined my seat as far back as it could go, trying to withdraw from the fierce afternoon heat. I looked at Mr. Bloom's flushed face.

"I'm roasting," he said.

We traveled slowly from Esperantina to Santa Rosa in the highlands. Along the way I saw mules tied to wooden posts and wearing straw hats; I saw men carrying sacks on their backs. Black women walked with large water jars on their heads and men without shirts worked in the fields or rested their dusty boots against crumbling walls in the shade. I even saw a man with dead rats at his feet, selling poison; hawkers—some with stands, most without—sold roast corn and snake charms, just like home.

We pulled up across the street from the address Nathan gave in his letter. It was a large house with a narrow brick walkway on the left side. The walls were peeling, the gate rusted at the hinges.

"This is it. You're sure you don't want me to come with you?" asked Mr. Bloom after he had parked the car.

"I'm sure," James said and got out. "Could you open the trunk?"

Then, Mr. Bloom did a funny thing. He got out of the car, too, and offered his right hand. James took it and first Mr. Bloom shook his hand firmly and then he pulled James close and hugged him.

"Let yourself breathe in there," he said.

I didn't know what he was talking about.

James struggled free from his embrace.

"Where will you be?" I asked Mr. Bloom.

There was laughter on his face when he said, "I'm going back south. Maybe I'll check out the *mumita* at the car rental, maybe I won't. If you need me leave me a message at the hotel, I'll check in every few hours. Either way, I'll be back here in a couple of days. You have money, call me if you need me." He pulled away from the curb and blasted the horn as he drove off.

I took one of the two heavy bags and the cake box and slowly James and I walked toward the iron gate. It creaked a shrill song when I opened it, the hinges scraping against their spring. Those across the street who seemed familiar with the sound looked up as I knocked on the brown door.

And then, I saw a woman and a boy who was bouncing a yellow plastic ball, standing there watching. She carried two shopping bags full of fruit and cut flowers. Her soft, dark eyes reminded me of a leading lady in one of those old black-and-white African films: narrow neck, dark skin, slender legs, wide hips and small full breasts completed the illusion. She was dressed simply in a white linen dress, a wide-brimmed hat and sandals. I wasn't sure how long she had been standing there. She looked alarmed. I saw her turn to look at the plume of dust that hung in the air from Mr. Bloom's car. She looked at James, at his trainers, at his new jeans.

"*Oi, Carla, tudo bem*," shouted somebody from across the street. It was a postman, a fat man, well over six feet, in shorts and a blue shirt, holding a sheaf of letters. "*Tudo bem*," said Carla. The postman paused to check through his handful of letters, and then waved and continued on down the street. I looked up at the sky when I heard a flutter of bird wings. Four crisp leaves circled against a wall in the breeze and drifted to the ground.

I then found I could not take my eyes from the little boy. He had dropped his ball but still stood with his mother, fingering his pockets. He looked like James. He had inherited the prominent Morrison lips. He had the same shape of skull, the same broad forehead. He watched James closely. Then, the boy peered at me as though he couldn't quite make me out and he huddled closer to his mother and nestled his face behind her dress, close to the back of her thighs.

James wiped away a tear as a great red truck shot past. It left a strong smell of fuel and a cloud of dust.

He paused and seemed to gather his strength. "My name is James Morrison."

The woman walked slowly, hesitantly, toward James and stopped when she was very close. She tilted her head as she stared at him and tears appeared in her warm brown eyes. She smiled at me and then she opened her arms and wound herself around James, holding him to her body. "James," she said. And then she turned to her son, Ricardo.

"*Você é amigo do meu pai*," said Ricardo.

James pursed his lips, straightened himself, making himself taller. His gaze fixed on his nephew.

James shrugged and looked at Carla. "What did he say?"

Carla hesitated. "He wants to know, are you a friend of his father?"

James smiled down at the boy. "I am your uncle."

Ricardo frowned indignantly at James and turned to his mother. "*Quem ou um uncle?*"

Carla laughed and then said gently, '*Esse é irmão do sev pai.*'

"*Irmão do meu pai*! . . . my father's brother!" He looked at James intently for a moment and then flung his arms around his neck and squeezed.

Carla turned to me. She shut her eyes when we embraced. She smelled sweet, flowery—rosemary or lavender, I couldn't decide which. Her arms, soft and warm, had a bluish hue from the sun.

James held Ricardo tightly for just a moment, and when he released him he turned around, looked at me and then at the sun over the land behind the building.

"Please," said Carla. "Come inside." She spoke as if the thought had just occurred to her.

James smiled at me, and then breathed in deeply. He leaned back and put his arms around my waist.

"After you," he said.

# FOREST OF A THOUSAND DEMONS

## An Essay by the Author of *Forest Gate*

I grew up in the East End of London, in an area called Forest Gate, where you could get your ass kicked if you didn't learn fast to keep your mouth shut and your eyes constantly averted. My best friend, Alex, and I spent our free time hanging around, robbing bus conductors, breaking windows, stealing cars and challenging people to fight on the flimsiest whim. When I was fifteen, I bought a gun from a dread in Notting Hill Gate, and Alex and I committed an armed robbery. Alex got caught and went to prison. I got away: I hid under the loose slats of my old school building for a few hours until I spotted one of my older sister's friends and begged her to walk hand-in-hand with me to the train station, where I caught the train to Oxford Circus.

My parents, Nigerians, found out about the robbery from Alex's mum and vowed never to let me out of the house again; I could study and go to church, but that would be it. Nigerian culture doesn't allow for parent-child negotiations, so I complied— perhaps because I always wanted to be a good catholic Nigerian boy, but also because I was terrified they would make good on their threat to hand me over to the authorities themselves.

Like many black men, I had reached a place from which there seems no way out, only the fear that all our efforts will come to nothing, that our whole lives may fall apart in our hands. It is the point at which we easily forget any allegiances, feeling instead as useless as unstrung beads. I have felt like this twice in my life. Ambition dulled, aspirations exhausted, my frustration became so all-consuming that I felt compelled to lash out against the system that I was convinced had been set up to make me, and others like me, fail. I had friends with older brothers who had tried to live by the book. I watched many of them fail miserably. Breaking the law made sense; it felt like an easier option.

In Britain we're not generally honest or open with each other about racism, even within black families. When I was five, I spent the first of many summer holidays going to work with my father at Chelsea Barracks on the Kings Road. I would eat lunch with the soldiers in the mess hall and toward the end of his shift we would walk around the beautiful grounds switching on the dim lamps before it got dark. My father, tall and shiny, would lift me up and tell me bogeyman stories about the IRA (who nail-bombed his beloved barracks in 1981) and whenever he passed a soldier he would get all stiff and address him as "sir." I loved the camaraderie of the soldiers, the way they saluted each other. I was going to be a soldier just like my old man.

I was twelve before I realized my father was a security guard. He didn't lie about his job, but for some reason I had always assumed he was the same as the soldiers I so admired. I felt so embarrassed. In the general confusion of adolescence, this discovery (and the feeling that I had been betrayed) made me lose all respect for him; I couldn't forgive him. Our relationship became quarrelsome and violent, and we grew apart. How could my father, who spoke to me of nothing but education and gainful employment, end up as a security guard?

It was only after I left home that I learned that in Nigeria he had been the governor of twelve schools. He came to London with the spirit of African independence blowing behind him, but was refused teaching positions because he had a hard edge to his Nigerian accent. At some point he gave up his idealism. But at twelve I doubt this knowledge would have meant much to me— or made a difference.

I would find out how hard it was by sixteen, when it came to finding a job for myself. Almost thirty years had passed since my father arrived, but not so much had changed. I wasn't sure what to do after I left school. I wanted to write a novel, but in the meantime I was working Saturdays in Topman on Oxford Street, selling suits to my mates at inflated discounts on the side. One day my mother, ever a believer in progress through the usual channels, sent me trussed up in a suit to a career advice center on Hoe

Street in Leyton. The room was heavy with the smell of piss; discarded ticket stubs littered the floor. In a corner was a huge binder, full of jobs for school-leavers.

I noted the three or four that looked interesting. One was at HM Treasury Chambers. Then this chubby white woman with a Leo Sayer "afro" called out my number. She spoke at me for twenty minutes before concluding with the offer of a job at the local McDonald's in Walthamstow, north London. "It's very popular," she said. "Ideal for boys your age."

"What's wrong?" My mum asked when I got home and burst into tears.

"Fat bitch said I should work in McDonald's," I sobbed.

"Don't say 'bitch,'" she said.

Then, having listened to what happened, she wiped the snot from my nose, half embraced me, and said, "Where's that piece of paper, the one with the jobs you were interested in? There is nothing to stop you from applying for those jobs yourself. And don't let me catch you crying over something like this again."

By this time I was sixteen. It was 1988, seven years after the riot in Brixton, only three years after the Broadwater Farm and Handsworth riots. I had spent more than ten years in school, but not one teacher had asked me what I wanted to do. Not one had offered me a book that I could relate to, nor spoken openly about race and social justice. My school was mixed but all the more confusing for it. The rugby team was mostly white; the soccer team mostly black. Rap music was not allowed at the summer disco and we all spoke urban slang. I wasn't bullied, but I grew up with a sense that I was less than "black." I was an African, laughed at by everyone because starving "Ethiopians" were always on the telly, and because of my surname, my father's tribal marks, his accent, and my mother's "funny" clothes. When I left all I knew was that I wanted to leave the area where I had grown up.

After taking A-levels, I read law at university to please my mother and then worked at HM Treasury Chambers in Westminster for five years. To some this might seem like a turning point, but I don't believe that education saved me. Lots of well-educated black men I know are unemployed or in jail. For me staying out of trouble was more about listening to the voice inside that says you don't want to end up where you know you could, where lots of people expect you to end up. My motivation has always been to resist the image that many people have of black men.

For a while I felt I had arrived. I was earning decent money, bought my first suit (Kenzo) and a tacky Ford XR2 (white with all the trims). I got married. I thought I was the business. On Gordon Brown's first day at work as chancellor of the exchequer I was one of the few hundred or so HM Treasury staff who, still riding high on the promise of New Labour, lined the marble steps to welcome him. I even shook his hand. The political landscape had tilted and everything felt right and proper. But of course it wasn't. When I looked around at all the anodyne black men in that fancy building it scared me to death.

I soon became bored of office life. I was terrified of turning into one of my black colleagues, who had been working there for decades making the same complaints about the illusions of equality within the civil service being worse than the obvious inequality. (Yes, there are lots of black people in the civil service, but they'll spend a lifetime waiting to be promoted, unlike their white counterparts.) So I wrote a letter to Tony Elliott (founder and publisher of the Time Out Group) about a fantasy I had to start a magazine for black men. After a year of an internship (after work, I would take the tube from Westminster to Tottenham Court Road), he agreed to invest. He gave me £100,000 in instalments, and I launched *Untold,* an i-D magazine for black men, the first of its kind. It sold 30,000 copies a month and ran for five years. Advertisers paid top dollar for pages. I interviewed Tony Blair, Nelson Mandela, Quincy Jones, Youssou Ndor. But the £100,000 didn't go far. Soon I was on my own, trying to extract money from reluctant advertisers.

It is not only because of their small circulation that so many magazines aimed predominantly at black people collapse. It is also about racism. I ran around London trying to sell advertising space for five years and mostly got nothing but absurd excuses. It was like banging my head against a jagged wall. Then one day I turned up for work bright and early as usual, and a bailiff—tall white dude in a bomber jacket and scuffed boots—greeted me at the front door. "All right, Pete," he said, smug as you like. He knew my name because he had come knocking so many times before. Bollocks to all this, I thought, and I never went back.

Then for the second time I found myself in that dark place. Only this time it was much worse than when I was fifteen. Like all company directors who lose their businesses, I felt a huge sense of failure. My magazine had banged on about successful black men. Now I couldn't afford a travel card. I was thirty-two and immersed in anger. I had lost my business and my home. I was made bankrupt. I was divorced and finding it difficult to come to terms with my absent/weekend father status. My world was falling apart. I started making bad decisions under stress. I was tired of constantly being reminded that I was not good enough, of having to be better than average just to be considered normal. I went into freefall, tempted to do things I had never dreamed I could contemplate doing. Instead of simply reacting to what was happening I wanted to act: Think I'm a thief? I'll show you a thief. Think I'm violent? I'll show you violence. I wanted to fight everyone, to repudiate all allegiances, morals, values, loyalties and sentiment. I just wanted to lash out.

But what I really wanted was to curl up like a dead leaf and allow myself to go wherever the wind blew. To me it seemed that the systems—those historical conditions that shape advantage (government, economy, judiciary, education, mass media, pop culture), so drenched in racism—were geared to make me fail.

I had to get out of East London fast. I spent a year living in West London, four months in Paris, a year in Nigeria. Whenever I spoke to my mum she reminded me (nicely) just how much of a bum I was. Then, two years ago, I moved to Brooklyn. It was like taking a deep, warm bath. America has always had its problems dealing with race. Accepting black men into positions of power isn't necessarily one of them. I'm no expert; I just prefer my chances here, where I've met more than enough assertive black men still full of ambition to lift the lid on my kettled anger.

I had my first proper punch-up in Chingford; I scored my first goal over on Hackney marshes on a Sunday morning; I lost my virginity one spring among the hyacinths by the pond in Victoria

Park; I could buy you a beef patty from a Jamaican spot in Dalston that might be the best in the UK, if not the world. I haven't known anything but a multicultural Britain. Yet the echo of all we have inherited from the postwar immigration era rings loud and clear in my ears and in the ears of young black Britons of the fifth and sixth generations. But I can't walk around London without wondering what has happened to all the black men of my generation.

The lack of any significant social reform in Britain is disappointing. The country should look back and reform the Race Relations Acts of the 1960s. Some of the companies that are all white at management level should be forced to hire and promote black people. The arbitrary powers to exclude that are too often deployed against black boys in our school(s) need to be overhauled. Bank managers should be encouraged (subsidized) to help black businesses. Britain needs black universities like those in America. It feels to me as if black men are being denied access to the credentials that enable us to compete. In some respects it is as if we are in the process of being wiped out.

I still go home from time to time, and whenever I'm back in Forest Gate, amid the drone of souped-up engines and the rank odor of KFC, I see groups of young men milling at street corners. I always get a sentimental sense of connection. They stare at me like they could kill me and I stare back at them, with their wild hair, sagging jeans and asses hanging out, and I understand them perfectly. Rebellion feels like the only way to escape the deadly boomerang visited on us. Not all but lots of my friends do bad things as a matter of survival. I don't necessarily agree with anyone breaking the law, but in our country, the way things are, I don't judge.

Just before I left for New York I met my old friend Alex again. We had a Guinness in the Princess Alice in Forest Gate. He is now a businessman of sorts. He sells heroin, morphine, methamphetamine and cocaine around a large slice of East London. "We would've made great partners me and you," he said. Alex spent years in prison because of something we had both done. He got caught and in that great East London tradition, he never spoke a word to the police about me.

When we were kids, Alex's little brother Isaac used to try to hang out with us. Specifically, I remember Isaac begging to come out with us one Friday night, when he found out we were going to rob the man who collected the money from our parents for the soccer pools (modern-day numbers runner). We followed that man for most of the night around the estates. He was white, in his mid-forties with a Barbour-style jacket and a flat cap. We took him for £80 and put the money toward a gun.

I asked how Isaac was now. Isaac was dead, Alex said. He had jumped off a tower block when he was sixteen, and he hadn't left a note.

For months after learning of Isaac's death I used to hear his thoughts in my head. Still I picture him often, looking scared and beaten, leaning over the edge of the deserted tower, with the harsh world rolling around in his mind. He must have known he didn't stand a chance—at anything. I picture Isaac looking in concentration over the tops of the sycamores, watching streams of tail-lights disappear down familiar perilous streets. In my mind I am always the first to arrive at the scene, and when I look at the body, I see that he is me. Alex the dealer, the ex-con, the desperado, could have been me, too.

It has became fashionable for black and white people in Britain to act as if they don't have the slightest idea about racism, about why black men reach the point of massive gravity—when inertia sets in—where we can't seem to connect properly with the world—why we are absent, why we end up unfocused, directionless, trying to rob and kill. In 2007 thirty teenagers, mostly black, were reported murdered. A recent police report on London's gang culture identified 170 separate gangs, with more than a quarter said to have been involved in murders. According to a 2008 study by Queen Mary University, London, suicide is proportionally more common among young black men than white; but more alarmingly, most of the suicides that occur among black men happen within twenty-four hours of being in contact with a professional therapist.

Black men in Britain remain almost invisible, at the lowest of the "racial hierarchy." Yes we get jobs, but not often enough in boardrooms; 37 percent of black men in the UK are on the police's national database whether they have been found guilty of a crime or not (compared to 13 percent of Asian and 9 percent of white men). This racial disparity hardly ever works in our favor. Even if we play by the rules we are twice as likely to be unemployed. White men are the gatekeepers to the roles we could use to redefine ourselves: in politics, television, radio, newspapers, even club promoting. Let us not pretend we can't see.

Prime minister Tony Blair came into power in 1997. His "New Labour" and "we deserve better" slogans sent us all into a bit of a frenzy. He gave birth to an idea of "cool Britannia," a play on the old imperialist song "rule Britannia." I voted for Blair and for an idyllic vision of Britain—of people living together harmoniously despite their differences. A number of phenomenally successful novels came out on the back of this ideal, playing upon the fantasy of a progressive multiracial Britain.

On July 6, 2005, the face of "progressive multicultural" Britain—a face at ease with different religions and races—won the bid for the 2012 Olympics, and on the following day, July 7, came the London terror attacks. Suddenly everyone was talking about race, culture, religion, immigration and identity again. How do third-generation UK-born boys become radicalized? It's a question for which the characters in this book might have some quick answers.

I had lived in London all my life and I could never fully relate to this dreamy idea of groups of multiracial teenagers walking hand-in-hand around London with no reason to notice their differences, oblivious to their race, their culture or their history. The British idea of multiculturalism is in fact a dangerous myth. In London, different races may live on top of one another, but we remain separate and often alienated communities.

I began to jot down my memories and impressions of Forest Gate when I was thirty. At the time I did not know why or for whom I was jotting these memories down. Once the manuscript was complete, I wasn't sure what I had done. I had guns, gangs and terrible violence in my story, everything that flies in the face of the most conventional, asphyxiating British literary establishment. In Britain, these are subjects that are rewarded with a certain contempt, that relegate writers to less than writer's status. I sent it out eventually because I knew *Forest Gate* represented a certain truth. Ironically, the backlash came not from the establishment but from some of my old friends in Forest Gate, people whom I grew up with and love said it made them feel uneasy. Others said they recognized themselves in the novel and have taken umbrage at the things I have said about drugs and growing up on the estates.

I knew I couldn't answer all the questions, but by writing *Forest Gate* I felt I could show a truer picture of what it feels to be young, black and male in contemporary Britain. I thought I could tell a story that showed how the people who arrived in London were changed by it, as were the natives, whose community was altered drastically in turn. It is a story that is relevant for every major city, not just London.

*Forest Gate* was heavily influenced by Sam Selvon's *Lonely Londoners*, C. L. R James's *Minty Alley* and Farrukh Dhondy's *East End at Your Feet,* all of which center on social transformation in Britain—new modes of human relationships in the lives of the city's British immigrants as they struggle to prosper and assimilate. I was also heavily influenced by African writing and Daniel Fagunwa's *Forest of a Thousand Daemons,* which I bought for 20p at a garage sale in 1985. The book haunted my imagination and taught me that literature could have rhythm and sound. James and Ashvin's experience in the home of a griot is one instance in which I was able to draw from the depository of my African heritage.

Even though I was born in London and I bear many of my parents' Nigerian idiosyncrasies, in my heart I have always thought of myself as a writer in that I do not want to belong anywhere. In 2006, when I learned of the fiftieth anniversary celebration in Paris of the First International Congress of Black Writers and Artists, I knew I had to be there. I spent most of the three days with a dreamy expression on my face staring up at the massive stone walls, trying to connect with the spirits of all the dead writers I so admired. I did meet a Somali woman who was making a film about female mutilation. I ended up staying with her and her friends for three months, roaming Paris trying to relate my experience of London with theirs. I enjoyed the bistros and visited the Banlieux areas, including Clichy-Sous-Bois, where the deaths of two teenagers, Zyed Benna and Bouna Traore, had sparked riots the previous year. The voice of my Somali friend became Armeina's, and those two teenagers who died—electrocuted as they hid from the police—only stoked the anger in the voices of James and Ashvin.

I came to Brooklyn in 2007, initially to edit a novel I had completed, but I kept being interrupted by the stronger voices of my childhood. As one memory after another presented itself the idea for *Forest Gate* grew and took shape.

"You'll see a lot of white people walking up and down this street," said the African-American real estate agent when he took me to my first apartment. I wasn't sure what he meant but moving here felt a lot like being in Forest Gate. Here's what Henry Miller said of one of my cross streets:

> *But I saw a street called Myrtle Avenue, which runs from Borough Hall to Fresh Pond Road, and down this street no saint ever walked (else it would have crumbled), down this street no miracle ever passed, nor any poet, nor any species of human genius, nor did any flower ever grow there, nor did the sun strike it squarely, nor did the rain ever wash it. For the genuine Inferno which I had to postpone for twenty years I give you Myrtle Avenue, one of the innumerable bridlepaths ridden by iron monsters which lead to the heart of American emptiness. If you have only seen Essen or Manchester or Chicago or Lavallois-Perret or Glasgow or Hoboken or Canarsie or Bayonne you have seen nothing of the magnificent emptiness of progress and enlightenment. Dear reader, you must see Myrtle Avenue before you die, if only to realize how far into the future Dante saw.*

To me, Bedford-Stuyvesant, the neighborhood where I live in Brooklyn, New York, is the same as the urban areas of Paris I visited or Forest Gate: a crowded residential area, an inferno of defeating streets; faded signs for long-closed stores and restaurants, African braiding shops and the twenty-four hour fried-chicken joint that always seems full, dingy laundrettes and loud cars with spinning wheels. Some nights Bedford-Stuyvesant even reminds me of the chaos of Lagos, a city where 18 million Nigerians are crammed.

My book was always intended to be more than a ghetto parable. It is a chronicle of the new energy of Britain and a means of political dialogue to counter the real paranoia, fierce prejudice and delirious fantasy presently running through Britain and cultivated by the mainstream media. My characters are tired of being told who they are and what they stand for; of feeling separate and alienated, muted; tired of being misrepresented. I didn't see or meet anyone who shared my views even though I had encountered people just like me wherever I had travelled. I decided I didn't want my story to be friendly, I didn't want clever human universals. I just wanted to get this story off my chest.

I love Britain because it opened its doors to my immigrant parents. And yet I can relate to boys who join gangs and inflict terror in their communities. I can relate to boys who sell drugs in order to earn money to feed their families. Young black men go through years of personal questioning as they turn inward and come to terms with the systematic order of white racism. As a result, many don't want to face up to their bleak futures, lose their balance and, predictably, many black men end up dying angry violent deaths. This is not fiction; this is happening in the UK at the moment at an alarming rate. People need to start looking at this seriously because radicalism is not confined to, nor did it ever solely belong to Muslims.

I wanted to visit this complex state of mind particularly in my character Ashvin. I wanted carefully to give him a dignified voice, one that resonates with pain. With Ashvin I wanted to focus on the family dynamic to give him heart. Anyway, I remembered telling myself to keep calm, to continue to write something truthful, to sneak my personal convictions into the frame. A book that would be grouped with a number of daring works of icy prose that helped to form a picture of the black man in extremis, that is to say, submerged in anguish, heavily weighed upon. I wanted my book to reflect the rage surfacing in young black men based in London in response not only to racism in British society but also the trauma of surviving our dead-end personal lives. I wanted to do it in a way of a story that peeled away at the layers wrapped tightly around young black men from different backgrounds lumped together in estates in London, who, together, had reached the point where they no longer cared whether they lived or died.

I have been in Brooklyn for almost two years now, and I am glad I came. I still have a lot of things to put right, but today I have found a way to value myself and to look in the mirror without flinching. I have a two-month-old son. Despite the promise of Obama I'm gutted that I will have to fly him 3,000 miles if I ever want him to see the Arsenal soccer team play at the Emirates Stadium, and I'm sick he will say "Mommy, can I have a cookie?" instead of "Got any biccies, mum?" as I did.

When he's old enough I will talk to him about my failures and the failures of British society. I'll give him the books that triggered all the questions in me, and when he gets angry I'll chill him out, take the time to answer all the difficult things he asks, and hopefully he won't ever have to contemplate buying a gun.

*Forest Gate*


# Reading Group Guide


Set in the slums of contemporary London, *Forest Gate* chronicles the lives of the dual narrators—James and Armeina—in the wake of a double suicide attempt that James survives but Ashvin, Armeina's brother, does not. Through the heart-wrenchingly human voices of Armeina and James, we learn about the extraordinarily sad family history of both narrators. Armeina, called Meina, was forced to flee Somalia with her brother, Ashvin, after the two witnessed the brutal murder of their intellectual parents by Ethiopian soldiers. Meina and Ashvin, with the help of their white benefactor, Mr. Bloom, move to the "estates" of London where they meet James, the youngest of six warlord and drug-dealing brothers and the son of a crack-addicted mother. James and Meina are brought together by the tragedy of Ashvin's death and James's survival and fall in love in the shadow of their shared sorrow. Poignant and breathtaking, tragic and captivating, *Forest Gate* takes the reader on a journey that reminds us all of the fragility of human life and the possibility of hope in spite of unmistakable tragedy and loss.

# Discussion Questions

1. The novel opens with a double suicide attempt that is only halfway successful. Meina, as the narrator, describes the two boys preparing to die: "they were quiet as they emptied their minds, as they tried to forget life, to blend with their frail place in the universe" (page 10). Discuss each of the boy's reasons for wanting to die. What would have happened if Ashvin had survived instead of James? What if both boys had died?

2. In many ways Ashvin and Meina's parents stand as a symbol of progress in the novel. They are educated, successful, political and modern. Meina is given the choice, for example, whether she would like to be circumcised or not (page 53). What are other examples of the parents' open-mindedness? How do the parents help shape the lives of Ashvin and Meina even after their deaths?

3. Consider for a moment the structure of the story. What effect does the variety of narrators have on the story overall? Meina begins and ends the story, and is, by far, the most popular narrator employed by the author. To what extent does the story become Meina's? Why do you think the author made use of a fractured structure with several narrators? Is it successful?

4. A theme of the novel emerges on page 18 when Meina muses, "life is ultimately what you carry around in your

heart." Do you think it was worthwhile for Ashvin and Meina to leave their country for London? Consider the question from both Ashvin's and Meina's positions. How did James carry the burdens in his heart? How did Mr. Bloom? Was any character more successful at "carrying" than the others? How so and to what extent?

5. Revisit the brutal fight scene between Ashvin and Nalma, starting on page 116. Easily one of the more difficult pieces to read, this scene is also a very important moment to the novel as a whole. We as readers at last have some insight into the extremely sad and complex feelings Ashvin has been coping with since he witnessed the brutal murder of his parents. James captures well what we feel as readers when he says "I couldn't understand why Ash was crying" (page 116). Discuss the ways in which this scene is important to the novel and especially to the character of Ashvin. Do you believe Ashvin's actions were meant to be cathartic, vengeful or both?

6. On page 51, Meina says she does not have any ideas of her own that are "strong enough to want to die over." Is this what makes Meina different from her brother? What are other differences between the siblings? Are their differences due more to circumstance or fundamental differences in their personalities?

7. At the onset of the story, Meina explains that she was named after the river Armeina that glistened and was never disturbed (page 2), according to her mother. But Meina does not share the peaceful existence of the river and therefore prefers her nickname. In comparison, James's six brothers are referred to throughout the story by numbers rather than names, and 5's suicide letter at the end of the novel is the first place where their birth names are listed. Consider what a name means to the characters in Forest Gate. Does the use of numbers symbolize that James's brothers are somehow subhuman?

Why do you think the author used this technique of numbers instead of names? Why are the numbers out of chronological order? How does the use of numbers compare to Meina's given name?

8. Why do you think Meina asks James to live with her? Do you think it was her only option? Do you think Meina is in need of James or do you think James is in need of Meina? To what extent do the characters depend on one another?

9. Depression and mental illness factor heavily into the novel. Ashvin is diagnosed as bipolar after his death, and 5 goes on his shooting rampage as a result of not taking his medication. Do you think it is significant that these characters suffered from mental illness? What do you think the author may be saying about the stress of living in Forest Gate? Does the mental illness of Ashvin and 5 present a binary of guilt versus innocence?

10. Can you find any symbolism in the title *Forest Gate*? How does the image of enclosed wilderness help determine the parameters of the story? How would you have titled the novel?

11. African-American writers such as James Baldwin, Langston Hughes and Richard Wright are heavily referenced in *Forest Gate*. Ashvin and his father in particular often recite the poetry of Langston Hughes. Do you think the author meant poetry to stand as a form of freedom and escape for Ashvin and his father? How do literary role models challenge stereotypes of slum life? What does poetry symbolize in the story?

12. What role does Mr. Bloom play in the novel? Do you consider him a just character or not? Do you believe he had Meina's best interest at heart?

13. James asks Meina: "Do you blame me for what happened to Ashvin? Be honest" (page 143). Do you think Meina forgives James? Do James and Meina forgive Ashvin? What role do you think guilt played in the suicide attempts? Does James feel guilty for surviving? Does Meina feel guilty for her brother's death?

14. How does the sojourn to Cornwall change Meina and James's relationship? Do you think the shift in setting— from the enclosed slums to the open sea—is responsible for James and Meina finally sleeping together and opening up to one another?

15. James describes listening to Meina read Richard Wright's book as "one of those stories you read and you never forgot, one that made you feel for your ancestors, one that made all your own troubles pale in comparison" (page 147). Do you think this is a fair way to characterize *Forest Gate*? Did the voices of James and Meina bring alive for you what it means to be Somali? What it means to be victimized by circumstance? What it means to be trapped?

16. Discuss the ending of the story. Do you think it was a happy ending? Do you think there is a future for Meina and James? For James's nephew?

# Additional Activities:
# Ways of Enhancing Your Book Club

1. *Forest Gate* lets readers get a glimpse into the world of a Somali woman living in London. Explore further what it means to be a young woman in Somalia and a young Muslim Somali woman living in London by having each member of your book club read *Infidel* (Free Press, 2008) by Ayaan Hirsi Ali. Can you find any comparisons between Ayaan and Meina?

2. Have a movie night with your book club and rent *The Class (Entre Les Murs)* (2008). Is this school similar to the school James and Ashvin attended? How so? Does the slum life in the film remind you of the slums of *Forest Gate*? What are the differences between the book and the film?

3. In the novel, Meina visits the Somali restaurant Zudzi (page 59) after she learns of Ashvin's death. Meina is reminded of her lost home, and her lost mother and says the food was "so delicious . . . I almost wept" (page 63). Host a book club meeting in a local Somali restaurant or have a potluck with traditional Somali dishes. Over lunch, discuss what it means to be displaced. What would you miss most? Can you relate to Meina's story?

4. Explore Langston Hughes's poetry further by picking up a copy of *The Collected Poems of Langston Hughes* (Vintage Classics, 1995). Select a poem and have each

member of your group take turns reading the same poem aloud. How does the poem make you feel? Is there a difference when several voices read the same poem? What effect did reading poetry aloud have on your group? Did reading aloud allow you to relate better to Ashvin's love of reciting poetry?

# Questions for Peter Akinti

1. **You were born in London but lived briefly in Nigeria before settling in Brooklyn. Describe how the various places in which you have lived helped you write this book. Was living in London your primary influence? Why did you decide to set *Forest Gate* primarily in London instead of Somalia?**

Living in London was definitely the primary influence on writing this book. I moved to Nigeria because I was fed up complaining about London, then to Brooklyn after complaining about Nigeria. I am thankful that I did. I used to say, once you're an East Londoner you just can't live anywhere else. I thought it was part of the fabric of who I am. By traveling, I was lifted into new worlds, where I began to think, see and feel differently, extending the boundaries of my mind and eventually my writing, looking at parallel lives of inventive young people who are practically the same yet divided by money, ethnicity and class.

2. **You mention several African-American writers such as James Baldwin, Langston Hughes and Richard Wright throughout *Forest Gate*. Are these writers your influences? What is your background and how did you decide to become a writer?**

These writers mean a great deal to me. Ultimately, and this is difficult to explain, they gave me the courage to honestly depict what I felt rather than portray what might please a specific audience or what might be financially rewarding. I am heavily influenced by all proletarian fiction, that which springs out of the direct experience of the working class. I grew up longing to be a journalist. I have spent an awfully long time scribbling words in notebooks, even before I realized what I was doing. I signed up for a writing course once. My classmates went silent, just sort of looked at me sideways when I took my turn to read something out. I never went back but I knew I was on to something.

**3. Why did you decide to write this story? Describe the journey from conception to publication.**

I had just had my first manuscript turned down by every major publisher in the western world. I was feeling pretty low, unsure what to do with myself. I met with an old friend for a drink who told me his brother had died by suicide. He was just a kid; his death shook me up a bit. I couldn't get this image of him standing at the edge of a tower block, a project, out of my mind. I asked myself the question: what he was thinking? And I was shocked when I realized I knew.

**4. Were any of the characters based on people you have known in your life? On people from history? On yourself?**

Lots of black men are dying in London at the moment. We have started to believe lazy journalists who say these deaths are all to do with drugs and gangs formed in inner cities. This is just not true. James is based on a few people I have known and some who are fictional accounts of people who make the news. Of course James is also part of me, a part of the group of young men who are dying spiritually; James is also the nephew of James Baldwin whom the letter "my dungeon shook" was addressed to.

Poor James. The character Armeina is based on a Somali woman I met in Paris who was making a film about female circumcision.

5. **Who is your favorite character and why?**

My favorite character is Mohamed, Ashvin and Meina's father, a quiet and formidable presence in the book. A man who loved his family and his country; a brave and principled man murdered for strong political beliefs.

6. **Your novel depicts a part of slum life that we don't often see in popular culture; that is, those who are victimized by their circumstance, such as James. Was it important to you to present an alternative point of view?**

I didn't set out to depict this or that. I wanted to be included in the political dialogue that seemed to be taking place in London about people like me without people like me.

7. **Why did you decide to tell the story from various narrators' points of view? What effect do you think the structure has on the story overall? Why was Meina chosen as your primary narrator?**

Honestly, I thought people would tire of the black male voice. Also, it sounded very much like me, Peter. I would often find myself writing passages and working myself up more and more, drifting further and further away from my plot. In the end I asked myself: What could I say about growing isolation, meaninglessness and moral decay from a black male perspective that hadn't been said already. I tried using the voice of a black woman and, oddly enough, it worked for me. I was able to detach, concentrate more on the creative process.

8. **Describe the research that went into the making of this novel. Was it a lot or a little? Would you say this book is more from personal experience or from history and current events?**

I remember reading about Faisal Wangita, son of the late Idi Amin, who got five years for killing Mahir Osman, an eighteen-year-old Somali boy in London. Then a seventeen-year-old boy was convicted at the Old Bailey of murdering Kiyan Prince in London last May. He stabbed him through the heart several times. Hannad Hasan, a sixteen-year-old Somali immigrant, claimed the stabbing was an accident. I remember he said the knife he used was "a little toy." I found hundreds of stories that highlighted how some young men from war torn countries are fuelling the violence in Britain. Ignorant journalists were blaming "black men" despite the huge differences in our make up—we may look, dress and even talk the same but culturally, we are very different. I got fascinated with Somalia (their civil war has been ongoing for eighteen years. It is one of the few countries in the world that is officially ungovernable). I studied the Somali immigrants who were arriving in the East Midlands then moving to London and being housed mainly in the inner city estates, just like Forest Gate. (Academic studies estimate there are now 100,000 Somalis in Britain. Officially the figure is 20,000.) The story just grew from there.

9. **Do you hope to break any stereotypes with this novel?**

I don't know if my little book can break stereotypes, especially in London where the divide is difficult to overcome. Hopefully it will be included in the ongoing debate.

10. **Who are you reading now? Who is your favorite author? What is next for you as a writer?**

My favorite author is a Nigerian writer named Daniel Fagunwa. I read him at a very young age; he made a great impression on me. I am working on another novel. I have finished with the creative work; now I'm doing the editing. The book is set in East London. It has Yoruba mythology at its core.

# ABOUT THE AUTHOR

Peter Akinti was a seventies child, born of Nigerian ancestry, in London. He read Law at a London University. He has written for the *Guardian*, and worked for four years at HM Treasury Chambers before founding and editing *Untold* for five years. *Untold* was the first independent British magazine for black men and had a wealth of gifted contributors from all over the diaspora. Peter spent eighteen months in Nigeria, running a restaurant, beer parlor, and cinema in Ondo Town, Southwest Nigeria. He currently lives in Brooklyn. *Forest Gate* is his first novel.